# DEATH TAKES A KNIGHT

# DEATH TAKES A KNIGHT

## A COTSWOLD CRIMES MYSTERY

## SHARON LYNN

*To Dave, for everything, always*

# Contents

# Praise for DEATH TAKES A KNIGHT

"Each new entry in this series raises the bar, and *Death Takes a Knight* is a standout. The story unfolds with a delightfully twisty plot that showcases the author's remarkable storytelling skill. What truly elevates the book, however, is the cast of characters—one of the most engaging ensembles in contemporary mystery. Their lively, intelligent banter had me laughing out loud one moment and leaning in to savor the subtlety of their exchanges the next. Beautifully written, skillfully plotted, and irresistibly entertaining—an absolute delight to read!"—Valerie Biel, award-winning author of *Beyond the Cemetery Gate*

# Character List

Primary Characters:

- Maddie McGuire - American archaeology college student working at the Roman Baths
- Edward Bailey - Dashing constable training with the Major Crimes Investigation Team (MCIT) and Maddie's boyfriend
- Simon (aka Lord Simon Pacock, Earl of Comer) - Director of Volunteers and Tours at the Roman Baths Museum and Dolly's fiancée
- Detective Inspector Parikh - Trusted detective at MCIT and companion to Maddie
- Tori Gonzalez - Maddie's best friend from Arizona, currently studying in Washington, D.C.
- Dolly (aka Lady Gwendolyn De Valence) - Owner of the De Valence Medispa and Simon's fiancée
- Constable Douglass - Loathsome constable training with MCIT and Maddie's personal nemesis

Supporting Characters:

- Sam (aka Samantha Niven) - Maddie's mentor and former boss at the Roman Baths
- Lady Vivian, Dowager Duchess of Comer - Simon's aristocratic aunt and Fundraiser Volunteer Coordinator at the Roman Baths Museum
- Reverend Roger and Meryl Priestly - Kind couple in whose home Maddie is staying
- Roddy (aka Roderick) - The Priestly's beloved garden rabbit

- Dr. Daniels - Dig team leader at the Roman Baths Museum and Maddie's current boss
- Lily - Maddie's lookalike friend and server at the Pump Room
- James Bailey - Edward's roguish but (hopefully) reformed brother
- Donny - Lily's love interest, bartender at The Boater
- Fred - Retired taxi driver and friend to DI Parikh
- Milo - James's border collie
- Marcus - Member of Dr. Daniels' dig team
- Mac (aka Michael MacMillan) - Manager of The Boater, Donny's boss
- Harold (aka Gabriel) - Con artist, thief, and former Chedworth intern
- Yvette O'Leary - Sam's cousin from Galway and new Baths intern
- Hawthorne - Butler at Comer Manor
- Rupert - Hawthorne's nephew, young and happy dogsbody
- Rivers - Lady Vivian's rather enthusiastic driver
- Gilbert - Chauffeur and waiter at the De Valence Medispa
- DCI Bray - Detective Chief Inspector for the Avon and Somerset Constabulary and aristocratic friend of Lady Vivian
- Jeffery Dailey - Nosy reporter
- Silvia and Nancy - Detective Constables covering Glastonbury
- PC Jones - Bulky Police Constable with the Avon and Somerset Constabulary
- PC Linden - Police Constable with the Avon and Somerset Constabulary
- Heather McGuire - Maddie's brilliant mother

Mentioned Characters:

- Abuela - Tori's very religious grandmother
- Nicolas - A handsome intern at the Mexican Embassy in D.C. in whom Tori is quite taken
- Mrs. H. - Hawthorne's wife and cook at Comer Manor
- Ed McGuire - Maddie's charming father
- Thomas - Tomato seller at the farmer's market

# Chapter One: The First Discovery

When I read that the water from the Chalice Well in Glastonbury ran red with blood spilled from the Holy Grail, I never expected it to look so real. Crimson tendrils swirled in the rusty water as though from a fresh wound.

Drying my hands on my jeans, I squinted toward the rise, where a seating area framed a two-tiered pool that trickled to my location.  Something bobbed in the water, but I didn't have time to investigate. Instead, I exited the gardens the way I'd snuck in and headed around to pay the entrance fee. My friend Lily had told me that the closest restroom was by the exit, and I was in dire need of a bio break, so I bypassed the line

Not that there was a line. A peaceful tunnel of ivy and flowers welcomed guests into the gardens. When I approached the ticket kiosk, the woman chirped, "Reentry is included in the ticket price." She cocked her head to the side, examining me.

I grinned.

"Did you change clothes and grow?"

Lily and I have the same long, wavy, strawberry-blonde hair with a roses-and-cream complexion.  But she's a head shorter than my five feet nine inches, with blue eyes instead of green.

"And moved countries," I said, my Arizona accent clear.

"Oh my. You could be twins!"

Lily appeared by my side.  "A long-lost uncle must have run off to the colonies," she said.

After I paid, I mentioned to Lily how the water really did appear bloody.

"More of a rust, I'd call it, Maddie," guiding me to the trail and stopping to pose on the crest for a picture. "We need a picture to show our first adventure together."

Lily snapped upwards of a million pictures, her short arms unable to fit both of us in the frame. I pulled out my cell. "Here, let me."

After Lily seemed satisfied, I did a 360 panoramic shot around the garden as she said, "We can go to the top to see the well, then come down to the lion font, and finally the pool there." She pointed to each position, finishing with the pool in our background.

Since I didn't know if the water at the top looked the same as the crimson swirls I'd seen from the base of the garden, I insisted we start closer. "No. It looked like blood in water. Come on." I steered us around the hedge of the seating area in view of the restroom I'd used.

As we got closer, Lily screamed.

An Arthurian knight floated, the honed edge of a broadsword stabbed through his chest, glinting in the sunlight.

Hoping against hope that it was a mannequin from the Glastonbury Abbey Arthurian Fayre down the hill that someone tossed here as a practical joke, I pulled Lily into a hug and turned both of us away.

A high-pitched buzzing sound filled my skull, and I made an effort to slow my breathing before black dots formed. Counting backwards from ninety-nine by threes distracted my brain enough for me to realize that Lily was about to hyperventilate.

Turning away, we collapsed onto the grass by the path. "Inhale, two, three, four, hold two, three, four, exhale, two, three, four," I chanted a box breath. After a few rounds of calming breathing, I felt Lily stop shaking.

"Maddie," she gasped, "is that…" she paused to gulp in air, "is that—"

"Shh, shh." I made cooing sounds, knowing that if she articulated the horror, it would make it more real.

The ticket booth lady appeared, no doubt summoned by Lily's scream.

"My goodness," she said as she crouched by us, looking around, probably for the cause of Lily's distress. "That shriek curdled my blood, it did. Are you quite all right?"

"Call an ambulance," I said in a shaky voice, not able to form a better answer to her question.

Instead of pulling out her phone, she stood and peered over us toward the tainted pool. "What's that?"

"No!" I said too sharply, shooting a hand toward her.

She stopped her forward motion and narrowed her eyes at me.

"Nine, nine, nine," I instructed, emphasizing the emergency services number.

The ticket lady's gaze got very wide, and I recognized the edges of panic, but she slipped her cell from her pocket. Unfortunately, she stared at it like an alien artifact.

Much as I wanted to curl into a little ball and hide, someone had to get the authorities here. Juggling my cell without relinquishing my hold on Lily, I hit Edward's number in my Recents.

Knowing that I couldn't bypass calling the police by contacting my constable boyfriend didn't stop me from doing it.

"Maddie, my love," he said, his soft voice caressing the greeting with his thick Scottish burr. "How is King Arthur?" he asked, unaware of my current situation. He probably pictured me in the thick of the Arthurian Fayre, sampling Medieval food.

"He might be fine," I groaned, "but one of his knights isn't." I'd seen too many dead bodies not to recognize a lost cause when it floated into view.

"What happened?" Edward asked gently.

"It's not my fault," I said, failing at my attempt not to whine.

"Lassie," he said, encouraging.

Taking a deep, still shaky breath, I said, "A cosplay knight was stabbed with a broadsword. He's in one of the pools at the Chalice Well."

"Are you someplace safe?" he asked.

"Yeah," I squeaked, picturing the body I so wanted to block from my mind.

While I talked, the ticket lady had regained her mobility. Presumably, she had called the ambulance, and now helped Lily up and guided us toward the entrance kiosk.

"You're doing fine, lassie," he said calmly.

"Do you think DI Parikh will represent MCIT?" Drawing on my scant knowledge of how the U.K. police force worked calmed my mind. "Or is this a different tri-force area?"

My friend and, at times, protector, DI Parikh was Edward's mentor on the force. Parikh agreed to take Edward on at the Avon and Somerset Constabulary despite his background with a gang in Scotland.

Of course, Edward had been properly vouched for and vetted by an Edinburgh detective and had to meet certain conditions to stay on the force. But still, Parikh was there for him. When Parikh moved to Major Crimes, he went out on a limb to bring Edward with him. Edward was young for someone training for a detective constable position, but with DI Parikh's guidance, Edward was thriving.

The detective inspector always had a kind word for me, even in the worst of circumstances. I hoped he would appear soon.

"We're still in Somerset."

I screamed, whirled, and readied my fists to punch.

It took only a second to see Edward's dark hair and crooked smile before I flung myself into his embrace.

"I hate finding bodies," I groaned, my voice muffled against his chest. "Why are you here? I mean, not that I'm not grateful, but you said you had to work today."

Stepping back, I watched his shrug. "The DI sent an email granting early release, and the keys to Parikh's mum's SmartCar were on my desk with a note saying he finished using it." Another shrug. "So I came to you."

"Thank you," I said, hugging him again.

After a quick kiss on the cheek, he said, "I dinnae ken it would be so dire."

Cop mode snapped into place as he surveyed the scene, and along with it, a posh accent displaced his Scottish burr. "Where is everyone?" He'd gotten so adept at masking his Edinburgh accent that I don't think he noticed when the swap happened anymore.

I shook my head as the wail of a siren sounded in the distance.

He smiled, touching my cheek. "Nothing to worry about."

Soon, officers and EMTs arrived, but my detective inspector wasn't among them. Since their transfer to major crimes, Parikh and Edward had dismantled a drug ring in the Cotswolds. Even though the distribution had been stopped, Parikh continued to hunt for the mastermind behind the scheme. Personally, I thought the fiend had moved to a different part of the country.

The powers that be must have agreed because both the DI and Edward were between cases.

Edward pulled out his phone and dialed a number.

Shrugging, he said, "Parikh's mobile must be off. It keeps going to voicemail. No response to texts. Not like him."

"Maybe he needed a day off. You've put in way too many hours lately, so I imagine he has, too," I said reasonably, hiding my disappointment.

"Not like Parikh," he repeated quietly as he stowed his cell. "Let's find your wee friend."

After directing two tourists toward the entrance to wait and guiding the gift shop clerk to join them, we brought up the rear to the booth, where the ticket woman mothered Lily.

My companion cowered in a chair, knees to her chest, eyes overly wide. The opposite of adventurous, Lily craved quiet and a slow pace, which is why she chose to live in Bath rather than her native Manchester.

"I always thought your life was wicked exciting, but I don't want any part of this mither."

When viewed from a distance, my escapes from bad people sounded daring. Close up, it was just awful.

Hugging her shoulders, I agreed, "Neither do I."

Phone in hand, she said, "I tried calling Donny, but no luck."

"There's a lot of that going around. Maybe we're in a dead zone," I said, immediately regretting my choice of words. "I mean, uh—"

Lily clutched my hand, stopping me from further babbling. "The police are here," I said, hoping authority equaled rescue in her mind.

Constables from the Somerset and Avon Police Force cover both Bath, where I have my shiny new student worker position on the dig team at the Roman Baths Museum, and the rest of Somerset County. Which

Glastonbury is in, according to Edward.

My inability to navigate via maps put me at a disadvantage, so I never looked at them. I silently vowed to commit at least my corner of England to memory.

Since arriving in England last semester, the only traveling I'd done was walking a portion of the Cotswolds Way and assisting in winterizing the Chedworth Roman Villa near Gloucester.

The journey from Bath to Glastonbury required stopping and changing buses in Wells, and Lily led the way. The experience felt like traveling to a different world. To be fair, Edward arrived here fast enough, so it might be closer than I think.

With the arrival of the local constables, Edward introduced himself before returning to us.

"Aren't you in charge?" Lily asked him.

Shaking his head, Edward replied, "No, although I might work the case. Everything has to go through official channels. MCIT will be called in because it's a homicide, but I'll only be assigned if DI Parikh is put in charge."

The local officers, who introduced themselves as Silvia and Nancy, took our statements.

"I can use your first names?" Surprised, I wanted clarification. Edward didn't offer his name until halfway through my first police interview. And that was after meeting him the night before in a bar.

"After what you've seen, love, you can call me anything you want," Silvia said with a smile as Nancy and Lily moved to a different part of the garden.

"You're handling this a lot better than other officers I've met," I said, recalling the constable at Chedworth who insisted on driving duty to avoid the crime scene.

"We've worked the festival twice. Nothing surprises us now."

When Lily first suggested going to Glastonbury, I thought she meant the world-famous music festival. Over 2000 acts on one hundred stages sounded awesome to me, and I added it to my bucket list.

Lily had other ideas, which was how we ended up at an Arthurian reenactment day at the Glastonbury Abbey.

Referred to as a tumble down, the Abbey was destroyed when King Henry VIII dissolved the monasteries. Unlike the light and airy, beautifully restored Bath Abbey, Glastonbury had only a couple of walls and outbuildings left standing. Despite being in ruins and covered by cosplayers that day, it was awe-inspiring.

Local legends claim that King Arthur was buried at the Abbey until the dissolution in 1539. After that, the monks weren't quite sure where his body went—or they weren't saying.

Either way, it was a great topic for my Legends and History class that I started this spring semester. Since my internship at the Roman Baths ended in December, I started taking online courses with my university in Chicago to complete my archaeology degree as a stipulation for working on the dig team. And after this morning's discovery, I was ready to focus on school and put dead bodies out of my mind.

The Medieval Fayre and Arthurian reenactment provided the perfect introduction to the subject of religion and legend. The gardens at the Chalice Well played into King Arthur's quest for the Holy Grail, including a thorn tree, supposedly grown from Joseph of Arimathea's staff.

"Miss?" Silvia's voice cut into my musing.

"Huh?" Eloquent, that's me.

"Your full name, place of birth, residence here, and reason for visit?"

"Maddie, or Madeline, I guess, McGuire, Tempe, Arizona, but currently at Ash Tree Cottage on Greenway Lane in Bath, and I'm not visiting; I live here now." Despite the present situation, I couldn't help the note of pride coloring that last statement. My one-semester internship, which brought me to the Roman Bath Museum, landed me an official position on the archaeology dig team this semester.

"I rent a room from Roger and Meryl Priestly." The kind couple treated me like one of their own, and I couldn't dream of living anywhere else. Their terraced home included my princess tower, complete with a microwave and dorm-sized fridge, but they usually invited me to join them for meals.

Once the Baths and the Priestlys had confirmed where I would work and live, I allowed myself to hope for a normal life. But no. Here was another body popping into my view. At least Lily spotted it at the same time I did. It was somehow comforting to have someone with me to explain things.

Any hint of comfort dissolved when Lily's wail tore across the gardens.

Officer Silvia and I exchanged a glance before racing to her.

Another constable arrived—a mean, officious constable who aimed his wrath at Lily. She burst into tears.

"Forgive me, miss," he said, "I thought you were a different young lady who finds bodies far too often. Why don't I get you a cuppa to settle your nerves?"

Although he apologized, my temper still raged at how poorly he treated my friend.

Silvia and Nancy agreed. "Hey there, we had the statements under control," Nancy said. "No need to browbeat our witness."

"As I said—" he began. His superior tone did nothing to stop Silvia from interrupting.

"These young ladies have seen something quite horrific. Have a care."

"Yes, I agree. I just thought she was…" he trailed off as I went to Lily and hugged her shoulder.

"Her."

Constable Douglass, a recent transfer to the MCIT unit and my personal nemesis, pointed a stubby finger in my direction.

# Chapter Two: The Douglass

"Honestly?" I buried my face in my hands. I mean, it was nice that Constable Douglass, who inexplicably hated me, apologized to Lily for being gruff. But the fact that he could be pleasant and, for some reason, had it out for *me* personally made his presence worse. What did I ever do to him? Besides discovering a body, which he unjustly accused me of orchestrating the death of.

*Twit*. Or jackeen, as Samantha Niven, my former boss at the Roman Baths, referred to him. I still needed to find out what it meant in Irish.

So much had happened since Christmas with my work and school that I felt out of control. Being at the scene of another murder did nothing for my mood, and I readied a tirade to launch at Douglass.

"Listen, you—" I didn't get very far before the two local constables laid into him.

"How dare you speak to either of our witnesses that way," Silvia started.

"These girls have seen a nightmare, and you yell at them? What is wrong with you?" Nancy added.

My anger dissipated instantly, and I instead formed a fond kinship with the women.

Until one said, "Even if they're guilty, they deserve professionalism on our part."

"We're not guilty," I protested in a dull voice.

"We'll see," Douglass answered with a sneer, before noticing Edward and affecting an affable expression.

"I was not aware that other MCIT had been called in already," Douglass said to Edward, proffering a hand.

"Not here officially," Edward assured Douglass.

Edward introduced Douglass to everyone as the SOCO team arrived, interrupting further discussion. Scene of Crime Officers collected evidence and took photographs before the detectives showed up.

I still wished DI Parikh would be assigned to the case, even though it was clear that the detective working with Douglass would be in charge. Parikh's calm demeanor and analytical mind solved problems quickly. As an added bonus, he never assumed I was a serial killer mastermind like Douglass did.

Once the officials were done with Lily and me, Edward walked us to the car he'd borrowed. Edward drove a motorcycle, so when he wanted to transport me, DI Parikh lent him his mom's.

A SmartCar.

A tiny, two-seater car.

The three of us stared at it.

"I could fit in the trunk," I offered. I'd done dumber things with worse drivers on Phoenix freeways.

The slight tilt of Edward's head indicated the answer was no before he said, "I am not stuffing my beautiful girl into the boot of a car. And, it is illegal." The last he emphasized by drawing out each word.

Lily had started to shake again, so I took Edward aside. "Take her. I can grab a ride share."

His face went blank, a sure sign of internal trouble, but he eventually nodded. "Text me every step of the way."

Hugging him fiercely, I drew in as much support as I could gather before putting on my best everything-is-okay face.

"You look shattered. Are you sure?" Lily came out of her stupor long enough to express concern for me.

I needed to work on my poker face. "Yeah, no, really, I'll be fine," I answered. "Off you go."

As I watched them drive away, I refused to feel sorry for myself, especially as leaving me was my idea. The wait for the ride share app to find me a driver was taking forever, so I walked back toward the abbey and the center of town.

A wave of dressed-up knights and Medieval ladies flooded the streets, making me realize I'd never find a ride in this crowd. I checked the app to be sure. After ten minutes of searching, it told me no drivers were available and to try later.

The screech of a bus braking cut through the noise of excited chatter.

I ran to the stop, hoping it was the right line, and hopped on board. "Are you going to Wells or Bath?" I asked.

"Wells, aye. There's a connection to Bath fifteen minutes after we arrive."

I thanked him and sat near the door so I wouldn't miss my stop. I texted Edward about the bus and my route. When he first asked me to make him aware of my location at all times, I balked. But considering the amount of trouble I got into, I agreed with the wisdom of it.

'Waiting,' he texted back. Edward's texts were often cryptic, made more so by his Scottish nature, which left a lot to interpretation. Was he still with Lily? Was he at Ash Tree Cottage where I had my room, or was he waiting at the bus stop?

Whatever the answer, it warmed me and kept me moving forward. I couldn't afford to relax yet, or I might break down on public transport. *Stiff upper lip, McGuire*, I told myself.

Without getting on the wrong bus, I made it.

A cool breeze whipped at my face when I stepped off, but the butter-colored limestone of Bath's Georgian architecture never failed to make me happy. *You're home*, it whispered to me.

"I need a beer," I said. Still under the legal limit in America, I made the statement in England without a guilty conscience.

"A nice cuppa would suit me fine," Lily said, appearing at my side with Edward.

"She insisted we wait," Edward said in answer to my perplexed glance. I thought Lily would be in her cozy flat under a pile of blankets by now.

"Don't want to be alone, do I?" she said. "Donny's still not answering."

Even though we were only a couple of blocks from our favorite pubs in the Abbey Green, a sports bar featuring the rabbit logo from Bath Ales overlooked the station. Close sounded better right now. Plus, the house I stayed in came complete with a pet bunny, and I'd become quite fond of them.

Upstairs, the view of Southgate settled me. Edward stood to order at the bar, but had to take a call and went out on the balcony for privacy. Before I could take over the ordering, a server surprised me with table service.

I eyed the menu suspiciously. "When you say nachos, what exactly do you mean?" In my time in Bath, anything resembling Mexican food paled beside Arizona's fare.

"Tortilla chips, cheddar cheese, and jalapeños," he responded with the correct recipe, although he pronounced two of the ingredients wrong.

"Okay, those, a Bath Ale and a pot of tea." I didn't know if Edward would have to leave, so I didn't order him anything.

The malty scent of the caramel-colored ale hit my nose when it was set on the table. It triggered a memory of sitting in The Boater, a pub on Pulteney Bridge where Donny bartended. He hadn't called Lily yet, and she kept checking her phone.

"Maybe he ran out of battery," I suggested.

"Maybe." She stared glassy-eyed, so I poured her tea and added a generous heap of sugar and milk.

"Here. Drink."

She did so, slowly at first, then in gasping gulps. I stood by until she relinquished the cup and then refilled it.

"Ta." After finishing the second, color returned to her face. I made eye contact with the server and ordered another pot.

Edward returned, gave me a hug, and kissed me on the forehead, a rare display for him in this kind of setting.

"You have to leave, don't you?" I asked.

"Only if you are okay. The station called, but I understand if you'd rather I stayed."

Conflict clouded his deep, dark eyes. Working with the police saved him in more ways than one. He wanted to support me, but needed to be perfectly reliable for his job. Proud of his dedication, I kissed him. "I'll be fine. I made it here by myself, didn't I?"

"I'll call later," he said and left.

The server arrived with the additional tea.

"I don't need any more," Lily protested, although quietly.

"Yes, you do. The first pot was to settle your nerves. This one is for comfort."

"You're the expert," she sighed.

As I opened my mouth to apologize for her finding a body, indignation took over. It's not like I find bodies on purpose, and I'm certainly not the only one to do so, despite what Constable Douglass thinks. "I don't like this stuff any more than the next guy, and it is not at all even remotely my fault that these things happen. Anyway, this time, you screamed before I saw it, so technically, you discovered this body, not me, although I do admit that I saw the blood in the water first, but you're the one who snuck me into the exit so I could use the bathroom and..."

I trailed off when a tear trickled down Lily's cheek.

"I'm sorry. I rant when I'm freaked out."

She reached across the table and squeezed my hand. "I see why. It's wicked awful."

"Wicked," I agreed. "But really, for me, I have to eat, otherwise I get weak and can't control my emotions, so use lots of milk in your next cup of hot tea," I instructed.

The color drained from her face, replaced by a mask of tinted green.

Leaping off my stool, I guided Lily to the restroom. After giving her some privacy, I entered and helped her clean up.

Having someone to take care of made it easy to ignore my own queasiness. An illusion of strength, I supposed, but in reality, I was clinging to the adrenaline that kept me from losing it. With Edward gone, I didn't have my rock to keep me calm.

The nachos arrived, and Lily sampled a cheesy chip after carefully flicking off the jalapeño. "Good," she admitted.

"What have you gotten yourself into this time?" a posh male voice said behind me.

I turned to find Simon, my upper-crust coworker from the Baths, sneering down his nose at me.

"It wasn't my fault," I squeaked in protest.

"Chin up, old girl," Simon advised in the most stoic form of comfort on the planet.

It was enough. Underneath Simon's pompous exterior hid a sweet guy who always had my back. Now that Simon was here to support a breakdown, I had one.

Bolting to the bathroom, I purged the violence of the day.

Grateful for not having touched anything I ordered yet, I washed my face in the sink and stuffed my head under the hand dryer. Which is how Lily found me.

"It sneaks up on you," I explained as she patted my back.

"Y'alright?'

I waggled my head, and she hugged me as we walked to the table.

My beer was gone, replaced by something frothy and chocolaty. I sniffed the concoction, smelling a hint of coffee. Simon appeared indifferent ninety percent of the time, but appearances are deceiving.

As I sat, I leaned into him, bumping shoulders. "Thanks."

"Chili peppers seemed like too much," he said with a glance at the nachos, "but Arizonans do have odd notions about food."

"They're dead tasty," Lily said, helping herself to another gooey chip.

Relaxing for the first time in hours, I asked Simon, "How did you find us?"

"Edward texted that you were in distress." A considerable pause before he added, "Again."

There was a time when Edward wouldn't have dreamed of contacting a member of the aristocracy. I was glad he did. Simon provided the perfect mix of solace and motivation to not wallow. Edward understood the bond we three had, and while neither of them would say it, we were grateful for one another.

"To that point," Simon continued, "you could have these moments while your paramour is still here to take care of you.

Horror-struck, I said, "That would be way too embarrassing."

Lily yelped with joy, interrupting Simon's rebuttal.

Stumbling off her stool, Lily ran to Donny, who stood in the doorway.

"My phone ran out," he said as they grasped hands. "I came as soon as I got your," he paused to check his screen, "thirty-two texts."

"Oh, 'ello, Maddie, Simon," Donny said, spotting us. "I'll get a round."

Instead of explaining that we had a server, we sat while he chatted with a fellow bartender.

"Simon?" Lily asked meekly, still shy around him. As Simon ran the volunteers at the Baths Museum, Lily, who worked at the Pump Room next door, viewed him as a superior who ordered lunch and tea from her. More often than not, the food didn't come from the fancy restaurant where she worked, but the manager allowed the dig team to borrow her for food-based errands.

"What do you do at the museum?" she asked.

About to jump in and answer for him, I pulled up short. It was a great question. The dig team, headed by Dr. Daniels, borrowed volunteers from the Baths but was funded separately. I knew this because of the paperwork I filled out when I was officially hired.

"My family is a protector of the past, helping to preserve artifacts," he said, sounding lordly, which was appropriate because he was, in fact, a lord. "My parents were Egyptologists, but I chose to focus on the Classic era, closer to home."

"What?" I asked, not because I didn't understand, but because Simon divulged more information about his private life to Lily with one question than he had to me after months. "I didn't know any of that."

As one with only exquisite breeding could do, he elegantly lifted a shoulder in a shrug. "You never asked."

Gaping like a codfish, I stared. Every single solitary time I asked him anything directly, he ignored me. Including for work.

Before I could complain, Donny arrived carrying a tray with assorted goodies. We sipped and nibbled, listening to Simon.

"At the Roman Baths, my aunt Vivian coordinates the fundraising efforts, and I go where I am needed. While obtaining my degree, I volunteered to train in all positions directly involved with artifacts. Currently, I coordinate the volunteers and staff of the dig team as they uncover a newly discovered room."

Tesserae, small ceramic mosaic tiles, were found when I first started my internship. Their placement marked a threshold or entrance to a room. Since their discovery, I'd been helping by sifting dirt. Not as glamorous as conducting tours, but closer to what I wanted to do with my life.

"I still can't believe I'm an official part of the dig team," I said, allowing a sip of the creamy, sweet mocha to warm my body. "Thanks for the refills, Donny," I said, turning to him and noticing a glop in his chin.

"What is attached to your face?" I asked, then realized how forward I sounded. Good old American straightforward questions didn't always go over well.

Fortunately, he laughed. "Spirit gum. I dressed as a merchant for the Arthurian reenactment today," he explained as he peeled the gunk off. "I'm not knight material," he added, indicating his slight frame.

With his tawny skin, I wasn't sure if he would have gotten far as a salesman in medieval England, but I grinned at his ingenuity. "That's a great idea," I said. "How did it go over?"

"You were there?" Lily asked, making an excellent point. Why hadn't he told us?

"Mac gave me the day off to be with you and helped me with my costume," Donny said, referring to the manager at The Boater. "But my phone ran out of battery along the way. I spent the whole time looking for you," he added, looking guilty.

Lily eyed him. "You found a magician, didn't you?"

Donny liked to do card tricks at the bar, which is how he got to know Lily.

"He was brilliant!" Donny proclaimed, admitting to not looking for Lily. "He gave me a tip on rolling a ball over my hand."

Picturing David Bowie manipulating a crystal ball effortlessly in the old movie *Labyrinth*, I commented, "I thought magicians never revealed their secrets."

"Oh, we don't. But this isn't a secret. It's balance, practice, and hard work."

Glancing at Lily, he said, "But the rest of the time, I looked for you. Do you want me to walk you home?"

Lily nodded, and they left Simon and me.

"How did you find King Arthur?"

"Until the whole body fiasco, it was really cool," I said. "I thought the event might be goofy, but they put a lot of care into it, so I can use it for my paper."

A man of few words, at least when talking to me, Simon raised a questioning eyebrow.

I continued, "The class I'm taking is about legend and history, you know, like how the Iliad was used as a basis for archaeological digs to discover the real city of Troy."

He made a circling motion with his hand as if to say, *Obviously. Get on with it,* so I did.

"I'm studying how various places in Great Britain lay claim to Arthur."

Our server appeared to clear the dishes. "But Glastonbury was Avalon. There's no question about that," he said, referring to the legendary castle where King Arthur was taken after his last battle.

"Well, Tintagel in Cornwall also claims to be Avalon," I said, "And—"

Before I could explain the theory that Joseph of Arimathea never came to Britain, making Arthur way off track with his pursuit of the Holy Grail, Simon kicked me under the table.

"Ow."

Joseph and the Grail may have gone to Esseda in modern-day Turkey to a fortress called Britium, thus the confusion. But I heeded Simon's warning to be quiet.

"Everyone knows Cornwall wanted something important, so they tried to take Arthur from us. But Arthur was buried at Glastonbury," the server said with a passion I didn't understand. It's not like I went around Arizona defending jackalopes or thunderbirds.

He leaned forward threateningly. "And don't you Yanks forget it."

# Chapter Three: Epic Fail

I didn't know what to react to first—the server's vehemence or being called a Yank.

Turning to Simon, I thrust my chin at him, willing him to explain. "Arthur is no legend."

"Well," I said, about to spew facts from my research that there probably was a warrior who fought the Romans and defended Britain, that morphed into the Arthurian legend.

Then stopped. That visceral reaction of our server had proved the power of myth in history.

"Maybe I should change my thesis to focus on the importance of legend."

"Perhaps," Simon agreed and jerked his head toward the exit. I gathered my things, and we walked downstairs into the fresh air. "So?"

"I don't want to think about it," I said, understanding that he wanted me to talk about the knight at the Chalice Well.

"And, yet."

"Fine. It was horrible. He just floated there, a broadsword sticking out like Excalibur in a stone." I shuddered.

The sword, glinting in a shaft of light, should have been displayed behind glass.

The image reminded me that knives were illegal in England. Edward had gotten me a Swiss Army Jetsetter with all the tools, but no blade. "It will be a clue, though," I said. The draw of solving a crime lessened the impact of finding a body. It was a perfect distraction. "There can't be many swords."

"I don't see why not. They're quite legal."

Staring, open-mouthed again, I processed the information. "So, anything three inches long threatens national security, but three feet of honed tempered steel is a-okay?"

He shrugged. Again.

"You know what? Lily saw him first, and I want to stay out of it," I claimed, despite the pang of regret I felt when I said it. Toughening my resolve, I added, "Every time I try to help, I get in trouble. I'm going to keep my head down and do schoolwork."

"A good plan," he said with a knowing smirk. He enjoyed a good mystery as well. Holding his arm out to his car, I headed toward it. "Edward asked me to convey you safely home."

"Thanks, buddy."

Sighing dramatically at my Americanism, he asked, "How many classes do you have?"

"Two right now, and I'll have two more in the second half of the semester. I love this one I'm doing the Arthur paper for. The other is Earth Science or something." I thought knowing a little about geology might be helpful on digs, but I checked the assignments, and they were all boring essays.

Parking on Greenway Lane, Simon got out of the car to walk me to the door of Ash Tree Cottage. I loved having a room in a house with a name.

"I can make it through the gate," I told him.

"Edward insisted."

It was my turn to sigh.

"You've had mishaps before," Simon reminded me.

The memory of a crazy man threatening me, the Priestlys, and Roderick the Rabbit inside this very gate sideswiped me, and I stumbled. Simon placed a hand under my arm, steadying me.

The problem with compartmentalizing emotions about bad things is that sometimes they pop out and ambush me when I don't expect them.

Stuffing that experience and the image of the knight back into dark boxes in the corner of my mind, I assured him, "I'm okay."

"Hmm."

"No, really," I insisted, trying to convince myself. "But, thanks." As he left,

I punched him gently on the shoulder, treating him like the brother I never had.

Scents of Meryl's freshly baked bread greeted me when I opened the door. The multigrain seed loaf smelled safe, comforting, and like home.

Tears stung my eyes. I loved this place and this wonderful couple who invited me into their family.

I'd put them in danger before, although technically not my fault. It's not like I invited the deranged druid to invade the sanctity of the garden.

My impending confession of having found another body froze me in my tracks. What if someone else found out where I lived and came after me?

On the other hand, why would a murderer leave a body in such a public place if they didn't want lots of people to find it? I have no connection to the event, other than as a witness. And the second witness, since Lily saw him first. No problem.

"There you are," Roger said from the top of the first flight of stairs.

"Is that her, darling?" Meryl called from the kitchen down the hall.

"Yes, yes. She seems to be cowering in the boot room."

Realizing I still clutched the doorknob between what I would call a mudroom and the Priestlys' entryway, I closed the door.

Meryl bustled through the dining room as Roger descended, and they engulfed me in hugs.

"Edward phoned to let us know of your latest adventure, as it were," Meryl said.

"You do lead an exciting life."

I lost it. Sobs shook my frame as the carefully buried trauma surfaced, begging for solace. Meryl mothered me while Roger made tea.

Shuffling me onto their Queen Anne-style living room, they cooed and fussed until I settled.

Teacup in hand, I gulped air a few times before taking a sip.

"Wow, sorry," I said. "That came out of nowhere."

"Emotions are bigger in a small space. Release them, and they become manageable."

So much for stuffing trauma into the dark recesses of my mind.

"That's so true," I said to Meryl. "I never thought of it that way."

Smiling warmly, she said, "I'm sure your mother said it to you, too. But my daughters never heard it when I said it to them."

Laughing, I thought of how I never let my mom, a font of knowledge and sage advice, believe that I was listening.

"Dinner is in forty-five minutes," she said, pushing up from the white, jacquard couch.

I endeavored not to spill my tea on the upholstery.

The Priestlys told me that I was responsible for all my food when I first applied to stay in the top-story room of their home. Since then, they've invited me, and often my friends, to join them for every meal.

"Let me know if you need help," I hollered after her before climbing the two flights of stairs to my very own personal princess tower.

The house, built into the slope of a hill, had four stories, including a basement and my room at the top. Opening the window, I crawled onto the roof, one story above the road to one side and rising over the ash tree that dominated the garden and a ravine on the other.

The view, so different from Arizona's wide open expanses of tans and reds, never failed to lift my spirits. After taking a deep breath, I crawled back inside and got to work on my King Arthur paper.

"School, not solving murders," I said out loud, and set to work.

Since the King Arthur festival spilled out of the abbey's grounds, I never felt any connection to the legend. Much as the thought of returning turned my stomach, I should experience the area properly.

Again, tamping down unwanted emotions, I swiped through my photos. On our walk from the bus station, I snapped a picture of a wizard, Merlin, I supposed, complete with a pointy hat and a blue robe covered with stars.

Through the gates, we delighted in the number of white, round tents dotting the abbey grounds.

Arthur's tomb was more difficult to see, as everyone at the Fayre crowded around it in droves. When I finally got a peek, it was just a wooden sign saying the monks moved the body in 1539.

Continuing to swipe, my shoulders relaxed as the delightful memories of the morning pushed the frightful images of the afternoon out of my mind.

Something in one of the pictures caught my attention. Reversing direction, I carefully reviewed each photo. Shortly before we left, Lily went to a stall to buy a souvenir, and I raised my phone above my head and turned in a circle, taking a dozen shots of jousting, axe-throwing, and archery. In one image was a man who looked like Detective Inspector Parikh.

"No wonder he didn't answer his phone," I said.

Although if he knew Edward was coming to see me in Glastonbury, and he was there anyway, why didn't he offer to drive?

Odd.

"Not important," I reminded myself. It was Parikh's day off, so he didn't need to spend it with his constable or the constable's girlfriend. I imagined that the detective had a life outside of police work, but I had never seen it.

Refocusing on school, my priority as I had a student visa, I made outlines in my notebook for the three projects in my Legends and History course.

I'd finish my essay by discussing the various parts of Britain that claimed King Arthur as their own. But, I would not mention that fact to anyone in Somerset now that I knew how important Glastonbury as home to Arthur was to the locals.

The next project would involve the importance of legend to cultural heritage, as evidenced by our server's reaction when I mentioned Cornwall. I'd need to do more research, and I wondered if Father Michael from the Bath Abbey had any information. It would be fun to have him help me with homework, instead of always asking for my best friend Tori Gonzalez, who was back in the States getting a Religious Studies degree to appease her very Catholic abuela.

The criteria for the final included a practical aspect. "Armor?" I mused. *Or weapons like broadswords*, my mind suggested unhelpfully.

Puffing out air, I moved to my science course. The first essay was so easy I could have done it in my sleep. I knocked out notes for the second one, then turned on my computer to start typing.

Before I got far, I heard Meryl calling, and I scampered downstairs for dinner.

"How are you doing, dear?"

"Better, thank you," I said, carrying Brussels sprouts to the pass-through window between the kitchen and the dining room.

A fish pie came next, and I eyed it warily. Tempe didn't have much seafood, and when we did, it wasn't great.

However, Meryl never steered me wrong, so I tried it. Flakey, buttery crust covered fresh white meat, rich with herbs and a hint of cream.

"This is amazing," I said.

Roger made muffled sounds of agreement as he happily chewed.

Finishing our meal, we moved to the living room for afters: a Bakewell tart. Filled with raspberries and marzipan, I relished the unique combination. At home, my mom and I skipped dessert except for special occasions when we drove to Scottsdale for gelato.

"Would you care to talk about it?" Roger asked gently. A minister from a church down the hill, Roger, possessed calm compassion. His height and thick silver hair commanded respect, but during my stay, I discovered a strong sense of goofiness in him.

My head wobbled about in a waffling motion. "I'm not sure," I admitted.

"Don't pressure the girl, Roger."

"No, it's okay. Like you said earlier, if I keep it inside, it might grow."

After explaining the ordeal, Roger and Meryl looked contemplative. They never took events at face value but dug, searching for deeper meaning.

"What do you think, my dear?" Roger asked Meryl. He often sought her advice and appreciated her insights.

"Do you know anything about the victim?"

Shaking my head, I said, "No. The detective asked us to leave after the constables took our statements. He could have been local, but I heard a lot of accents at the festival."

"What are you thinking?" Roger prompted.

"It's symbolic, isn't it?" Meryl continued. "The sword, in a knight, in the waters of the Chalice Well."

"A sacrifice, perhaps?"

"That doesn't fit in with the Christian heritage," I offered. Having recently interacted with Druids, I acquired a lot of knowledge about sacrifices. Mostly, that the Druids didn't do them. Or Christians, for that matter.

"A strategic move, perhaps," Meryl said, losing me.

Nodding, Roger said, "Chess. Placing a knight in a sacrifice position provides cover for the pieces behind it."

As we cleared the table, Roger described chess ploys and gambits. I knew how the pieces moved, but I always got too caught up in mathematical possibilities to finish a game.

Brain full of theories about something I promised myself to forget, I headed upstairs to my computer.

After transferring my written outlines into documents, I opened my Learning Management System. The LMS portal housed the lectures and reading materials for the course and provided drop boxes for submitting assignments.

The dashboard had important announcements, links to the courses, and also displayed my current grades.

In red, my Earth Science grade displayed fifty-eight percent.

My chest clenched in panic.

Flashing, my inbox included one message.

'Progress Status," the subject line stated menacingly.

'In light of your failing status in Earth Science, both your scholarship and continued acceptance in this major are in jeopardy.'

# Chapter Four: Sherlock Holmes

"What?" I shouted at the computer screen. How did I go from an honor student to failing, losing my scholarship, and getting kicked out of the program?

My ability to handle problems was completely and utterly depleted.

Without checking for time differences, I called my best friend Tori from the computer's app.

"The great thing about my internship is that we're only five hours different now," she opened, not bothering with traditional greetings.

Seeing her calm face and sparkling dark eyes, I felt a tug of guilt for calling with my problems and not to see how she was doing.

"How is DC? Does Scott miss you yet?"

Scott, Tori's high school boyfriend, had a controlling streak that I could do without, but he calmed down enough to allow Tori to spend a semester away.

"He's flying out this weekend. Washington is amazing but very gray. Like, gray trees, gray bushes, gray buildings. Also, not enough sky." She paused, squinted, and rubbed a hand over her face. "Did you find another body?"

"Yes, but that's not important right now. And I really do want to hear about your internship."

"First off, how on earth do you do that? Second, what could possibly be more important? And, third, as much as I want to tell you all about it, I feel a *but* coming."

"But, what the actual heck is up with my science class?" I blurted.

"Seriously?"

"I'm failing!" I cried. The importance of the situation needed emphasis.

My cell dinged with a message from Samantha Niven, or Sam, my mentor and former boss at the Roman Baths. I ignored it.

"Did you read the grading to see why?"

Refusing to make eye contact, I shook my head no.

Ever patient, Tori stared into the camera, willing me to open the assignment.

"Fine," I said, clicking on it. The hideous twenty-five percent score that lowered my overall grade to failing glared at me. I stuck my tongue out at it.

"What did I do?" Tori said, reacting to the gesture.

"Sorry. That was meant for the stupid grade." I squinted at the comment. "It says, 'Under word count,' but that can't be right because I double-checked it twice, and I'm over by forty words." My breath sped up.

"Do not panic." The sharpness in Tori's voice cut into me.

"But—"

"I know you've never failed anything ever, except for the one time you got a C on a math test and I had to take you to the school nurse."

"You don't have Dr. Heather McGuire, Shakespeare Professor and scholar, as your mother." My mom was awesome, but having a PhD for a parent put a lot of pressure on me to succeed, particularly since she wasn't crazy about my chosen field. The fact that I excelled in school played a huge role in her support of me moving to England in my sophomore year.

"I'm pretty sure if I failed an assignment, my mom would call your mom, and Heather would rain fury on me," Tori reminded me.

"True," I said, my breath slowing.

"Our moms expect brilliance, and we will deliver."

"If you say so." I sighed, but felt better knowing we could fix this together.

"I do," she said, smiling. "Did you read the syllabus?"

"Well, yeah, for the due dates."

"Look to see if there is an instructor comment."

Scrolling to the bottom of the four-page document, after the course catalog description, lurked the note in question.

"It's just a bunch of the adjunct's writing credits in scholarly journals," I said as I scanned. "Wait. OMG. I quote, 'All papers and discussion posts have a 1000-word limit even if the assignment says less.' And again, I say, OMG."

"Part-time faculty aren't allowed to change the courses, so they add things to the syllabus. It happened to me once. Withdraw from the class and find a better one next term."

"You lived through that nightmare and didn't tell me?" I asked, now able to be compassionate since my problem was potentially fixable. "I'm a crap bestie sometimes."

She brushed away my comment with her hand. "It's when Scott was in his jealous phase. He wanted to be my everything."

*And keep you away from your friends,* I thought. He was making huge strides with his controlling nature, so I said, "Even though he's perfect now."

"He is," she said with a smile that didn't quite reach her eyes. "So, body?" she asked, before I could delve into the look.

"Not my fault."

"Never is."

"This time, I didn't even see it first; Lily did."

She widened her already large brown eyes, willing me to continue.

"It was a knight in a pool of water at Glastonbury."

Blinking, she took in the description and knit her brows together in confusion.

I continued, "We went to see King Arthur. There was a reenactment, and one of the knights wound up at the Chalice Well Garden with a broadsword in his chest." I trembled, the image invading my mind in technicolor.

"That's weird and disturbing." With her uncanny ability to always know when to distract me, she added, "Hey, you finally left the Cotswolds."

Shaking my head, I said, "No, Glastonbury is still in Somerset."

Tori rolled her eyes. "Not everything in Somerset is in the Cotswolds and vice versa. They extend almost all the way to Stratford-Upon-Avon."

"How do you know more about where I am than I do?"

"I'm better at maps," she said, typing.

Pretty much everyone was better at reading maps, so I turned my attention to what she was searching for on her computer.

"Are you looking at Sherlock stories with knights?" I asked.

Because the first unsettling thing I found in England was a severed human ear that reminded me of a Holmes story, we looked for help from Doyle as a way to make sense of things.

"I am, and there aren't. Doyle was knighted, though."

"A few centuries too late to coincide with my Arthurian discovery," I said. "Meryl and Roger thought it might have to do with chess."

"Ah ha! *The Adventure of the Retired Colourman* has chess in it," Tori said, typing furiously.

"What's a colourman?"

"Focus."

"Fine. Anything useful in the synopsis?" I asked as I watched her eyes scan across the screen.

"Holmes thinks chess players have scheming minds."

"Great. That's all we need—a particularly clever villain."

The conversation derailed me from spinning out of control, and I was able to ask about Tori's adventures.

She regaled me with stories of Washington, D.C. Her internship at the Embassy of Mexico and the Mexican Cultural Institute allowed her to toggle between public administration and translation duties. Along with her degree in religious studies, Tori planned on a second, more practical major, but hadn't landed on which yet. This experience let her practice.

Listening to her tales calmed my mind, and when we said our goodbyes, I was motivated to get things done.

Step one, drop the science course before it ruined my GPA.

Step two, read *The Adventure of the Retired Colourman,* since I now only had to deal with one class, and it might offer a chess-based clue.

Not that I was planning on solving what happened to the knight, but because knowing more might help with closure for me. The excuse to waste time sounded lame.

Step three, return the text from Sam at the Roman Baths.

Honestly, step three sounded easiest, so I started there.

'I miss your smilin' eyes, I do!' Sam's thick Irish accent came through, even in instant message form. 'Can you help me interview the intern applicants tomorrow?'

Thrilled and honored to be asked, I leaped at the chance. 'What time?'

'9:00 a.m.'

Grateful for the distraction, I made a list of questions to ask the candidates. I also considered creating a specific job description for the new interns to follow.

Now that I was a part of Dr. Daniels' dig team, I had the experience to select a suitable replacement for my former position.

* * *

Even though I adored the walk down from Bear Flats to the Baths, the January weather was unpredictable, so I caught a ride with Roger. The Manvers Street Church, where he served as minister, was only a couple of blocks from the Bath Abbey Square and the entrance to the Roman Baths.

Confirming my choice, the sky opened up, and rain fell in sheets. With the windshield wipers working frantically, Roger navigated the streets and zipped to the drop-off/pick-up zone by the Abbey Hotel. We sat for a few minutes, hoping for a break in the weather, but no luck.

I jumped out of the car with a wave and splashed to the Georgian building housing the Roman Baths. Unassuming from the square, once inside the building, a magnificent window-lined white plaster dome welcomed visitors.

Bypassing the lines, I ducked into the Oversight Office to find Simon waiting with Sam.

"You're late," Simon commented in what I now knew was his ritual greeting no matter the time. I winked, taking a seat opposite him and behind Sam.

"You'll be blurred so the interviewees can't see ye."

Disappointed at not having a more active role in the process, I turned to Simon. "Did you sit in on my interview?"

He nodded.

"You recommended me?" I asked, surprised, considering he did his best to sabotage my success when I started.

He shook his head and answered, "Outvoted." At my confusion, he added, "Cliff, rest him, had a say as well. I believe he worded it, 'The fit ginger.'"

"That he did," Sam confirmed.

Wringing water from my strawberry-blonde, not ginger ponytail, I scowled. Not only did my looks, not my qualifications, help land me the internship, but now my pride at being asked to participate in the selection process had greatly diminished.

"Chin up, old girl," Simon said fondly. "I was happy to be proven wrong about you."

Possibly the nicest thing Simon had ever said to me, I almost teared up as Sam hit the call button on the first interview.

A French guy from Paris had all the charm of a week-old baguette. After our miserable experience with the French interns at Chedworth Roman Villa, none of us included him on our list of possibilities.

The next was competent but painfully shy and barely audible. "I can't see her doing tours," I commented to general agreement.

A couple more made it to my possible list before Sam announced the final candidate. Yvette O'Leary from Galway came onto the screen, bursting with Irish personality.

"Sam, me darlin'! How's your mum?"

Cutting my eyes to Simon while Sam and Yvette caught up on family news, I mouthed, "Related?"

A brief nod, and we were brought back to the interview.

"Cousin Sam has someone hidin' in the background, so she does. Trying to trip me, are ye?" Yvette asked.

I thought Sam's accent was thick, but it couldn't hold a candle to Yvette's.

"Let me introduce ye to me team," Sam said, removing the blur setting on the conferencing software.

After introductions, Yvette said, "The famous Lord Pacock, Earl of Comer. Holy Mother of all that's holy. I wish I hadn't asked. Now I'm all nervous. Sweatin' like a nun in a cucumber patch, I am."

The rest of the interview was peppered with similar phrases, and by the time we wrapped up, my sides hurt from giggling.

A foregone conclusion, Yvette was offered the internship and accepted. She would join us in two weeks.

With a smile, I headed to the elevator to the Undercroft. I sent a quick text to Edward, letting him know I'd be offline since no signal reached the site under the streets of Bath.

As an intern last semester, I had been honored to sift debris brought out from the dig. I had a cozy sifting table in the utility stairwell, and Sam and Lady Vivian added a lamp and a stuffed chair for breaks.

Now that I was counted among the official employees of the archaeological team, I moved away from sifting, the job shifting to one of the volunteers. I didn't know what I'd be doing. Holding onto Yvette's enthusiasm and joy, I approached Dr. Daniels.

"Yes?" he asked, as if he'd never seen me before.

*Honestly?* He joined us for drinks on New Year's Eve. Geez.

"Howdy," I said with a broad smile. If you wanted someone to remember you're an American, go with Texan.

"Ah, yes, miss, uh. The American."

"Maddie McGuire," I supplied, and he nodded.

"That's right," he said as though he were quizzing me on my name.

The archetypal absent-minded professor, Dr. Daniels, at least no longer mistook me for Lily and ordered tea.

"We will miss your keen eye on the sifting table," he said, and I immediately forgave him for every time he forgot my name.

"Uh, Matt," he called over his shoulder to a thirty-something man on the team.

"Marcus, sir," the man responded without a hint of exasperation.

"This is, uh?" he flapped a hand in my direction, and Marcus and I took over the introductions.

"Right-o, Maddie. You'll be upstairs, cleaning and photographing. We saw your pictures of the Roman coins at Chedworth. Fine work."

"Thank you," I said slowly, processing the information. I'd hoped to dig on the site, but because of classes, my hours for the team were less than last term. Maybe they only permitted full-time team members to brush away layer after layer of ancient dirt, each with its own story.

"I'll get you settled. Back in a mo, Doctor," Marcus added as we strolled to the elevator.

Cleaning artifacts and bits of stone from the discovery would provide an amazing experience. Another skill to add to my growing resume. I nodded, happy with my conclusion.

"And thanks for taking the time to show me around," I remembered to tell Marcus.

"My pleasure. I admit to being a bit jealous. Revealing the intricacies of a tesserae is my favorite part of the job."

This assignment sounded better and better. As we traveled up to the lab, one level above the street, excitement bubbled in me.

Marcus showed me the cleaning room and the photography area, which included some illustrations by Lady Gwendolyn De Valence, also known as Simon's fiancée, Dolly. Exquisite, like everything she did, Dolly's drawings captured the essence of the pieces as well as their details.

Just as Marcus opened a cabinet with toothbrushes, skewers, and sponges, his phone rang.

"Yes, sir…Marcus, actually…" He rolled his eyes. "I took Maddie to the cleaning lab… McGuire, the American…yes…yes…be right there."

"Dr. Daniels?" I asked.

"He really is quite brilliant."

Grinning, I said, "I've seen flashes of it. He'll learn our names someday."

"Listen, you just look around for today, and I'll train you formally tomorrow. Right? Right."

Without waiting for an answer, Marcus hustled away.

Carte blanche to poke in cabinets sounded alright by me, but it only took twenty minutes to see everything.

"Only three and a half hours to go 'til I'm off," I said, plopping into a chair and letting Edward know my current job included connectivity.

After only two games of solitaire, I decided to head downstairs to see if

Sam needed any help, but I didn't get very far.

To my delight, Edward tapped on the hallway window and came through the door.

Pale, he stood stiffly.

Greeting him, I invited him to sit. The last time he looked this emotionless was when I'd been questioned by DI Parikh for murder. Not a good look for a constable to be dating a felon.

I hoped that whatever had him so intense this time didn't involve me. "What's happened? Is James okay?" I asked, referring to his former gangland brother who hadn't completely accepted his new life on the straight and narrow.

"James is good." The posh accent informed me that whatever he wanted to tell me had to do with work. The way his jaw clenched indicated he kept a lid on his emotions.

"What happened?" I prompted.

"DI Parikh," Edward began, stony-faced, but didn't continue.

Police in the UK didn't have to contend with open carry gun issues like in Arizona, but they still encountered plenty of danger.

Waiting isn't something I'm good at. I fought back a torrent of questions so as not to interrupt.

It seemed like an eternity before Edward spoke.

"Detective Inspector Parikh has been arrested for the murder of the knight."

# Chapter Five: Wait, What?

Sure I heard Edward's declaration about DI Parikh wrong, I shook my head. "Wait, what? That can't be right. Have you seen him? What's he saying? Does he have a good lawyer? What does he need?"

"He says he's not guilty and the evidence will prove his innocence." Edward's expression gave nothing away.

Still, I detected a hint of something in his voice. Skepticism, maybe.

"What evidence do they have?" I asked.

He finally looked me in the eye, and I hunched my shoulders, retracting the question. I knew he wouldn't tell me.

"It's a mistake," I asserted.

"What if it's not?"

I couldn't believe what I was hearing. "You know it is," I said.

While DCI Bray worked with the Edinburgh police to get Edward vetted and started with the force in Bath, DI Parikh mentored Edward, ensuring his success. Parikh shepherded his transfer from the local constabulary to the Major Crimes Investigation Team.

"How could you doubt it?" I continued, my ire growing. "I mean..." Clenching my fists, I counted to five.

Then, ten.

Then, I counted by perfect squares until the rant spooling in my brain uncoiled. The last thing Edward needed was for me to lose it.

My fingers relaxed, and I scooted back, took his hands, and studied him. The short waves of his black hair stuck out at odd angles. Dark circles ringed his intense brown eyes.

I always counted on Edward to have everything under control. Never one to share his emotions, he kept a tight rein on anything that betrayed his thoughts.

In contrast, my easily read, cartoon-level expressive face displayed everything going through my mind. Including annoyance at his lack of outrage at this situation.

Which, admittedly, wasn't helping.

Drawing on my middle school acting lessons, I recalled the title role in *The Ice Queen* and channeled her calm, take-charge demeanor.

"You will tell me what you think happened. Do it now."

Edward's face twitched in an almost smile.

Maybe I should dial back the Ice Queen.

"Sorry. But we are going to figure this out. What was the proof?"

"Maddie, me love, you know I can't discuss an active case with you."

"And why not?" I countered. "You're not on the case. That jackeen Douglass is." I still didn't know what the Irish word meant, but it felt right to use it then. "Parikh needs all the assistance he can get."

Ever the rule follower, Edward drew his lips into a thin line. They might as well have had a zipper.

What he needed was a lesson in the artful disregard of guidelines.

"During the last case, didn't Parikh himself say I could be included?"

A slight nod.

"And didn't I help?" If by "help" I meant getting caught by a psychopath and thereby identifying the killer, then yes, I helped.

Edward sighed.

"No one on the force understands Parikh better than you, so you're duty-bound to investigate."

He shook his head, his expression defeated.

Could he possibly believe Parikh was guilty?

Sweeping an arm around the empty lab, I said, "I'm stuck here for three more hours, and no one has trained me. I'm bored. Give me a task."

His crooked smile appeared.

"It beats moping," I suggested.

"I will not reveal police evidence or details you shouldn't have," he warned.

I slapped on a neutral expression so my triumph wouldn't show.

"Don't gloat," he added.

Reviewing the cabinet contents in my mind, I went to the drawer with graph paper and mechanical pencils. "Okay, let's start with a timeline. What do we know about the knight?"

"Maddie."

A single word was all it took to remind me that he wouldn't voluntarily divulge police procedures. Yet.

"Scratch that. What do we know about Parikh's movements?"

Edward shrugged.

"Oh, come on. He must have told you something off the record."

"Fine," he said in a fairly good imitation of me. "DI Parikh overslept."

"Honestly? Why won't you tell me anything? Why aren't you calling in the cavalry to protect him? You think he's guilty, I can tell by the way you're not saying anything. I got more out of you last time, but now that it's personal, you've clammed up. I don't understand."

Despite the personal attacks, Edward let my rant wind down.

"Madeline McGuire, you are a force of nature, to be sure. Please, let this one go."

Not ready to admit defeat, I drew a timeline in perfect, even chunks, starting at 5:00 a.m., and added 'asleep.'

"What time does Parikh normally wake up?"

Palm up, Edward gave me a 'How should I know?' look.

"Estimate," I suggested.

"Six."

At six, I wrote, 'overslept.'

"Did he say when he woke up?"

Edward shook his head. "Maddie—"

"Why didn't he go to work that day?"

No response.

As a responsible grownup, I figured Parikh would be out the door early. I put 'left' on the 8:00 a.m. slot on the line with a question mark after it.

"Let's focus on what he did next. Even if he didn't work, he must have gone to the station to leave you keys."

My matter-of-fact manner did not extract facts from Edward. I soldiered on.

Edward's expression gave away absolutely no information.

The more stoic he became, the more determined I got. Deep in Edward dwelled violence, which he channeled into a dedication to make something of himself. Why didn't he want to use that now?

Well, if he wasn't willing to fight for his mentor, I was. We needed a more exact timeline and Parikh's movements. I would keep at it until something clicked.

"When did you get your email giving you the day off?"

"You have to let this go. These people are dangerous."

I held up my hands. "So? It's not like I'm going to go traipsing into their lair and dragging them down to the station. I just want to help."

"Help by staying out of it."

Ignoring him, I went back to my timeline. "What time did you get the email giving you the day off?"

He narrowed his eyes at me.

"It's not evidence," I argued. "I'm just asking for information from my boyfriend, which has already been partially revealed."

Checking his cell, Edward scrolled and then handed it to me.

The names on the message were correct, but I checked the DI's to see the address just in case it was a fake. Rather than coming from a police.uk domain, Parikh's email originated from Gmail.

"This isn't from his work address," I said, returning the phone.

After glancing at it, Edward confirmed, "Aye, but it is his personal one."

"You're sure? Double-check it. Is it all spelled right?"

He took the cell back and nodded.

"But that's odd, isn't it? Parikh strikes me as a by-the-book kind of guy."

The DI's methodical nature made him an excellent detective, able to follow clues down multiple branches.

"Aye, that he is." Gently, Edward laid his hand on mine. "Maddie, enough.

Leave it."

"But—"

"Don't you have a paper you should be working on? Keeping your visa should be your priority."

Edward echoing my thoughts from last night only annoyed me. "Then why did you give me the email information?"

After closing his eyes for a moment, he opened them with renewed intensity. "Because I had already told you about it, ye stubborn…"

He trailed off, no doubt editing a stream of Scottish words I probably didn't want translated.

Straightening, he said, "DI Parikh asked me to give you a message."

"Wait, what?" I said again. "Why didn't you open with this? How could you keep vital information from me?" I readied my pencil to make an exact copy of what could be a clue. "What did he say? Exactly."

Edward cleared his throat. "Please check on Fred as I am unable to do so this week."

"Fred?" I asked, confused. The only Fred I knew was a retired taxi driver who liked to spout odd facts to anyone walking by. "The elderly gentleman who hangs out at The Crystal Palace?"

Edward agreed. "Fred mentioned you to Parikh a couple of times."

"What does check mean?" I asked, suddenly concerned that I didn't have the necessary skills.

"Don't panic. Fred just needs someone to have a good chat with once or twice a week. Give the bartenders a break."

"Oh, well, that's sweet. So, not at his house."

"No," Edward said. "Stop by the pub."

Police orders to hang out in a bar. What would my mom say? I grinned, thinking that I wouldn't give her this little tidbit of information. When I remembered that the order was because DI Parikh was behind bars, the grin faded.

"And that, me lovely, is plenty to keep you busy." Standing, he said, "I have a case. Promise me you'll let this go."

Flipping the timeline over, I glanced up with what I hoped was an agreeable expression.

Edward opened his mouth, but was interrupted before he could insist.

"Miss Madeline?" Marcus had appeared without me noticing.

"Huh? Oh, hi." Impressive response while I was hanging out with my boyfriend at work. Just the kind of thing I wanted to get back to my new boss. Improvising, I said, "I had a question about caliper calibration. Are artifact measurements taken at every stage of cleaning or only after?"

"Calipers?"

Guessing his confusion came from the fact that I didn't see such a tool in the lab, I said, "To measure the finds."

"Right, of course. This way. Rulers are with the photography equipment."

Marcus led me to a cabinet while Edward slipped down the stairs before I introduced him. Or agreed to his request. Probably for the best.

My mind wandered until Marcus opened a wide, shallow drawer with various rulers and explained what to do. "Put the ruler and the artifact on the grid paper and photograph them on one page." Pointing to a pile of what looked like boxes of rubble to the untrained eye, he said, "Start by taking pictures of those."

"One shard per shot?" I asked, noting that most of the pieces looked like fragments of tesserae, a ceramic base with a blue glaze.

"They came from different layers and grid sections, as indicated by the box's label. Keep layers together."

During a dig, dirt is removed horizontally, in layers. A layer is defined by the materials around it. In the Roman Baths, many layers consist of foundation components used by subsequent residents. Below that, dirt and sometimes mineral deposits.

Marcus showed me the standard label for the grid paper, including the artifact's original location, date, and photographer, and then left me to take pictures.

Unlike sifting through kilos of debris, taking pictures allowed me to touch honest-to-goodness ancient Roman remnants. I couldn't help but try and piece the fragments together in my head to form a full tile.

Fascinated by the tiny shards of history, I managed to forget DI Parikh's arrest, and I lost track of time.

A knock at the door pulled me back to the present.

Sam and Simon stood at the entry.

"More interesting than filing, is it?" Sam asked.

Not wanting to admit the number of times I played a game or fell asleep while transferring the Oversight Office records from paper to digital, I changed the subject.

"What time is it?"

"I believe you Americans would say, 'Quittin' time,'" Simon said, coming in and helping me stow the materials for easy access the next day.

"Join us for a pint, Maddie, me darlin' girl," Sam said.

"Okay. Can we go to The Crystal Palace?" I asked, figuring I could check in with Fred once we were done. I snatched my cell off the desk and stuffed it into my jeans jacket pocket.

Resistance was futile in the face of an after-work beer. We strolled around the corner to the Abbey Green, headed to the pub, ordered half-pints of ale at the bar, and settled at a table near the fireplace, which was now filled with candles.

"Have ye learned anything new?" Sam asked.

I assumed the question was about finding a body and not about archaeology.

"DI Parikh was arrested," I said, my voice dull. I didn't add that Edward showed signs of believing the detective was guilty.

After shock and disbelief were processed, Simon asked, "What did he say?"

"Edward told me to stay out of it, but I managed to get a couple of facts. I've started a timeline of events, but I didn't get very far."

Sam and I continued to chat while Simon pulled out his phone and made a call.

"Aunt Viv, I need a favor."

# Chapter Six: The Big Guns

Sipping our drinks, Sam and I listened to Simon as he spoke to his aunt, Lady Vivian, Dowager Duchess of Comer.

The first time I found a body, a ridiculous statement that no one should ever have to make, Simon and Lady Vivian swooped in to handle the press and, to my surprise, the police. The aristocracy's reach far outstripped the good-old-boy network in the US.

Today, Simon used those connections to provide help without my asking. A warm glow of gratitude bubbled up in me. Squelching the impulse to thank him, I hid my smile behind my beer.

Only having access to his side of the conversation, I deduced that his aunt would make arrangements to visit Detective Inspector Parikh. Simon had called in the big guns.

When he disconnected, he said, "Give Aunt Viv a list of questions. She will find a way to get the information you need."

"Right-o," I said in my horrible British accent.

"Do be quiet," Simon responded.

"We need to discuss the candidates," Sam announced.

"Why? I thought Yvette started in two weeks."

Sam nodded but said, "Aye, that she is. But since she's my first cousin once removed, I need you two to fill out a form that says we aren't showing favoritism."

"I'm totally showing it. She was my favorite," I said.

"A darlin' girl, to be sure."

"Me or her?"

"Both," Sam said, raising a glass in a toast.

With that out of the way, Simon asked, "What shall we have Aunt Viv ask?"

My initial pleasure at Simon's involvement turned to suspicion. "Why are you being so helpful?"

He looked down his nose at me.

Unblinking, I stared back until he slumped.

"Wedding plans. They are relentless. Dolly had me download an app to keep track of tasks." He leaned toward me. "An app," he repeated, sounding appalled.

"That's a perfect idea to keep things straight. What's the problem?"

When Simon and Dolly first announced their engagement, I pictured a beautifully appointed small ceremony at the De Valence Medispa, which Dolly owned and managed. But no. This was to be a grand affair instead.

Simon handed me his phone. The app's checklist loomed.

Looking over the admittedly relentless list, I asked, "Where's Cheltenham?" The name came up next to booking hotels for guests.

"North of Gloucester."

"A spa town, Regency era. You'd like it," Sam added.

"That's what Bath is. Why not have it here?" Lady Vivian had a flat in the famous Royal Crescent, and Simon, steadfastly private, had one somewhere.

"Because Bath does not have Sudeley."

"What's Sudeley?"

"A castle."

"You're kidding me." It's one thing to know actual lords and ladies. It's another thing to think they needed a castle for a wedding. The only castle in Arizona was a cliff dwelling.

"Alas, no," Simon sighed. "Dolly is friends with the family. Ancient ties and all."

In the face of overwhelming British history, I agreed with Simon's plan of avoidance. "Yeah, right. What we need from Lady Vivian," I said as Simon took notes, "ask Parikh for a timeline of his movements starting with oversleeping and where he was during the, uh, time in question."

The picture I found last night flashed unbidden into my thoughts.

Someone who looked very much like DI Parikh had been at Glastonbury during the time of the murder. Rather than revealing that piece of damning information, I stared at my beer.

I needed to examine the photo more closely to confirm that the man had Parikh's dark hair and olive skin, glasses, and a neatly trimmed beard. But a second look could prove me wrong. No need to mention it until I was sure.

Withholding details niggled at me. My friends were trustworthy and had helped me through some awful situations. But Edward's seeming acceptance of Parikh's guilt held me in check. What if our combined brain power proved a verdict we didn't want?

For now, I'd keep it to myself.

"What aren't you telling us, me girl?" Sam asked.

I swiped a hand over my face. "Believe it or not, I've been getting better about not letting every emotion show."

The two chortled, and I hoped they would forget the question.

Based on their expressions, they didn't, but were gracious enough to let it drop, mostly because Simon got a call, and we transferred our attention to him.

"Yes, Aunt Viv?"

There's nothing more frustrating than wanting to eavesdrop on a conversation and only hearing a string of yeses. Sam and I pounced when he hung up.

"Don't keep us waiting, boy. What's the news?"

"What did she say?"

With deliberate, annoyingly slow movements, Simon stowed his cell and took a sip of ale.

I ground my teeth.

"DCI Bray will escort Lady Vivian to Parikh in the morning. She will also suggest a lawyer."

"I thought you used barristers over here," I said, having heard the term in a movie.

"Barristers are for family law, lawyers for criminal."

The word "criminal" gut-punched me. If ever there was a noun that did not describe the meticulous detective, it was that one. But then, why was Edward convinced of Parikh's guilt?

Shaking my head chased away some of the disquiet, but not all, so I changed the subject. We wouldn't get further until Simon's aunt got information out of Parikh.

Since broadswords were on my mind, I asked, "Other than the Beau Street Horde, there hasn't been much metal found in Bath. Why not?"

Archaeologists discovered the Beau Street Horde in 2008 when the Gainsborough Hotel, located next to the Roman Baths, added a swimming pool. The horde consisted of over 17,500 silver coins fused in a block. Unlike the gold coins we unearthed at Chedworth Roman Villa, which shone like the sun, the tarnished Beau Street Horde had been crammed into a box, causing them to tarnish. The wooden box later disintegrated.

"The curse tablets are metal," Simon pointed out, referring to the appeals townsfolk presented to Sulis Minerva to right wrongs. Or simply because a neighbor annoyed them. People haven't changed much.

"And the baths are lined with lead," Sam added.

The lead's reaction to sunlight gave the Great Bath its iconic green color. I knew this, but it wasn't what I was thinking about.

"Weapons and armor. Why aren't there any?" My question came out more forcefully than I intended, but knights and swords were on my mind. I hoped that if I understood more about them, I could protect myself from the onslaught of negative imagery.

Delicately, Sam said, "Bath's always been a spa town, Maddie. You wouldn't house an army here, would you?"

About to argue for the sake of it, I thought for a moment instead. Surrounded by rolling rises, Bath sported lovely views, but its valley position made it vulnerable. Quarries removed so much limestone that the hills were unstable. As a military location, it was a bust.

"No, I guess not."

My voice must have sounded defeated as Simon offered, "We do have our Viking sword."

"What? When were the Vikings here?" While researching my adopted town, I never came across any mention of a Viking invasion.

"They probably weren't. No one knows why the sword was here. It might have belonged to a medieval tourist."

"Not really relevant then, is it?" My mother would describe my tone as "waspish," and I regretted it. "Sorry. I'm a mess tonight."

Fortunately, Fred wandered into The Crystal Palace in the form of a perfect distraction, and I waved him over.

"Aye?" he asked, peering at me.

"Hello, Fred. Detective Inspector Parikh wanted me to tell you that he won't be visiting for the next couple of weeks or so," I said.

"Ah, my American friend," he said, removing his flat cap to reveal a fringe of fluffy white hair. "Why is that?"

"There's been a misunderstanding, and I'm afraid he's been arrested."

Fred's gasp of unbelief would have been comical if the situation weren't so awful. "Never in all my years did I meet a man so dedicated to protecting the public," he said, scrunching his hat and looking dismayed.

Simon jumped up and maneuvered Fred into a chair.

"I'm sure it will be fine," I said. Amazed at my inability to handle the situation with any kind of grace, I added, "It's okay."

His hand lashed out and gripped my wrist with a sudden ferocity. "You must get him free. See to it," Fred said.

Before I could agree, Edward walked in.

Pulling away from Fred, I asked, "Do you want me to get you something?" but Edward shook his head no.

"I came to see if you wanted me to walk you home."

"Yes, please," I said, working on making my responses more civil. "Sorry, everyone," I said again as I stood.

"See to it!" Fred's voice quavered with intensity.

"I will," I said to calm him down.

Sam got up to hug me. "It'll be alright," she said, then added, "I'll look into Roman armor and build a lesson for you. There's a resource in Chester."

As part of my internship last semester, Sam set aside time each week to tutor me on aspects of Roman archaeology. Her vast knowledge guided my understanding of the Romans. Happy that she planned on continuing the ritual until the new intern arrived, I thanked her.

As Edward and I navigated with cobblestones, cold wind swirled around. Huddling together, we headed up Manvers Street toward the train station. Over the Avon River and under the highway, we entered the park and climbed the steps to Bear Flats, all in silence.

Edward took my hand and lifted it, pressing his lips to my palm in a gentle kiss as we walked.

So many emotions crashed into my system. The thrill I always felt whenever Edward kissed me. Empathy for his situation. Plus, a healthy dose of frustration at being unable to do more to help.

I wanted to tell him it would be okay, but I didn't know if it would be. Until he told me why he was so quick to believe Parikh was guilty, I couldn't be sure of the outcome of this mess.

Not to mention that if the detective were convicted, it might reflect on Edward's career.

Unsure if the news would depress or excite him, I chose not to mention Lady Vivian's impending visit to DI Parikh. But it was the only thing I could think of, so the silence continued until we reached Greenway Lane and Ash Tree Cottage.

"Do you want to come in? Meryl always has extra food."

He drew me into his arms and held on tight. Without another word, he kissed me on the forehead, turned, and walked away.

With a sigh, I went in.

I greeted Meryl and told her I wanted to be alone, so I wouldn't join them for dinner. Between Parikh's arrest and Edward's reaction, I didn't trust myself to keep quiet and not wildly speculate.

At the top of the house, my room welcomed me, bright and friendly. I took one of the lace-covered throw pillows off my bed and hugged it to my chest.

Checking the time, I subtracted the difference and risked calling my mom on the chance she wasn't teaching yet.

"Hello, my beautiful child!" Heather McGuire's voice sang from halfway around the world.

"Hi," I squeaked, having failed to preplan my conversation. Tears welled in my eyes.

Years of angsty-teenage training kept my mother's voice calm and free of probing questions. "As ever, your call permeates my soul with utmost delectation."

The absurdity of her vocabulary had the desired effect, and I giggled. "Delectation? Honestly, mother."

"I freely admit that one is new. I have a grad student who likes to test me."

It sounded like English-nerd flirting to me, but I wasn't about to go down that road.

"Elation, happiness, joy, pleasure. It all works when referencing you," she continued.

I pictured her sitting in her office on campus: strawberry-blonde hair in a French twist, a pale pastel blouse complementing a pink silk skirt. She dressed to perfection, even when she taught all online courses while I was in high school. Now that she saw students face-to-face, her wardrobe went up a notch.

"I miss you," I said.

"And I you, darling girl." I heard clicking, most likely her perfectly manicured nails tapping impatiently on her desk.

I paused for a beat before saying, "The suspense is killing you, isn't it?"

"Oh, my goodness gracious sakes alive. You're teasing me now? What is it? Bad? Good? Tell me!"

Laughing, I said, "It's bad, but you're making me feel better."

After relaying the story of Glastonbury and the knight, I felt sorry for myself. "Why does this keep happening to me?" I whined.

"It runs in the family, apparently," she answered, distracted.

Obscure references never made me happy. "What? Mom, are you okay? Did something happen?" My concern was not unwarranted. During my freshman year, when I was away in Chicago, a very bad man stalked her.

"Oh, it's nothing. Rita and I are having an adventure is all." Before she explained further, an ear-splitting yowl interrupted.

"Is that Oberon? Aren't you at work?" I had Tori get my mom a Maine coon cat to keep her company when she moved into a condo. Mom, of course, named the cat after a Shakespeare character.

"I am, but he has a vet visit shortly, so I brought him with me. He is not best pleased."

"Let him serve as a watch cat. With that voice, no one could sneak up on you."

After a couple more pleasantries, she hung up as the veterinarian appointment drew close. Even though I didn't get words of wisdom, I felt better.

As I contemplated a meal of chocolate hazelnut spread on crackers, I regretted telling Meryl I wanted to be alone.

After the first cracker, I considered rethinking my life choices, but a gentle knock on the door delayed me.

"I won't stay," Meryl said as I welcomed her into my room. Setting a plate of ham with peaches and a side of roasted potatoes on my desk, she added, "But you do need decent food."

"You're so kind. You didn't need to do that." My stomach growled so loudly when the scent hit my nose that she laughed. "Thank you."

My phone rang as I tossed the second cracker into the trash. The caller ID filled me with dread.

Unblinking, I whispered to Meryl, "It's Jeffery Daily. The reporter."

Most visitors to quiet Cotswolds towns don't have a local reporter in their contacts. This reporter, however, managed to sniff out every crime in the area, especially if I was involved.

"Let it go to voicemail," she advised as she pulled her cell out of her dress pocket and searched for something.

"How did he know?"

"He is a reporter, dear. It's his job." A crease formed between her brows. "I do think it is important you see this," she said, handing me her phone.

A replay of a local news broadcast boasted the tagline, "TOURISTS FIND MURDER VICTIM."

Eyes glued to the screen, I listened to the reporter, praying that she wouldn't say my name.  Lily and I were lumped together as "two girls," but no further information was given, so I paused.

"Of course, he thought it was me," I said, referring to the reporter. Wishing his instincts were wrong, I extended the phone to Meryl, but she shook her head no."You should watch to the end," she said, atypically ominous.

# Chapter Seven: The News Report

Watching the news report in my serene, safe, secure room felt surreal, and I had to reach for the comfort of my pillow again. Concerned, I listened carefully. The phone trembled in my grip when the broadcaster described the victim, Dan Raibead, as connected to both theft and drug crimes.

Meryl supported my hand and slipped an arm around me. She understood the implication of the fake knight being involved with drugs.

When Parikh started working for MCIT, he made it a quest to eradicate drugs flowing through the Cotswolds. He and Edward almost succeeded, with only one or two perpetrators still at large.

If the costumed knight was one of those who escaped, Parikh's motive skyrocketed. Still, Edward's conviction of the detective's guilt seemed like an overreaction.

Handing Meryl's cell back again, I asked, "What do you think?"

"Probably something close to what you think. Edward spoke at length about Parikh's frustration that the drug ringleader got away. This information gave him a reason to hunt for Raibead, I imagine."

"Yeah, that's pretty much what I decided."

With a hug, Meryl left, and I dithered, as my mother would say, not knowing what to do with myself.

I called Lily, but she was getting ready for a date with Donny, so I exchanged a few texts with my old dorm mate back in Chicago.

One message to Edward didn't elicit a response, so I stewed, wanting to call Tori but not wanting to bug her.

Fortunately, the phone app on my computer flashed her name, and I attempted to answer without sounding desperate.

"How's D.C.?"

"We have rats, but that's not why I called. Did you hear that report about Dan Raibead? Is he the one Parikh is in trouble over?"

Relief at not having to introduce the subject myself made way for curiosity. Curiosity always won. "Are you monitoring the news in Bath to keep tabs on me?"

"Of course," she said, like stalking me happened every day. "Oh, don't look at me like that. I don't trust Washington enough to walk around at night. I need a distraction, and you're it."

"Reading about murder isn't going to make you feel more at home."

"Nothing will make me feel more at home," she said, her forehead wrinkling in distress.

"Yes, it will! Honestly. Everyone feels homesick for the first few weeks. Go to the museums or the zoo. Aren't they all free there?"

The hint of a smile appeared. "You're right. The city is pretty impressive. I'll try the Natural History Museum tomorrow at lunch and report back."

"Perfect."

We mapped out more plans to avoid ennui, and then Tori turned the conversation back to me.

"It's a weird name, don't you think?"

"Dan Raibead?" I shrugged. "It sounds Irish, but lots of things over here do."

"Remember the Dead Rabbit Gang?"

Tori and I wasted a large part of our youth watching old movies in the spare room at my house. It kept us quiet when my mom was working, and we were out of reach of Tori's obnoxious older brother.

"From *Gangs of New York*? So?"

"In Irish, it's Dead Raibead and got warped into dead rabbit. Anyway, it means something like 'strong man' or 'hulking'. I thought it was too much of a coincidence that he sounded so close to both a gang and an excellent hitman name."

My face scrunched up. "It's a bit of a stretch. I mean, if a gang were actually involved, they wouldn't advertise it with a guy's name like that."

Tori slumped. "I know. At least it's Irish, and so it wouldn't be related to Edward's past at all."

The tattoo that scarred Edward and James, an angry unicorn's head with a bloody knife in its teeth, blazed through my mind. "No, he has a different animal.  Although" I paused, puzzling together pieces that didn't quite fit, "Irish Gaelic and Scottish Gaelic both come from the ancient Celtic language."

"And you're wondering if there is a similar phrase in Scottish," Tori finished.

"Yeah, but I'm also thinking it doesn't matter. Except that Parikh is his mentor, Edward isn't involved in this mess."

I didn't mention how Edward hadn't fought to defend Parikh.

"So you think I should keep looking into this mess?" I asked.

Tori's brows furrowed.  "Only to the extent of what we're doing now. Don't go looking for trouble, Maddie. It finds you well enough on its own."

* * *

Photographing shards and fragments brought up from the Bath's dig site the next day took a lot more brain power than sifting to find them. After finishing the first set of artifacts for the day, I realized I didn't include the correct ruler in the shots.

The second time through went more smoothly. Concentration kept my mind from spinning about things I couldn't control, so when I got multiple layers containing several bits of blue tesserae, I searched for a pattern.

Tracking which of the three bags each piece came from, I took chunks and placed them together to create a single tile. The photo turned out perfectly, even after I enlarged it to look for errors.

Once everything was back in its proper place, I texted Simon to come and look.

"I say, well done, old girl."

Some English phrases made no sense, especially when uttered by a young twenty-something to a nineteen-year-old. Still, I grinned at the compliment while he called Sam in to look.

"Shouldn't you call Dr. Daniels?" I asked Sam after she arrived.

"Me? No, darlin'. That's for you to do."

Shyly, I squeaked, "Really?" The assembly struck me as a natural thing to do. But what if I had overstepped? Simon and Sam appeared impressed, so this might be something that could further my career.

My lack of education stared me in the face again. I'd applied for the internship as a sophomore instead of a senior. The position was awarded despite my class standing due to some behind-the-scenes shenanigans I didn't know about at the time. Now, I saw the wisdom of a student who had almost completed an archaeology program for the job. What I didn't know became glaringly obvious.

Puffing out the breath I'd been holding, I grabbed the picture and went to the Undercroft, where Dr. Daniels oversaw the dig.

Marcus noticed me first and asked if I required assistance.

Rather than showing him the photo, I told him it was important that I speak to Dr. Daniels. While Sam and Simon were all about supporting my assembly skills, I didn't know Marcus well enough to trust that he wouldn't take credit somehow. He struck me as nice, but I had been wrong about people before.

That said, I didn't want to be accused of jumping the reporting structure or exceeding the bounds of my current job description. Why couldn't adult decision-making be easier?

"The American?" Dr. Daniels said when he saw me.

Not my name, but he consistently identified me—a definite improvement.

"As you know," I said, although I wasn't sure he did, "Marcus has me photographing the cleaned fragments."

"Quite right. Carry on," he said, turning away, already bored.

"I assembled this," I almost screeched, waving the picture of the tesserae tile in his face.

Eyes focusing, he took the image. "I say." Ignoring me, he turned to

Marcus. "Did you see this?"

*Uh oh.* I didn't want my new teammate to hate me, so I jumped to his defense. "Marcus set up clear parameters for me to follow, and I bent the guidelines. If you were mad that I moved artifacts from different layers, I didn't want to get him in trouble, so I came to you first."

His look went from focused to laser-sharp, and I shrank back a step.

"Did you say pieces came from different layers?" he demanded.

*Dang dang dang dang! Why didn't I show Marcus first?*

A babble of excuses created a bottleneck at the base of my throat, fighting to see which one would blurt out of my mouth first. Thankfully, none did, and my head bob answered enough.

"How did you see that they fit as one?"

Not expecting that question, I simply shrugged, making me look simple.

*Say something brilliant, McGuire,* I told myself, wrestling my brain to the floor.

"I'm, uh, good at geometry and spatial relationships. It's why I want to specialize in Roman architecture. I visualize how the rooms flowed, and I excel at finding inconsistencies that lead to hidden nooks." I shrugged again, regretted it, and closed strong. "The tile designs stayed in my head as I photographed. Everything was returned to its proper bag, marked, measured, and documented. I made sure nothing got misplaced."

Handing the photo to Marcus, Dr. Daniels said, "Right," and left without another word.

Not knowing if "right" was about not mixing up the bags or the work I'd completed, I turned my wide eyes at Marcus.

He nodded once.

Back in the US, I would have taken this to mean that I might not be fired. However, after months of working with Simon, I interpreted the nod as "Impressive."

Or, "You're screwed." I couldn't tell which.

I wanted to go back upstairs, but needed to check Marcus' reaction and get the photo back. Rocking back and forth, I waited for him to do something other than stare at the assembled mosaic tile.

"What?" he asked, although I hadn't said anything. Adopting the absent-minded professor role in Dr. Daniels' absence, Marcus saw me linger but didn't move.

"Are you mad at me?" I asked, even though it was too bold a query to be answered.

"What? Right," he muttered, not answering. "I find reassembly tedious," he admitted, which I took as a good sign.

"Really? I thought you liked working with the shards."

"I do, but individually. The jigsaw puzzle aspect is not my strong suit."

We moved to the elevator, and he spoke rapidly, forming a plan as we returned to the lab.

"Keep photographing, but also watch for artifacts you can piece together. I'll make a chart to track them, and add notes when they're from different layers in the dig."

He pulled out graph paper and sketched a 3D square with corresponding numbers to mark each layer.

Placing the graph in front of me, Marcus said, "Identify the quadrant from two axes."

Understanding, I took the paper and marked it in two places, one showing the vertical layer, the other the horizontal section of the grid, and said, "Pieces from here and here. And on this side, I keep a written tally."

"Quite right."

He left me to it, and I felt I'd made a tangible contribution to the team.

Holding on to that sense of accomplishment, I pushed away any worrisome thoughts about murdered cosplay knights.

Sam entered the lab to let me know that Yvette was arriving early, since I had already moved on.

Suitably proud of me, she offered a quick hug before saying, "Yvette will be joining us for those talks on the Baths ye seem to like so much, so you'll have a chance to get to know her."

Grinning, I said I would be there. "Dr. Daniels has already cleared time for me to study, so I'll count that." My outburst about armor came to me. Sam had promised to find information for me, but I blushed over my previous behavior and didn't want to ask if she found anything.

"You'll be thinking about Roman armor, swords, and blacksmiths, then," Sam said, reading my mind or my expression, which tends to be the same thing.

"The Baths are amazing, absolutely no question about that, but a lot of Romans spent more time at war than hanging around in spa towns. It's like my education is getting lopsided." And knowing more about swords allowed for investigating the death of the knight without getting too close. That should satisfy Fred.

"It's true that history is oft associated with battle and war," she said, a faraway cast in her eyes.

The tension between Ireland and England still permeated many relationships in a way I couldn't comprehend, and I made a connection, understanding why she loved her job so much. "We're lucky here to have sites like this and Chedworth that let us explore everyday lives instead of battle."

"You're becoming perceptive, so ye are." She smiled. "Chester is where you'll be wanting to go to see the Roman army in action."

"In action?" That took hold of my curiosity. "Where is it?"

"Far outside the Cotswolds, closer to Liverpool." She grinned. "But the blacksmith is not up and running yet."

For someone who had lived in England for months, I hadn't done a lot of traveling. The only time I saw London was from the air and then a train window on my way to Bath. The distance to Glastonbury covered my second-longest trip. Considering the island, including Scotland and Wales, almost fit in my home state, I wondered if I should explore more. Except, the two millennia of history under my feet could take a lifetime to delve into.

Still, stepping out of my comfort zone sounded like an exciting idea.

"They do reenactments," Sam continued about Chester. "You can get there by train. But if you want to see a blacksmith in action, there is one near Glastonbury."

I was tempted by a trip to Chester. My dad bought me a BritRail pass that allowed me to use the railroad whenever I wanted. "Maybe I could do it as a field trip there for a class project," I said. "You wouldn't happen to know how long it takes?"

Pulling up the Great Western Railway app and tapping, she said, "Anywhere from three and a half to five hours."

An all-day adventure, there and back. I couldn't ask Lily to come with me after what happened at Glastonbury. Maybe I could lure Dolly away from the spa by promising train time as wedding planning assistance. But it would be faster to go to Glastonbury.

"I'll see if I can get a day off by doing twice the work the day before."

"By my calculations," Simon said from the door, "you've done that today."

Startled by his sudden appearance, I let out a little screech of surprise, which he ignored, followed by, "Why? What time is it?" A glance at my phone confirmed the fugue state I slipped into when photographing and thinking about jigsaw puzzles.

"Geez. Just a second." I texted both Edward and Meryl to let them know my whereabouts. The Priestlys didn't ask or pry, but I liked having a parental unit looking after my well-being. Enough life-threatening things happened to me here that I took comfort in checking in.

"Do you think Dolly would come with me to look at Roman blacksmiths if I promised wedding planning time?"

Chin in the air, the better to look down his nose at me with his watery blue eyes, he surprised me by saying, "I might. For the same price."

"Honestly? Cool, dude." Simon hated hearing my Americanisms, so I threw them in to keep me from expressing mushy feelings about our friendship. "When?" I asked, while I texted Marcus that I worked a double today and if I could have tomorrow off.

Despite the reasonable request, I panicked that I overstepped my boundaries again, and I added, 'I'll of course come in first thing so that you can inspect the quality of my work, and I will cancel my trip if I need to do more.'

"Not till Saturday, I'm afraid," Simon said.

"Saturday," I repeated, regretting my ask for the next day off. As I typed in,

'Never mind,' which made me appear inconsistent and flighty, I got a return text from Marcus.

'No problem at all. I checked with Dr. Daniels, and he assured me your time off for school should be flexible.'

*Wow!* I cheered silently. That was nice. 'Thank you so much,' I messaged back, erasing the three exclamations I originally included and instead adding, 'I am taking a field trip to learn about ancient blacksmiths.' I hoped it made me sound dedicated.

'You will learn much.'

A long, suffering sigh came my way, and I realized Simon needed my answer. "Saturday, yes. Thank you! Can you drive us to Glastonbury? I want to see a real blacksmith."

He sniffed, but his aunt entered the room before he could say no.

Today's photography work took so much of my attention that I hadn't had time to think about Lady Vivian's excursion to see DI Parikh, so it was like an attack when she spoke.

"I'm afraid I have some rather upsetting news."

# Chapter Eight: Sham Castle

It is important to note that often when a British person says something vague and innocuous, they mean something monumentally awful. This axiom especially applied to Simon's Aunt Vivian. Understated and powerful, her compact, immaculately turned-out frame radiated perfection while her velvet-blue eyes commanded any room she entered.

"You saw Parikh?" I asked, the interruption agitating Lady Vivian.

Mentally, I slapped a hand over my mouth and waited. Patiently…ish. So many questions needed answering.

"As you know, I visited your detective inspector," she began.

In my head, I shouted, *We know!*

"He is holding up admirably but without much anticipation of being cleared."

"What?" I interrupted. Again. It earned me an imperious glare. This time, I physically covered the lower half of my face.

"I must remember to pick up a pair of glasses for him. He seems to have lost his and is getting headaches." Pausing, she pulled out her mini rose-gold purse notebook and made a note with the matching pen before continuing. "The evidence collected by Constable Douglass is quite compelling."

My hand moved from my mouth to support the weight of my head. Bad enough to be accused and arrested, but to have your own team corroborate your guilt was awful.

"Did—" I began, but shut myself up. For some reason, something Edward said came back to me, but I didn't want to go there yet.

"He does not know why he overslept, does not remember offering

Constable Bailey the day off, but said he had been considering it, so it was possible he sent the email."

I groaned. Why couldn't he be sure? Without Edward reporting to work that day, no one could verify Parikh's whereabouts as they tended to move around where they were needed. Instead, Edward brought Parikh's mother's car to Glastonbury to the scene of the crime, where lots of people could see it.

Even though Edward came to see me in the car, it didn't mean Parikh hadn't used it earlier and sent it to Glastonbury later to confuse the timeline. Parikh often drove the little SmartCar as it got such good gas mileage. If I figured that out, his colleagues likely did, too.

"The note received," Lady Vivian continued before I cut her off. Again.

"What note?"

A glare, followed by, "As for the note he received asking him to meet him, it was printed on plain paper and left with his milk delivery. The milkman did not place it with the bottles."

Pausing, she raised her eyebrows as if inviting me to interrupt. I chose not to, and she glanced at me approvingly.

This news was hard enough without testing my manners. I attempted not to scowl.

"The note itself said, 'Meet me at Sham Castle at 9:30.'"

"Doesn't that mean he has an alibi?" I asked, hope spurring the question.

"It would if a hiker had seen him or the note had been signed. But…" She let silence fill in the blanks. No one had, and it wasn't.

"Why did he go? Did he know who it was from?"

"Apparently, the castle is where he often met informers from the drug ring."

I gasped. "Was he meeting Dan Raibead?"

"Alas, no one appeared," she said, which did not directly answer my question.

Had Parikh met the victim that morning? Or intended to? Was Raibead an informer, and that's why he was killed? But if so, why had Parikh been arrested and not a drug associate?

Nothing made sense.

Lady Vivian finished, so I got up and paced around the lab. "Where did you say this castle was?"

"Sham Castle," Simon supplied.

"What's a sham?" I asked, thinking it might be connected to shamrocks or some local family.

"A fake," Simon answered.

"Yeah, I know that." *Obviously*, I didn't say. "But what is Sham Castle?"

"A fake castle."

"What, like two feet high or something?" I pictured a miniature golf course set piece.

"No, it's castle height. It's a folly."

I sighed. Dolly used the term 'folly' in reference to a garden element, but it didn't make sense in this context.

Pursing my lips, I tried to come up with a question that would produce a sensical answer. I failed. "What?"

"A facade. It is along the Skyline Walk and abuts a golf course."

Not too far off from my mental image, just full-sized. Curiosity about the Skyline Walk took a back seat to wanting to know more about the Sham Castle. "I think I'll take a stroll up there," I mused more to myself than my friends.

It sounded interesting, and I might find something useful.

Marcus entered the lab, his eyebrows hiking into his hairline. "My lady," he addressed Simon's aunt with a little bow, which she acknowledged with a dip of her head.

While Simon was a lord, he did not encourage the use of his title or formalities. The same did not hold true for Lady Vivian, who expected and received respect from everyone.

The poor man looked so flustered that I took pity on him. "Marcus, good you're here. Could you check my work and let me know what I need to do differently?"

Leaping at the chance to do something, he went to the cabinets where the artifacts were stored and scrolled through my corresponding photos.

While I said goodbye to my friends, he made notes. Once the room cleared, he showed me two techniques to better define shadows and improve the sense of depth in the images.

"Should I redo what I did today?"

"Not at all. You've done quite well, and I wasn't expecting you to get this far. Enjoy your blacksmith." With the aristocracy gone, he returned to his regular, efficient self.

Rather than explaining that my day off would be spent exploring the Sham Castle, I said, "Thank you so much for teaching me that lighting setup. I appreciate it so much. It's such a huge help."

"Quite right," he said, his lips forming a line.

Too effusive, I decided, and reminded myself to be reserved around this guy.

* * *

Roger offered to drop me at the trailhead for Sham Castle. As we sped through the charming neighborhood, I saw the familiar form of Fred hobbling along and asked Roger to pull over.

"Do you need a ride somewhere, Fred?" I asked.

"I've got two fine legs," he said, peering at us. When recognition dawned, he asked, "Have you gotten the detective released yet?"

I dowsed the urge to roll my eyes. I don't know how he expected me to do something that the police couldn't. "It's early days yet," I said, quoting from a TV show.

"It's up to you, it is," Fred insisted.

Rather than keep Roger from work, I thanked him, got out of the car, and waved goodbye.

Resuming my conversation with Fred, I pointed out that the police were working on it.

"The only copper that's worth anything is the detective, and he won't do anything to help himself. No, it's up to you."

"Why me?" I tried not to sound pitiful, but honestly. With Fred depending on me, the distraction part of the investigation went away, and it just became a millstone. Everyone else wanted me to stop investigating. Fred's insistence that I do made it distinctly stressful. "I have to work on my classes in order to keep my student visa," I explained.

"Why, because the police think they have their killer, and they won't look for anyone else," he responded to my question, ignoring my explanation.

That too sounded like it was from a television show. "I don't think that's true," I said gently. "They don't want to see one of their own accused."

The doubt that Edward had shown about Parikh's innocence crossed my mind, but I shook it away. "DI Parikh has every faith in the police."

We walked a block before I realized I didn't know where I was going. "Do you know how to get to the Sham Castle?" I asked.

Fred nodded and pointed up a street. "I'd show you, but I'd just slow you down. Go uphill when you get to Sham Castle Lane."

Unsure, I took a few steps before turning around.

"Turn right," Fred clarified. "Remember what I said."

As in, remember I'm supposed to solve a murder, or not get lost? I chose the latter, and pulled out my cell make sure.

The lane crossed onto a trail leading up to the main Bath Skyline Hike.

Hike was right. As I learned on The Cotswolds Way, England is much steeper than I originally pictured. Even with all the walking I do, I was puffing like a steam train halfway up, so I stopped and looked around.

What must have been a mass of green in the summer stood twisted and ominous this morning. Had I seen anyone on the way here? Other than a couple of cars on the road, no. Perhaps the area's deserted nature made it perfect for a meeting between DI Parikh and an informant.

Regretting my lack of preparation, I muttered darkly about being hungry. It wasn't like the trail was impossible, but I rushed out of the house without eating.

On the bright side, I clocked in at 9:30 a.m., so my experience matched my incomplete timeline of Parikh's movements.

No one stirred.

I continued to climb, no castle in sight. Pushing through a tunnel of tangled tree branches, I spied a tower. An honest-to-goodness castle tower.

Scurrying faster for a better view, I tripped and landed on my hands, scraping flesh from my palms. I chose to finish the walk at a more stately pace.

A boy sped past me in a fair imitation of a gazelle. If he went that fast over the uneven terrain, he'd done the run before.

With Fred's nagging voice in my head, I ran, pursuing the boy. "Hey! Hey, you running!" I shouted, very probably sounding like a crazy girl.

Happily, he paused and turned, so I hit the gas and caught up with him, looking more insane.

"Sorry, sorry, sorry," I said, panting. "Do you run here often?"

Hardly sweating, the teenage boy stared while I bent over and puffed.

"The reason, gasp, gasp, I ask is because, gasp, my friend walked on the trail earlier this week." Standing up straight, I puffed a couple more times and smiled. "We need to talk to people who might have seen him." There—a complete sentence without sounding like I needed an inhaler.

"Yes. Which day?"

I explained the day and timeframe, but he shook his head. "Not me. I can check with the other lads on the team and let you know. What's your number?"

Almost falling for it, I got three digits out before realizing I was giving my cell to a boy I didn't know. "Oh yeah, sure. Did you say a team? What's the name?"

He told me.

"And you have some friends who might have been by that morning?"

"A couple of mates, yeah."

"Can I have their names?" I held my cell between us, taking notes.

Each answer was accompanied by a step closer to me, his phone at the ready.

Inching back, I said, "This is great news. Really. I'll have a constable contact your coach to get the details."

That statement hit him like a bucket of cold water. The mischievous glint left his eyes, and his mouth turned down.

"Constable, yes, well. Must run." He did. Literally.

Pleased with my detective skills and ability to not give out my number without insulting a witness, I relaxed and took in my surroundings.

Sham Castle stood proudly on the crest of a hill overlooking the city. It looked like the real thing from the front, with the interior walls knocked down. Four towers, arched windows and doorways, and a crenelated top rose to take in the magnificent views. From the back, while still impressive, the different-colored bricks and flat surface ruined the illusion. For the golfers, it made a fantastic landmark.

The folly reminded me of castling in chess. I always used it when I played because it let me move two pieces at once. The move protects the king by swapping his place with a rook.

Shaking away the distracting thoughts, I took pictures of Sham Castle, hoping to find inspiration or a clue for the sake of Fred.

Using Marcus's advice about lighting, everything turned out better. "Things I didn't intend to learn as an archaeologist," I said aloud since no one could hear me.

The golf course appeared well-maintained, but no golfers were out that day. The constabulary would have checked tee times for potential witnesses, but I made a note to ask about them. Without Parikh in charge, who knew what slipped through the cracks?

Something rustled in a bush. I turned in time to see a grey squirrel jump onto a tree trunk and scurry up. With the zoom on, I caught him with his magnificent bushy tail in a photo.

Reluctant to leave, I searched the area again, looking for anything to help Parikh.

*If he isn't guilty*, a little voice in the back of my mind whispered. Edward's lack of faith had infected my conviction that he was falsely accused.

*Why didn't he think his name would be cleared?* the voice asked, poking another hole in my certainty. Lady Vivian's report on her visit with the detective hadn't been as helpful as I'd hoped.

Between Edward's doubt and Parikh's refusal to do more for himself, I wondered if Fred was forcing me into backing a lost cause.

I circled the facade one last time and trudged to the trailhead, my mind in a muddle.

A bug whizzed by my ear as I picked my way down the trail. Batting at it, I overbalanced, stubbed my toe on a rock, and pitched forward, landing on my hands and knees. Again.

Better than sliding down a cliff, but dirt pushed into my already scraped palms. Gingerly brushing rocks out of the open wound, I looked around for what must have been a healthy-sized insect. Odd, considering how cool the temperature.

I didn't see any flying or creeping crawlies. Wondering what flew by me, I stood, scanning the area. A slight movement caught my attention. A large black and white bird burst into the air as I stepped closer.

"Eek! You scared me," I scolded them.

It was beautiful—the size of a crow, with iridescent blue in the black and striking white markings. We didn't have them in Arizona, and I wondered what it was.

He zipped by me and landed on a branch, dive-bombing me as I fell. Mockingbirds weren't above such mischief, and I grinned at him, happy to have it remind me of birds from home.

My smile faded as I examined its perch—not a branch, but metal protruding from the tree.

Trudging through the leafless bramble, I paused a few feet from the bird, who squawked indignantly.

"Am I too close to your prize?" I asked it.

"Caw!"

"I'll take that as a yes. Okay. You win."

Taking out my cell, I took a picture and enlarged it instead of going closer.

My noisy companion clung to the hilt of a rondel—a replica of an early medieval knife with a round handle.

"Not an insect, but a knife?" My voice went up an octave by the end of the question, scaring the bird away.

"Wait," I pleaded with it, missing its companionship.

Skin crawling with the sudden awareness of exposure, I cowered and stumbled into a thicket of bushes before picking up the trail down to the road.

Once I reached a line of trees that screened the top of the hill, I texted Edward the picture. 'I think someone threw this at me.'

His immediate response said, 'Get out of there NOW!"

# Chapter Nine: Seed Bread

Edward's text insisting that I leave the area immediately had the opposite effect on my body than it should have. Rather than flooding with adrenaline to get me back down the hill, under the train tracks, and across the bridge to the safety of the Abbey or the Roman Baths, pain throbbed in my knees and wrists, intensifying with every step, slowing my progress.

If there was one piece of advice about traveling to England that I could give past me, it would be to wear knee pads. Having fallen on a sample of trails, stairwells, dark alleys, and brightly lit hallways, the wisdom was warranted.

Reaching toward a nearby boulder to steady my descent, I put too much weight on my hand, further opening the scrapes.

Thankfully, Dolly provided me with my very own scent of thieve's spray. Removing it from my jacket pocket, I gently spritzed my palms. Even if it didn't disinfect, it stung like it did and diverted my attention until I reached the road.

A flight of stairs stretched down before me. Endlessly. Into eternity.

Okay, maybe not that long, but neither knee wanted to bend. Leading with the right foot hurt, but so did leading with the left.

Instead of descending, I hoisted myself back up to street level and limped along the sidewalk toward the street that Roger and I drove up. It would take more time, but I wouldn't risk breaking every bone in my body by tumbling down the stairs.

The creepy feeling of being watched fled. Either my flight or fight responses were dulled to nothing, or I didn't sense any danger.

Or I needed to be face-to-face with a knife-wielding maniac to get a reaction.

That sobering thought got me moving while glancing over my shoulder. I was so intent on what might be behind me that the sound of a motorcycle near me didn't register.

When I finally glanced around, the rider raised his visor, exposing Edward's handsome face.

"Hi," I squeaked as he turned off the bike, dismounted, and hugged me.

"Despite my obvious conflict of interest, I have been authorized to take your statement and drive you home."

"Okay," I said, still squeaky.

"After another minute," he said into my hair, peppering me with small kisses.

My breathing calmed, and Edward pulled back, searched my face, then grinned. "Y'alright?"

"Thank you," I said, pleased my voice returned to its normal register. "I'm okay."

I winced when he took my hand to retrace my steps to Sham Castle.

He turned my hand palm up, kissed the scrapes, then weaved my arm through his, and we continued our walk.

"I found a potential witness," I said.

"Did ya now?"

"A track team that practices here around 9:30 a.m. on weekdays." I gave him the coach's name and contact information.

Edward nodded with a stoic expression etched on his features, but refrained from lecturing me about interfering in police business. We understood it wouldn't have the necessary impact to stop my curiosity from overcoming common sense. Besides, it was a good clue.

A clue I could offer to Fred to get him off my back about helping.

With Edward's help, I led him to the spot where I fell. "I tripped here," I said, indicating the matted grass like some sort of expert tracker. "Something whizzed by my ear. I thought it was a bug or a bird."

Edward scowled at the zoomed-out picture of the knife with the pretty bird on it.

"Magpie."

"He's gorgeous.  Why do they have such bad reputations?"  I asked, remembering all the stories about them stealing shiny objects.

"One for sorrow," Edward said cryptically. "Bad luck."

"Well, this one helped us because he found the knife."

Edward pulled flags out of a backpack and marked the area. "How close did you get?" he asked.

A SOCO (Scene of Crimes Officer) would comb the ground for clues. Edward wouldn't add his shoe prints anywhere but the perimeter, but he would need to tell them where I had been.

"Right here. My magpie complained when I tried to get closer."

Squinting, Edward said, "Which tree?"

As I pointed, my hand wavered. It had been obvious when the black and white squawking bird marked the spot.

The photo offered little context besides leafless nature, but I found a bent branch that matched. "That one," I said, triumphantly pointing, regaining my expert tracker status.

Except that no knife protruded from the trunk.

As I took a step forward, Edward's arm held me back.

"Really. It was that one." The confidence drained from my voice.

"It could have fallen," Edward suggested. He pulled out a camera with a telephoto lens and took some shots.

"Anything?" I asked, impatient for a report. In my picture, the blade was stuck up to its hilt. Falling out seemed unlikely.

A magpie flitted to a nearby tree.

"Good morning, Mr. Magpie. How is your wife?" Edward intoned under his breath.

That question needed a lot of unpacking, but I stayed focused on the problem. "Did the rondel fall? Is it on the ground?" I pressed. Shifting back and forth, I tried to peek over his shoulder at the screen, but he kept it close to his face.

Doubt flooded me. Maybe the magpie had buzzed me, and that knife had been there forever. But then, where was it now? The blade should still be sunk into the tree.

Each step caused a throbbing in my knees, so I forced myself to be still. My mom came to mind, gently placing a cool hand on my arm, calming me in an instant.

Biting off the impulse to ask again, I raked my eyes across the landscape, looking for the thrower's hiding place.

A bench with a solid back perched with a perfect view of the city. Behind it, a person would be hidden unless they moved.

"He probably threw it from over there," I said, flopping my hand toward the seat.

Edward eyed it and then the tree, no doubt tracking the trajectory of a projectile.

Without a word, he marched to the area and placed more little flags to cordon it off.

"Come on," he said as he started down the trail, "we need to meet the team on the street."

"Whoa, whoa, whoa. Did you find it?"

He paused, shook his head no, and continued.

"Slow down and let me see those pictures."

Instead, he took my arm to steady my descent.

Finally, I wrested the camera from him and flipped through the pictures until I saw the bent branch again and zoomed in on the tiny display screen.

Clear but almost camouflaged, there was a clean, straight wound in the bark. "Look," I said, handing him the camera.

He took two more steps before acknowledging it, then he stopped. "I see. That's fresh."

"Mmm hmm." I silently thanked my brain for refusing to admit I was wrong.

The SOCO team pulled up as we approached the road, and he showed them the picture. While I sat in the van, he took the team back up and then came to take me home.

Helmet in place, I rested my head against his back, holding on tight. In deference to my mother's wish to never ride a motorcycle, Edward borrowed a car, but he didn't have time today.

The thrum of the engine relaxed me, and as we wove the streets up to Greenway Lane, two thoughts struck me.

First, while I stumbled away, someone calmly removed the knife. A sudden chill between my shoulder blades caused my back to constrict.

With a shake, I focused on the second, happier thought. If that person threw a knife at me, that meant that Parikh wasn't guilty, because he was still in jail.

When Edward cut the motor, I said, "This means Parikh is innocent if someone else is after me."

Edward didn't respond other than to dismount and secure the bike.

"Doesn't it?"

Eyes pinched in distress met mine. "He was released on caution this morning."

* * *

Never in a million years could I imagine Detective Inspector Parikh throwing a blade anywhere my way. But the fact that the incident happened on the morning he was released didn't bode well.

Words failed. Despair robbed me of forming a proper rant. While blowing off steam tended to calm me, it didn't do anything for Edward's pain, which radiated off him in waves.

Once we were inside the gate, I stepped over the fence to the rabbit hutch.

"Roddy, come here, boy," I coaxed.

A pink nose twitched in my direction, followed by a white face, then long black ears. In two hops, he closed the distance and jumped into my lap.

Gathering the bunny in my arms, I indicated for Edward to follow me to the swing tied to the enormous ash tree that gave the house its name.

Seated, I passed Roddy to Edward. His impassive expression softened as he stroked the rabbit. Few things on earth are as comforting as a friendly bunny.

Tamping down the insistent and annoying number of questions that fought to burst from my lips, I sat quietly. My mom used this quiet technique on me when everything anyone said to me caused an argument. Granted, I was in middle school at the time, but I appreciated the space that quiet provided.

She would tell me about her day without asking about mine. I gave it a whirl. "I'm not going to be in the Undercroft anymore. They've moved me up to the lab permanently."

Edward kissed Roddy's head—a positive sign.

"It feels like both a promotion and a demotion at the same time. Photographing and cleaning are vital work, but I'm further from the actual dig. They let me assemble tesserae."

Edward passed the rabbit to me, put his arm around my shoulder, pulled me close, and kissed me.

"Bràmair," he murmured. We sat that way until my stomach growled loud enough to startle Roddy.

"Maybe we should get lunch," I suggested.

The house, while empty, still smelled of Meryl's freshly baked bread.

Setting Roddy at his now permanent food station by the pantry, I directed Edward to start slicing. Produce from the farmer's market in Southgate spilled over a basket on the counter. As I washed, Edward finished prepping bread and found cheese and chicken.

He wolfed his food and leaped at the chance of seconds when I indicated the fixings.

Again, zipping my lips tight against questions, I wondered how long it had been since he had eaten properly. His brother James, while a good cook, wouldn't provide food unsolicited.

After we devoured everything but the heel, I said, "We should probably go to the store and get a fresh loaf for Meryl and Roger."

"Or," Edward said with a faraway look in his eyes, "we could make one."

"Bread?" While not an absurd suggestion, my baking skills ended at muffins and cookies. "Do you know how?"

Grinning, he said, "My gran taught me."

As it was the first time he'd smiled in ages, I wasn't about to discourage him.

"What do we need?"

"Let's start by finding Meryl's recipe," he said, flipping through a recipe box I never noticed before.

"Here, right. I'll get the bowls and pan, you go to the larder for the flour, oats, and seeds."

I gathered the ingredients as he listed them out. While in the pantry, I discovered a well-worn bread machine. Meryl made fresh loaves so often that I figured she used the machine for kneading and rising and transferred the dough to a pan to bake in the oven.

Grabbing the loaf pan, I chose not to tell Edward about the machine. He needed something to do.

The only thing that flummoxed us was finding the yeast. My mom always kept it in the refrigerator, but that's because it's hot in Tempe. Meryl had it tucked away at the back of a cupboard full of cereal.

After handing it over, I boosted onto the counter and watched as Edward bloomed yeast and weighed flour. Concentration on the task smoothed out the scowl that had been etched on his features for too long.

"Oats," he said, looking up from his bowl, wooden spoon hanging in midair, "Did you see oats?"

"Forgot." Twisting awkwardly, I opened the cereal cupboard again, searching for a bag or box that looked familiar. Nothing did, so I relented and read the labels. A yellow bag boasted jumbo oats. I displayed it for Edward. "These?"

"Aye, that'll do," he responded with a spare glance.

The rich, slightly sour scent of yeast tickled my nose when Edward turned the dough onto the butcher block island. He sprinkled flour, moved the glob around, and added more until a ball formed.

Push, fold, turn. Push, fold, turn, he kneaded rhythmically, lulling me into sleepiness.

THWACK!

Spasming, I whacked my head into the cupboard at the sudden sound. "What the?" I demanded.

Thwack! Push, fold, turn. Thwack! Push, fold, turn.

Edward continued to work the dough with a noisy smack.

"Is that necessary?" I asked since he didn't react to my first question.

"My gran's was the safe place when James and I were wee. She baked bread. Nothing else. Never cookies. Too expensive to use the stove for just a snack."

His voice quiet, he continued to knead, revealing his past.

"William came for a while, until the gang took him."

The eldest of the three brothers, William, was an enigma to me. All I had been told was that he could beat a man to death in a fair fight and that he let James leave the Edinburgh gang last month after thrashing Edward.

"The gang lured me next, but not before I could make my own loaf. I need the seeds."

It took me a second to realize the last was directed at me, and I stopped trying to picture a life where gangs absorbed children one at a time.

Chasing away images, I found Meryl's mix of sesame, poppy, sunflower, and pumpkin seeds. After weighing the right amount, I handed it to Edward, who incorporated it into the dough.

Quietly, not to break the mood, I hoisted back onto the countertop.

"I dinnae believe the DI would throw something at you to hurt you," he began, changing the subject. "And he knows better than to try to scare you away. I don't know what he's playing at."

Questions flew through my brain, but I didn't want Edward to go silent again. I held my tongue and sat on my hands to keep from fidgeting.

Thwack, push, fold.

"The SOCO team found the note," he said while steadily kneading.

A frisson shot threw me. Finally, information on the case. I bit the inside of my cheek to hold my impatience at bay.

"Printer paper, printed on an office laser-jet."

"Well, that's no help. It's not like handwriting or a typewriter that's identifiable." My grandma told me she got in trouble at school because her teacher recognized the dropped capital S on the typed notes she passed in class. Mechanics are easier to identify than digital.

"Actually, it is."

"What do you mean?"

"Printer dots," he said, like that should mean something to me, and it absolutely did not.

A girl can be patient for only so long. "Please explain, in detail, what printer dots are. Please," I repeated for good measure.

"Steganography."

I sighed, audibly.

His grin faded almost instantly. "Most color laser printers include a unique pattern of yellow dots on every page to identify where it was printed."

"Wow. Talk about spycraft that no one knows about. That's crazy. Shouldn't they tell people these things?"

Thwack, push, fold, turn. Forming the dough into shape, Edward placed it gently into the pan and grabbed a tea towel to cover it. His hand waved about, testing various corners of the kitchen until he settled on the counter by the oven.

"Twenty-five minutes for the rise," he said, checking his watch.

Extending his hand, he helped me off my perch. We picked up Roddy and went back outside.

The wind howled, making our swing too cold, so we entered the boot room. Warmed by the sun, the antechamber offered views of the outdoors while sheltered by the house.

Roddy hopped from corner to corner, twitching and sniffing.

"Do you know where the note came from?" I asked, cautiously returning to our previous conversation. He didn't offer the information freely, and lately, that meant bad news.

"The One Stop Shop."

"The police station across from the church?" The aptly named building housed most of the city's offices. Two constables manned a window in the same lobby where residents also paid their water bills.

"Aye."

"So a policeman might be framing him?" Disturbing news, but it could be a clue.

"The current thinking is that he printed it himself to create an alibi."

Unpacking the logic behind DI Parikh printing an alibi took more time than it should have. The bread rose, got sprinkled with more seeds, and baked while I stubbornly refused to agree with "current thinking," as Edward described it.

"Wouldn't Parikh know about the printer creating a unique watermark and therefore avoid it?" I asked him.

"If he did know, it explained why he didn't use his home printer."

"Mrph!" I squeaked inarticulately. From the start of the investigation, Edward accepted that Parikh had killed the knight. So far, I hadn't asked why, but today I had to. "Why are you so convinced he's guilty?"

"Because I would have killed Raibead myself if I had the chance!" he snapped before storming out of the house and roaring away.

# Chapter Ten: Avalon

Unable to process Edward's declaration about wanting to kill the knight himself, I made hot chocolate and carried the thick-sided mug to the boot room. Wind swirled crumpled, gray leaves, creating a chaotic view. When the sun disappeared, I hid in my room, not knowing what to do.

* * *

The next morning, Simon showed up way too early to take me to Glastonbury, which I no longer had interest in. Chasing down Edward and making him explain sounded like a better idea.

Last night, I considered hunting him down on his boat, but since he had to change his mooring every three days, I couldn't be sure where he was.

"You look a bit peaky," Simon greeted me as I plopped into his Citroen.

Tamping down the urge to mimic him like a middle schooler, I chose silence.

He took off at a speed not intended for the streets we traversed. Arizona roads were huge and straight with turn lanes. Here, ancient stone walls raced by, inches from my window.

In addition, Tempe had 360 days of sunshine and zero boyfriends who threatened to kill someone. Geez. I needed a distraction.

"So, your parents were Egyptologists?"

"Yes."

I waited.

Nothing.

"Did you ever go on digs with them?"

He nodded. Once.

"Come on! You told Lily about it." The more he evaded my probing, the more I wanted to know.

"Her mind required a new subject. The poor girl had just seen a dead body."

I attempted to glower at him. "The first time I saw a body, you instructed me to be quiet."

"As I recall, you were rather noisy."

This time, I did mimic him before saying, "Of course, I was noisy. You should have been, too."

He cut his eyes in my direction.

"Fine. You would never be so un-lordly."

A hint of a smile from him.

Good enough for me to continue prodding. "How old were you when you were at the dig sites?"

Since I've known him, Simon has refused any job related to Egypt. If an opportunity came up to dig there, he passed it along to Sam so she could have the experience.

The inquiry dangled for so long that I almost forgot what I asked.

"Ten. Mother and Father took me to Cairo while they dug at Saqqara Necropolis." He glanced at me, and I indicated that I had heard of it.

Tales of untouched tombs and the mummy wrapped in gold were fascinating, but it was the ancient Romans that captured my archaeological interest.

"That day," he continued, although I didn't know what day he referred to, "my parents left me at the hotel. They never returned."

Orphaned at the age of ten. No wonder he never wanted to go back.

"I'm so sorry, Simon. Was there a cave-in or something?"

"Car accident, actually. Their jeep hit a pothole and flipped."

"How awful. That's worse than an on-the-job incident."

He looked at me. "I always thought so, too."

"Well, now that I've made you as depressed as I am, what should we talk about?"

Tilting his head my way was Simon's way of asking about my distress. Did a sad childhood trauma compare to Edward's parting words?

Probably not, but he asked. Sort of.

"You know how everyone assumes Parikh is guilty?"

Nodding yes to my question, he said, "Here we are."

We arrived in Glastonbury and parked near the Abbey Tea Room, which was within walking distance of everything I had on my list to see.

A squeal of delight came from the restaurant. Several women at a table were piling gifts in front of what looked like a bride-to-be.

"Go on," Simon urged.

Much as I wanted to unburden myself, I owed it to him to keep my promise of assistance. "No. I'm here to help with your wedding tasks. What's on your list?"

Sighing, he recited, "Flowers, stationery, photographer, invitations, and guests."

Based on the app he showed me, I thought his duties would be monumental. I avoided rolling my eyes.

"Flowers. Really? You're stressed about flowers when your aunt single-handedly wins the prettiest village contest every year? And you literally have acres of greenhouses. Ask her what she wants to use."

"I can't."

This time, my eyes rolled on their own volition. "Why not?"

"Dolly asked me to take care of it."

"Were those her exact words?"

Simon thought for a moment before confirming.

"That is code for 'Please ask your aunt to take care of this for us.' The bride can't ask the groom's family for stuff."

Looking relieved, Simon said, "Aunt Viv has been a bit snippy of late."

"That's because you haven't asked for her help. She is the solution for stationery and invitations, too. Lady Vivian's note paper is exquisite. Tell her that when you ask what to order.

"The photographer," I continued reading off the checklist. "We'll need to do some research for that. Do you know anyone? I'm getting pretty good at lighting," I offered.

"No," he said, more firmly than I thought warranted. But, I guess if he was going to have a wedding in a castle, a professional was called for.

I just hoped I'd be invited. Being friends with a lord and lady didn't guarantee a place at the ceremony. Plenty of rich kids from my old neighborhood only invited important family connections to the actual wedding and had a separate party for their friends after the honeymoon.

In fact, my dad started hedging his bets for being in control of the guests when he first saw me play bride dress-up when I was little. "I'll pay for the whole thing, but all daddy's work friends will want to see my Pumpkin on her big day," he'd say. I assumed as much for Dolly and Simon, especially after hearing about the venue.

I carried on with Simon's duties. "The Roman Baths must have a photographer for their marketing department. That's a good place to start. Want me to ask?"

"I'll do it." After far too long, he added, "Good idea."

"That leaves the guests, which takes us back to your aunt. With the other tasks, she might feel adding an invitation list to her plate is too much. On the other hand, she might already have one. Ask her for her address book and anyone she doesn't want to include."

"Quite right," Simon said as we strolled away from town. "List sorted except for one last detail. Let's head to the Tor."

The Glastonbury Tor, a natural hill terraced long ago, was topped by St. Michael's Tower. It was the highest point for miles and once rose above the once flooded plains of Somerset. Its height and proximity to ancient floods explained its comparison to Avalon, Arthur's home after Camelot.

Over 500 feet up, the climb took more out of me than I wanted to admit to Simon. Keeping my puffing to a minimum, I gasped when the wind howled. Which was a lot.

"Geez," I complained when an enthusiastic gust sent me stumbling. "Why is it so windy?"

"Nothing to stop it," Simon answered as we reached the top.

I'd been so focused on not getting carried off by the breeze, I hadn't looked up. In the shelter of the Tor's tower, I gaped at the view.

Patchwork fields of green and gold, bordered by hedgerows, stretched for miles. The path we came up sloped relatively gently compared with the far side of the Tor, which dropped away to more meadows, some dotted with clumps of snow.

"Going back to the guest list, I do have one additional, shall we say, favor to ask of you," Simon said.

Here it comes—the "You're great, but you can't come" speech. I understood, but I still needed a calming breath before I said, "Sure."

"You see, Aunt Viv and I have discussed it, and Dolly agrees." He stopped like he finished the thought, but he hadn't.

We entered the pointed arch doorway into St. Michael's Tower, the only part of the fourteenth-century church still standing. Rising to the heavens and open to the sky, the magnificence of the structure softened my prickly spirits.

I couldn't let Simon flounder because I knew the drill. Putting him out of his misery, I said, "Look, Simon, I get it. It's an aristocracy thing. You can't have a rebellious colonial mixing with the royalty."

"Maddie."

"Honestly, it's okay. It happens all the time back home. The ceremony is more for maintaining relationships than for friends. We can have a little get-together after you get back from the honeymoon. No problem. Where are you going for that, by the way? Do you have any plans? In the states, it's usually Hawaii or—"

"Do be quiet."

"What?" Annoyed by the interruption, I huffed. After all, I was giving him an easy out.

"I was not finished."

"You paused," I commented.

"That was not an invitation."

"More like an opportunity."

"Do you want to hear what I have to say or not?"

"Fine," I answered. Admittedly, kind of petulantly.

"Fine," he mimicked, also petulant.

At least we had that going for us.

"You are infuriating," he added.

"I think the word you're looking for is charming."

At this, he hung his head, despair written across his face.

Until he laughed.

"Really rather quite infuriating," he said, grinning, and we continued our survey of the area.

Sobering, he straightened and turned to face me. "On behalf of Dolly and my family, I would be honored if you would stand up for me at my wedding."

"Huh?" Eloquent, that's me.

"Like a best man…only, girl."

"Me?" The request was so completely opposite of what I expected that I wasn't processing it well.

"You did save my life, you know."

"Yeah, but—"

"And Dolly's sanity."

"Granted, but—"

"Who better to represent us?"

"Like a groomsman?"

"Best man," he repeated.

"Not on Dolly's side?"

"She has her cousin, whose wedding Dolly participated in. Rupert will be the ring bearer, and one of the girls associated with the family at the castle will be our flower girl. A small affair, all in all."

I wanted to be perfectly clear before I jumped to any conclusions. "You want me to be your best man?"

"You normally aren't this thick."

I launched at him, wrapping him in a massive hug.

Naturally, he tried to back away before anyone saw us, but I didn't let go, and he softened and hugged back.

"May I mark you down as a yes, then?"

I let go. "Yes, please. I would be honored." I curtsied. Honored, yes, but I couldn't wait to tell Tori I got to be in a wedding in an actual ancient castle.

"Do I wear a tux or a dress?"

"I am sure Dolly has a plan to make you look stunning."

"But not as stunning as Dolly."

"No one is ever as stunning as Dolly," Simon responded in a delightful show of affection. Since Simon's interests lay elsewhere, seeing him recognize Dolly as a catch was awesome.

"Ooo, does this mean I get to throw your bachelor party?"

"Please don't."

That haunted look Simon got when he was overwhelmed by wedding details surfaced, and he changed the subject. "What was it you said about Edward believing in Parikh's guilt?"

That question doused my spirits. I'd almost forgotten Edward's parting words. "It's not good," I began.

"Your mood earlier indicated that."

"Edward said he would have killed the guy himself if he had a chance."

Both Simon's eyebrows went up, the equivalent of shouting an obscenity.

"I know, right?" I said. "He stormed off before I could ask what he meant."

"Have you tried to contact him?" Simon asked reasonably.

The thing was, I didn't want to be reasonable. I folded my arms across my chest.

"Text him," Simon advised.

"Since when are you an expert at relationships?" I muttered. Childish, considering I had been inwardly scolding myself for not trying to get in touch with Edward.

"Which one of us is getting married?" Simon asked.

"That doesn't count," I answered, knowing the marriage was somewhat arranged. However, Simon and Dolly were content with the situation, so I gave up arguing, pulled out my cell, and texted Edward.

'You okay?' I asked.

'Sorry I stormed out. I miss you.'

I grinned.

"Happy now?" Simon asked rather smugly.

"Yeah, okay, fine. You were right."

I ignored Simon while Edward and I made arrangements to meet later. When I finished, I walked around the base of the tower again. Seven symmetrical terraces encircled the Tower. No one knew why they were carved there. Historians considered agriculture, defense ramparts, or even a three-dimensional labyrinth, but no theory had been entirely accepted.

Even in winter, green still dominated the landscape.

"So pretty," I sighed, watching folks brave the elements to reach the top.

Simon said, "Like a chess board. You can see how Lewis Carroll got his inspiration."

The comment struck a chord and resonated through me.

"Chess," I said, the puzzle pieces clicking but creating a fuzzy image.

"Or draughts," Simon said, clearly not experiencing the same epiphany as me.

"No, chess," I insisted, not wanting to lose my train of thought on what he was talking about.

Surprising me, he turned and waited. I had gotten so used to him playing the obnoxious older brother that I sometimes forgot how well he could read me.

Relaxing, I let the imagery below fill my mind. The people looked like they moved of their own volition, but from this angle, I imagined a force guiding their outcome, like in chess.

I looked at Simon once I felt certain. "Someone is manipulating us. All of us."

# Chapter Eleven: Chess

The idea of someone manipulating us made sense. Every move we made to help Parikh was countered almost before we finished.

When I explained the theory to Simon, he said, "Like a master chess player. That makes DI Parikh the king, correct?"

Wind whipped our clothing as we descended the Tor.

"Exactly. The ultimate goal was to take him off the board, not kill the other guy."

"I accept the premise," he said, like I had asked him for his opinion, but he redeemed himself by asking me to explain my logic.

"First, I had never heard of Glastonbury except as a massive concert venue before Lily invited me."

"Making Lily a pawn. And you."

I danced around, happy that Simon played along and let my creativity flow.

"Next, somehow, for the first time ever, Parikh overslept, making it possible for him to get the note."

"Sleeping pills?" Simon suggested.

"Maybe. I don't know how easy it would be to dose someone. But if someone snuck something into his tea, they probably took his car keys at the same time. And Lady Vivian mentioned his glasses were missing, too."

"Perhaps another pawn did so."

We went over the timing of Edward's email and the arrival of the DI's car near the murder.

"In this analogy, what piece is the victim?" Simon asked.

Pondering, I hurried us past the Chalice Well and back to Glastonbury Abbey.

"If we present it right, Edward may give us more information. We know Raibead informed on the drug ring. Let's be literal and say he was a knight in the chess master's arsenal. Meryl and Roger mentioned that sometimes a player will sacrifice a knight to protect the king."

"You're saying that whoever is manipulating you killed the knight to protect himself."

Agreeing, I said, "And the second I thought we had proof that Parikh couldn't have thrown a knife at me, it turns out he had been released that morning."

Simon stopped, touched my arm, and asked, "Knife?"

"Rondel, actually. I was at Sham Castle."

"Yes, I remember you mentioning it."

I had an unfortunate habit of telling everyone, including strangers, important details about my life in England. I still let it slip where I lived to anyone who would listen. It's so charming to have a house with a name, I just can't help saying it—Ash Tree Cottage on Greenway Lane.

We paid at the gate and entered the deserted grounds of the abbey. Following the trail toward the kitchen, we passed a man playing the penny whistle on a solitary arched wall. A haunting tune filled the air, a soundtrack to our conversation.

"You didn't think that was an important fact to relate?" Simon asked about the knife.

Touched by his concern, I played the nonchalance card. "You can hardly expect me to tell you every time someone tries to kill me."

"True," he said, straight-faced. "It might get tedious."

Smiling, I turned in a circle, my arms wide, allowing the aura to surround me.

Free of its medieval reenactment, the empty abbey's grandeur radiated through the few remaining arched walls and towers. Diamond shapes were cut into the field of grass, showing where the massive nave's pillars would have stood. No wonder Henry VIII thought the monks had too much power.

The abbey's size, glory, and beauty refused to be discounted, even now.

"Did the police retrieve the rondel?" Simon asked.

Shaking my head, I said, "No, but I got a picture of it. Still, it didn't help since I was only a few blocks from Parikh's house. One of the reasons I want to talk to the blacksmith is to see if weapons like that are still forged." In reality, I wanted to know about the murder weapon stuck through the knight's chest, but the rondel had been added to my list for obvious reasons.

We wandered the grounds, and I took much better photographs of Arthur's grave marker than I had with Lily.

Finding a bench, I pulled out my phone and took notes about Arthur and the local legends surrounding the Tor. Gwynn ap Nudd, King of the Welsh Fairies, lived in a magical castle on the Tor, guarding the gateway between the living and the dead. Before being banished by an abbot, Gwynn ap Nudd held sway over the countryside.

After his banishment, Morgan le Fay, Queen of the Fairies, continued to rule the land and the Tor, which was called Avalon. She brought Arthur there to heal his wounds and placed him between the realms of life and death after he found the Holy Grail.

"These legends are fascinating. I love it here," I told Simon. "I'd much rather study legends and plan weddings than investigate a murder."

"Then why do you?"

Contemplating, I said, "Good question. When I start, it helps to make sense of the horror. Then it just sort of snowballs. And there's Fred."

Simon nodded. "That was an odd encounter. Why does he think you can help?"

Torn between being offended that he didn't think I could help, and agreeing that I was an odd choice, I shrugged. "Maybe Parikh tells him fantastical things about me to keep Fred entertained."

I stowed my phone and quoted Winnie-the-Pooh. "How about lunch?"

Returning to the Abbey Tea Room and Restaurant, we had a delicious meal. Somerset brie and broccoli quiche was impeccable—creamy and crunchy, with a flaky crust. Since I didn't know how long we would be at the blacksmith, I ordered a Somerset cream tea to-go, which included two scones, clotted cream, and mouth-watering strawberry jam.

After stowing our food treasures in the car, we drove along a country road to the blacksmith.

The repetitive clank, clank, clank of a hammer pounding metal greeted us. Following the racket, we opened the gate on a white picket fence. A large, bearded man wielded a small, ball-peen hammer, beating a curl into metal that he held with what looked like giant pliers.

Looking up, he acknowledged us but did not stop hammering.

I stepped forward, drawn toward the process of creation. The final blow was followed by a twist that turned the metal into a lovely curve, then plunged it into water. Steam and sizzling filled the air.

"You must be Lord Pacock," he said, wiping sweat off his brow with a burly forearm.

Simon agreed in a lordly sort of way and introduced me.

"Thank you so much for letting us visit," I said, watching him retrieve the curved blade from the water.

Holding the knife to a shaft of sunlight, he said, "Gurt lush," which I chose to ignore.

"Is that a coal fire?"

"It is," he answered, feeling the heat emanating up with an open hand. "It's easy to build a coal forge, although it'll take you a while to get it hot."

"Do you ever make rondels?"

"Quite a few. Popular with the Romans in Chester."

"Have you made any for locals?"

He shrugged. "I don't ask."

Shorter answers indicated I was being too pushy, so I decided to take another tactic and ask about forging in general.

"Are you still able to buy coal? I thought it was banned."

"House coal is, but I just have the one. Not a whole village to heat."

"What do mainstream forgers use?" I wanted to know.

Explaining the differences between coal, gas, and induction forges, he lost me after about two minutes, but he enjoyed the telling. Next, he showed me six different types of hammers in various sizes, along with the massive assortment of tongs used to hold the metals. "Don't do no good to have a fancy hammer if you can't hold on to nothin'."

The tools displayed on every surface of his shed looked straight out of a torture dungeon movie scene. I thought it wise not to share this observation.

Unable to contain myself, I asked, "How about swords?"

This time, he grinned. "You'll be wanting to know about that broadsword at the Chalice Well," he said, suddenly ghoulish.

But the answers I needed were ghastly, so I didn't judge. "Yeah. My friend found him."

That statement proved to be a mistake. I spent more time fending off his questions about the murder scene than getting information about swords.

Helpfully, Simon stepped in and steered the conversation where I wanted it to go. He must have learned this skill from Dolly.

"I have one here like it," he said, referring to the murder weapon. "A constable came by and showed me."

"Douglass," I hissed.

"That's the one," he said, pointing to a long blade, but I wasn't sure if he meant the constable or the sword. "It weren't none of mine, though. Mass-produced."

When he handed me the hand-and-a-half sword, I almost dropped it, surprised by the heft. The blacksmith showed me how to hold it, and I was surprised again at how well-balanced it was.

"This is beautiful," I said, examining the etchings on the blade.

Beaming at me, he pointed out aspects of interest, including the shaft, hilt, and pommel. "This here's the fuller," he said, running his finger along a groove. "Some call it a blood gutter, but it's there to add strength to the blade. The blood runs off easy enough."

On that disturbing note, we left him and drove back to Bath.

"The thing is," I pondered as the countryside raced by the car window, "someone has to know about more than just my association with Parikh. I'm sure he has lots of cases, so why focus on embroiling me in this mess?"

"You are the strongest connection to Edward," Simon pointed out.

"True. I wonder if this ties back to that drug ring Parikh and Edward dismantled over Christmas."

"How so?"

"Well, if someone in the ring wanted to punish those two and not just the detective inspector, it would make sense to use me as a pawn."

"Or," Simon added, "it's simply because you have an appalling habit of finding bodies.'

"Lily found this one," I argued, but he had a point. Jeffrey, the reporter, contacted me right away after hearing about the knight. If someone that distanced from my circle of friends made that conclusion, anyone could.

We drove the rest of the way in silence, each lost in our thoughts. When he dropped me off at Ash Tree Cottage, I barely avoided tripping over Roddy on my way through the boot room.

"Hey, Sir Roderick," I said, lifting him for a cuddle. "Are you good at chess?"

The bunny's long ears came up, then lay flat.

"Didn't the white rabbit play chess?" I asked, not expecting an answer, but Roddy looked away, almost as if to say, "No."

"I need to do research, don't I?"

This time, Roddy's nose twitched in agreement.

Taking his advice, I brought him into the kitchen to ask Meryl if she had *Alice in Wonderland*. A note told me the soup on the stove was for me and that she and Roger would be out all evening.

I left Roddy in the kitchen and explored the bookshelves. As I remembered, almost all the Priestlys' books were mysteries, but in their daughter's room, I found a copy of *Alice*.

Unfortunately, I couldn't find anything useful. Frustrated, I video called Tori.

"We have rats." She repeated this fact about D.C. before I said hello.

"We had rats in Tempe, too," I reminded her.

"Those are fruit rats, and they're gray with fluffy white chests and are cute. This thing was as big as me."

"Granted, you are very small."

My petite friend growled.

"How big?"

"Like, two feet long! And I thought for sure it would scamper away as I got near it, but no. It stared me down. I had to go into the street to avoid it. Then, I saw a woman in sturdy pumps kick a different rat out of her way without pausing."

"Um, good for her?" I phrased it as a question, unsure if Tori approved of the behavior.

"Totally. For her, these creatures are a part of the landscape. Nothing to be concerned about. I adopted the attitude, and not a single person cut me off or stepped on me today."

"Hey, that's," I paused, deciding on the right word, "amazing, actually. La Camarón makes her mark."

While I would never call my friend a shrimp in English, I thought it sounded like a superhero in Spanish.

Tori disagreed.

"Why can't I find anything about chess in *Alice in Wonderland?*" I blurted out before she hung up on me.

"You mean *Alice's Adventures in Wonderland,*" Tori said with an air of superiority.

"No," I insisted, turning the book over and examining the cover more closely, "it's…" The title was exactly as Tori said. "Oh. Whatever."

"The other is a movie. And the reason you can't find it is that chess is in *Through the Looking-Glass, and What Alice Found There.*"

"No," I insisted again and then thought better of it. Tori devoured every children's book she could get her hands on in both English and Spanish when we were kids, which was why I called her in the first place. "But isn't the Red Queen in the first one?"

"That's the Queen of Hearts who plays croquet. The Red Queen plays chess, putting Alice on the board as a pawn." Tori tilted her head to the side. "Why?"

"Something Simon said when we climbed Glastonbury Tor today."

"You went to the top of the Tor? Was it awesome?"

"So awesome! And windy."

After filling her in on my tour of the Glastonbury Abbey, Tor, and the blacksmith, I explained my chess-based revelation.

"But if a chess mastermind is moving you around an imaginary board, wouldn't it have to be someone you know?"

"I thought of that, but it could be someone out to get at the police, and I am police-adjacent via Edward."

"They made a huge dent in drug trafficking," she mused, referring to the case Parikh and Edward cracked. "Was it connected to a gang?"

"The drug ring they picked apart wasn't associated with a group of people but had lots of distributors."

"Individual cells?" Tori asked for clarification, and I nodded. "Smart. That makes it harder to trace back to the person in charge."

"Parikh never did find the mastermind," I said, my eyes growing wide, mirrored by Tori's.

"Mastermind, like chess," we said together.

"The mind behind the murder could also be the one in charge of the drug ring," I expanded the theory. "They would be motivated to remove DI Parikh from the picture. And humiliate him."

"True," Tori agreed, "but someone would still need to figure out how to get you and Edward and, therefore, Parikh's car to the murder scene. Right?"

"Right." I dragged the word out, willing Tori not to go where I thought she was going.

"Which means it has to be someone you know."

"Not necessarily," I persisted, not wanting anyone in my circle to be implicated in setting up a murder to frame a detective inspector.

"Who suggested Glastonbury?"

"Lily. But she doesn't have a mean or manipulative bone in her body."

"You're sure?"

"Completely. Totally. One hundred percent."

The thing was, I had been wrong about many people since my arrival in England.

Dead wrong.

# Chapter Twelve: The Next Move

Putting aside disturbing thoughts about criminals whom I might personally know, I got ready for a date with Edward. However, once I started my walk to his boat, our arranged meeting place, I couldn't stop thinking of Lily as a criminal mastermind. After all, I only had her word that she didn't have brains. Why would someone come out and say that, unless they were laying plans for an intricate con?

And the same goes for her stay in Manchester after the bus accident during my first month in England. I didn't know her last name then, so how did I know what she was really doing? By the time she returned to Bath, she didn't even have a limp. Maybe the collision was a ruse.

Crossing the Parade Bridge over the cricket fields, I made my way to the river walk. Engrossed in my musing, I walked past someone sitting on a bench.

"Oi!" he called.

Unaccustomed to being catcalled, I turned, ready for a fight.

"Oi? You expect me to…" I said before recognizing the speaker as Edward. "Oh, hi."

"I thought you saw me. Let me begin again. Miss Madeline, please join me," he said with his posh work accent.

"I expected you to be further down."

He nodded at the narrow boat I just passed. "Latest mooring."

"Is James home?" While Edward's wayward brother wasn't my favorite, he sometimes cooked for us.

"With the police in Bristol."

"What?" I said, instantly worried that James got caught pickpocketing, conning, or otherwise causing mischief.

"What?" Edward asked, confusion plastered on his features.

"What happened? What did he do?"

"Suspicious little thing, aren't you?" Edward said, grinning.

Little was an exaggeration, considering we were the same height. "Well?"

"I told a DI there about James's drawing skills. They're using him for witness sketches."

My estimation of James shifted through several gears before I said, "That's awesome! I'm happy for him. And you."

"Aye."

Prior to leaping into my probably-not-well-thought-out theory of my friend as a criminal genius, I wanted to return to Edward storming out. Picking up his hand, I squeezed it in both of mine, feeling his warmth radiate through me.

"I suppose you want to hear about what I said earlier."

I nodded.

"Raibead was a key informant for cracking the drug ring," he began.

Squishing the myriad of questions bubbling up, I nodded encouragingly.

"We couldn't have done it without him. He and DI Parikh always met at Sham Castle, usually in the morning. That's how he knew the note was from Raibead."

One question answered without my interrupting—an important lesson for me.

"We knew he was close to the head of the operation, but he would not reveal the final key piece to clear out the drugs. Without knowing the leader, everything would start again with different players."

Edward ran a hand over his face before continuing. "The more we pressured him, the more he withheld. I'm convinced he started the Locksbrook Road warehouse fire on Christmas. There was evidence in there. All destroyed."

"That's why you would have killed him yourself?" A girl can keep her curiosity at bay for only so long.

"Aye. I dinnae mean it." He looked deeply into my eyes. "You know that, don't you?"

Violence dwells deep in Edward, coiled like a snake, but it only reveals itself when he needs to protect someone: a defense reaction, never offense.

"Yes," I answered truthfully. "It did kind of freak me out a little, though. Simon said you were blowing off steam."

Edward paused for only a moment before nodding, indicating he understood I talk with my friends about everything.

Drawing me to him, we kissed until I wondered how long James would be gone.

Turns out, not long enough. An inarticulate greeting broke us apart, and we turned to see James running toward us.

"I got a job!" he announced proudly. "A real job. With a police force. Crikey, what would the old girl think about that?"

"She wouldn't believe it," Edward said, picking up his younger brother in a bear hug. "I dinnae think she believes me."

I assumed the old girl in question was their grandmother, but since Simon used the same phrase to refer to me, it was hard to tell.

"Congratulations, James," I offered. "When do you start?"

"Tomorrow, och aye! Can you believe it? Let's celebrate. I'll make Cullen Skink. You two go back to whatever that was."

Ignoring his suggestion, we followed James's leap onboard, buoyed by his enthusiasm.

The small galley was well-appointed. I squeezed onto the bench at the table and awaited instructions.

None came as the brothers worked in tandem, seamlessly creating a deliciously smoky fish stew.

I could get used to being cooked for like this.

With nothing to do, my thoughts wandered to the criminal mastermind ruining DI Parikh's life.

"Fifteen minutes," James announced the remaining time dinner needed to simmer. Turning to me, he said, "You're not talking. That never happens."

About to protest, I stopped myself, as talking would prove his point.

Glancing at Edward for support, I noted his stony expression, a sure sign he didn't want his emotions showing.

"Okay, fine," I said, giving up. "At the Tor today, we talked about chess, and I have a theory that the goal of the murder wasn't to kill Raibead; it was to frame the DI."

They stared at me.

I carried on.

"We're being moved around the board like pawns to implicate Parikh. And the person with the biggest motivation for wanting him gone would be the leader of the drug ring you brought down." I rushed through the explanation, hoping speed would ensure acceptance.

Neither boy argued, but Edward asked, "Why kill Raibead?"

"Sometimes you sacrifice a knight to protect the king."

"That's true of all pieces," James pointed out.

"But Raibead was dressed as a knight," I countered. "An actual knight. Not a horse, like in chess."

James cut a sidelong glance at me as if to say, "Duh," which I deserved.

"Anyway," I continued, "another reason might be Raibead was getting ready to divulge more information."

Edward shrugged when I looked at him for confirmation.

"But the thing is, to maneuver us like we've been, it has to be someone we've met." I picked up steam. "And, hear me out, I think the leader might be Lily. She's the one who got me, and therefore you, to Glastonbury so Parikh's car would be seen there; she found the body, not me this time, her. We only have her word that she was recovering from an accident in Manchester when she could have been running a drug ring, and…" I ran out of steam in the face of James's incessant chortling.

"Lily," he gasped between guffaws. "Little Lily, ha ha ha," he fake-laughed until actual chuckling overtook him again.

To his credit, Edward did not crack a smile. He said, "I checked on Lily after the bus accident. Remember? I got her name and confirmation from the trauma center."

"Really?" Instead of embarrassment, relief flooded through me. "Good.

That's good." I nodded.

"James," Edward said in a way that cut his brother's laughter short before looking back to me. "The rest of your theory has merit."

"Really?" I repeated, sitting taller.

Nodding, he said, "But it doesn't need to be a friend. It could be anyone who's seen us in The Huntsman."

"Or The Boater," I agreed. I didn't add the Crystal Palace as I usually went there with only Lily.

"Aye. I spent a lot of time there until I met you."

A blush heated my cheeks, so I asked James, "When's dinner?"

"Grab a bowl, lass."

The stew, Cullen Skink, was thick with potatoes and rich with milk. A hint of nutmeg complemented the smoky haddock.

"Are you sure you want to be an artist? Chef suits you," I told James as I shoveled the concoction into my mouth.

Uncharacteristically, he smiled shyly, turning to hide his red face. "What evidence do you have on your governor?" he asked.

I focused on my dinner, expecting Edward to say something about not discussing an active case.

However, he surprised me by listing everything they had against the DI.

"Witnesses placed him in Glastonbury; he didn't report in for duty, his mum's car was in Glastonbury—" Edward held up a hand to stop me from interrupting. "Any objections I made were written off as me protecting my boss. The note from the supposed informant was printed at the local station, and most damning of all, his glasses were found in the pool with Raibead."

The glasses. I forgot about those. Lady Vivian said they were missing. "Circumstantial," I declared like a melodramatic lawyer. "Any citizen can use the printers at the station to print water bills or whatever. And it's obvious someone slipped sleeping pills in his tea, then lifted his glasses and the car keys."

"Douglass won't hear a word about Parikh being framed. He insists good police work leaves an irrefutable trail."

"Of course, he won't," I complained, then snapped my fingers. "What about the track team? Did they follow up? Did anyone see Parikh at Sham Castle that morning?"

Edward shook his head no. "They said the coach had them do time trials. Too focused on speed to look around."

"Drat. Has the DI said anything in his defense yet?"

Again, no.

"Why not? He's as stubborn as Douglass."

"Aye, that he is. And for the same reason. He believes good police work will clear his name."

"What about the murder weapon? They can't tie it to Parikh," I argued.

However, Edward did not jump to contradict me. Instead, he told us, "The DI has a weapon collection. Many coppers do, but he focuses on ancient swords." He paused, then added, "And rondels like the one thrown at you at Sham Castle."

Burying my hands in my face, I moaned. "But that means the true killer knew him well enough to choose the sword."

"That would be one way to look at it."

"I feel like a 'but' is coming," I said.

Edward puffed out air before saying, "But the blacksmith in Glastonbury picked his picture out from a lineup as someone who purchased from him."

Excited, I jumped, the spoon dropping into my bowl. "But I met him. The blacksmith. He said the broadsword wasn't one of his. That clears Parikh."

Instead of responding with happy exclamations, Edward frowned. "Unless the blacksmith offered names of other places a person could buy such a weapon."

Silence thickened. Finally, I said, "And he did."

Nodding, Edward confirmed, "Aye. The blacksmith recalled Parikh asking about something similar, and he provided a list that included online sources, including those in Europe."

I pushed my bowl toward James, who refilled it.

"If you ask me," James said, placing the stew in front of me, "he might be guilty."

Thrusting my chin toward him, I glared.

"Well, then. How did this mastermind you've conjured up do it?"

"I'm glad you asked," I said, shooting him a toothy smile.

James rolled his eyes. Very annoying. I made a mental note to stop doing it.

"Several things needed to happen, but with good planning, they all could have been carried out the week of the murder.

"Step one was to get Lily to ask me to Glastonbury because if I'm there, Edward will be there, and he'll want a car instead of his motorcycle to give me a ride home. So he would borrow Parikh's SmartCar. Easy. Anyone could put a flyer for the Arthurian Fayre in front of her, including the mastermind himself."

"How do we know she'd ask you and not Donny?" James asked, infuriatingly logical.

But I had thought this through. "The killer needed to plan it for a day when Lily was off, but Donny was working. Schedules are always posted. Easy," I countered. "The previous day, the mastermind needed someone, a pawn, to slip sleeping pills into Parikh's afternoon tea. Tricky, but if this really is someone who coordinated a drug ring across England, he knows people who would do something like drop a doctored tea sachet into a cup."

Before either boy pointed out more holes in my theory, I moved forward. "That was probably the part requiring the most faith. So not a pawn. More like a bishop. Someone who moved in unexpected ways to avoid cameras. They could have printed the note then, too. It might have even been Raibead. Parikh expected to see him."

Edward shook his head, but I didn't stop. "Table that for now. Once the DI made it home and drifted off to sleep, a simple break-in to snatch keys and glasses wouldn't be difficult."

"But—"

"And," I overrode him, "the email could have been sent from his home computer while he slept. Brazen, but easier than hacking."

"But your plan is way too risky and involves far too many variables," Edward pointed out.

"Not nearly as risky as killing a cop," I countered. No one argued, so I went on. "It's a snap to go in the exit at the Chalice Well. I did it to use the facilities, then went around front to pay. The thing I can't figure out is how the shop folks didn't see the body."

I waited, but no one offered a solution, so I thought aloud, "If the killer and Raibead went in the exit right after opening, the employees would be at their stations and wouldn't see the pool where he was stabbed."

With a sigh, Edward conceded that Raibead had been killed prior to being placed in the pool, which was why only a few tendrils of blood swirled in the water.

Shuddering, I put the image from my mind and suggested that the killer could have been mistaken for a groundskeeper carrying a bag of soil or mulch.

"You're forgetting one thing, lass," Edward said in that tone of voice my mother used when she didn't want to cause a fight.

Bunching my hands into fists, I waited.

"There were eye-witnesses who placed Parikh in Glastonbury."

Actually, I hadn't forgotten. But I didn't want to admit to a picture on my phone that proved it.

# Chapter Thirteen: Games

Rather than admitting to Edward and James that I had pictorial evidence placing DI Parikh in Glastonbury the morning of the murder, I said, "But that's just silly. Why would he stick around? Who kills someone, dumps their body in a public place, and then goes sightseeing?"

Shaking his head, Edward answered, "More villains than you might think."

Not the answer I wanted.

Growing quiet, I pondered whether I should show them the photograph of DI Parikh at the Glastonbury Medieval Fayre. I didn't want to be the friend who put the final nail in the coffin. The weight of the decision pressed on my heart, and I held back tears.

But Edward trusted me to help with the investigations that I somehow always became embroiled in.

It came down to trust. I couldn't hold back. Reaching for my phone, I said, "I have something to show—"

A loud beep rang from Edward's phone, and he stood. " Sorry, luv." He kissed me on the forehead. "Must run."

And he did. In a few quick strides, he was off the boat, on the dock, and racing away.

Dating a constable had its downsides, including sudden departures.

James and I stared after him until I finally offered, "Want help with dishes?"

The thing about the boat was that it looked like a disaster when anything was out of place. But the small size also meant there was never much to stow. Everything was shipshape in no time, and I headed back up the hill to

Ash Tree Cottage on Greenway Lane and troubled sleep.

* * *

The following day, I declined Roger's offer to drive me to the Roman Baths and instead allowed the cold wind to whip my thoughts into place as I walked. My knee still ached from my tumble at Sham Castle, so it took longer than usual, but my head was clear.

Rushing to the Oversight office out of habit, I was about to change directions to head upstairs to the lab when I heard a shriek. I flung open the door to find Sam and Yvette doubled over in laughter.

Both women clapped hands over their mouths like they'd been caught by Mother Superior.

"Maddie, me darling girl. Thank the good Lord, it's you," Sam said as she smoothed her hand over her short red hair. "I was going to start my Roman Bath lecture for Yvette. Let's go to your lab so you're not late reporting in."

My former boss said all this in a rush as she shooed me out, not giving me the opportunity to ask what was so funny.

The lab stood dark and empty, but Marcus appeared just as I got the lights on.

After everyone greeted each other, Sam invited him to stay for her mini-lecture.

Nodding as he pulled out a chair, Marcus asked, "What is the subject for today?"

"Sulis Minerva."

"Ah, yes," Marcus interrupted. "Created by the Romans, an amalgam of the Brythonic pagan goddess Sulis and the Roman Minerva. One of the few such crossover deities accepted by the Celts."

Brythonic? Geez. He sounded like my mom with her ridiculous vocabulary. "British" worked just fine. While Marcus seemed at home around Dr. Daniels, he needed pointers on how to work with Samantha Niven. Interruptions and showing off were not high on her list.

"Specifically, her statue," Sam continued smoothly. "And if it's okay with young Marcus here, let's go down and look at her."

Marcus nodded, and I gratefully thanked him. If he hadn't stopped by, we would have stayed in the lab rather than seeing the magnificence of Sulis Minerva's head during Sam's lecture.

The museum wasn't open yet, so we could cram around the lighted glass protecting her while Sam spoke.

"She was discovered in 1727. One of only three gilt bronze pieces in Britain."

"Gilt?" Yvette asked, leaning in close. "That's gold, is it?"

"We found she had six layers of gold originally. Two were fired on, with the remaining four applied as gold leaf."

"The bronze work is so beautiful," I said. "She was bigger than us, wasn't she?"

"She would have been an imposing sight to behold. We still don't have her body."

"Honestly?" I breathed. A fact I should have known. "But her head is so perfect."

Sam agreed with a wistful expression that I understood. *Maybe someday, we will find it.* "There are wee holes in her hairline where a Corinthian helmet was attached, making her even taller."

Picturing the statue, gilded bright, towering over her people, sent a frisson through me. "Was she wax cast?" I asked.

"The lost-wax method," Sam confirmed.

The method required an artist to create a positive of the subject, then a negative, between which would be packed with wax. Once the positive and negative were clamped together, bronze would be poured into it, melting the wax and replacing it with a detailed statue.

"That would have required a lot of heat to melt enough metal."

I related what I learned from the blacksmith. "He said you can make more products with induction heating, but he uses coal for authenticity."

Sam nodded and lifted a hand toward Sulis Minerva. "Our lovely lady here was the protector of craftsmen, including blacksmiths. The smith lucky enough to make her would have been honored above all others."

"He might have been the only layman to see her," Marcus added.

It took me a moment to remember why that would have been. "Only the priests were allowed in the temple where she stood," I said to Yvette, who was wide-eyed with wonder as she scribbled notes on a small pad.

We got a few more details, and after thanking Sam, Marcus and I returned to the lab.

Marcus checked my work from before and declared it passable, which I interpreted as the most amazing thing he'd ever seen, and he left me to photograph more artifacts.

No two pieces were alike today, so I couldn't form a mental picture to puzzle them together.

While my eyes worked, I allowed my mind to ponder DI Parikh's predicament. I'd been so relieved when Edward cleared Lily of suspicion that I didn't think about who could have manipulated her.

Donny came up as a possibility. After all, how much did we really know about him other than that he did magic tricks? His sleight of hand could throw us off the right trail.

All of the logic I used to accuse Lily held true for Donny. He knew their schedules and could have suggested to Lily that we attend the Glastonbury event.

I couldn't picture him lifting or otherwise lugging the knight uphill to the Chalice Well Gardens, though. Even if he had a van backed up to the exit gate, it was still a walk up to the pool, and Donny wasn't a muscular guy.

*But he was at the Arthur Fayre*, I thought, playing devil's advocate with myself.

"And in disguise," I said aloud, remembering the spirit gum on his chin. He told us he dressed as a merchant, but we only had his word for that. And why did he need a costume at all? Although, to be fair, Lily and I were two of the few who weren't wearing period clothing.

A knock on the lab window startled me out of my musings. Lily waved, and I pointed her toward the door.

"Look at you," she said. "From dungeon to tower in one promotion!"

"I guess that's a fun way of looking at it."

Squinting skeptically, she said, "You don't sound sure."

Grateful for someone to talk with, I invited her to sit.

"Can't. Lunch order time, innit? And you're on the list, all fancy-like."

I gaped. "Really?"

She grinned in answer.

"Wow. There are some perks to being up here," I said as I carefully stowed the pottery shard I'd been photographing. "But let me come with you."

I texted Marcus that I was going on a lunch break and followed Lily to the Bath Bun to pick up tea and sustenance.

"So, what is it?" she asked, not taking my vague answers.

"When I was under the stairwell sifting dirt, I was closer to the site. I thought once I was an official team member that I'd be able to dig."

"Leave it to you to want to be in the muck," she said, laughing. "Me, I like nice things." Displaying her wrist, she showed off a delicate gold bracelet.

"Pretty!" I said, suddenly jealous since all my jewelry was in a safe at my mom's condo. "Is that from Donny?"

A red blush crept from her neck to her cheeks as she nodded.

While I wanted to chat about my new position, I couldn't ignore a perfect segue when presented with one.

"How long have you and Donny known each other?"

"Well, there's knowing, and there's dating. It's officially two months now, but he's had his eye on me for quite some time."

Pausing while she placed the order for the dig team, I pondered. A bracelet at two months is a statement gift. At least, back home, it was. I'd broken up with boys for less extravagant gifts given too soon. I wondered how he afforded it on a bartender's salary.

As if reading my mind, she said, "The bracelet was his grandmother's. She apparently collected them, and now whenever she sees a family member, she gives one away."

I doubted Edward's grandmother had the same collection, but before I went down a rabbit hole of what my boyfriend's family was really like, I asked another question.

"Has Donny worked at The Boater long?"

"Oh, donkey's years. I was reluctant to go in at first."

Knowing Lily's quest for a quiet life, I asked, "Too rowdy?"

"By half," she confirmed. "But one day, I walked by, and this sweet smile through the window stopped me."

"Donny?"

"Donny! I ordered a pot of tea, and he did a card trick for me. If I'm honest, I was hooked right then."

Such a better story than how I met Edward in The Cellar Bar, now boarded up and closed forever. I thought he was a clod, and then he was the constable who showed up at my door the next day.

"He hopes to be manager one day," Lily continued to talk about Donny. "Sort of resentful of Mac when he just waltzed in, but I guess he owns some build—"

My phone let out an unholy screech, interrupting all my functioning brain cells. If I were home in the desert, it would be a warning of an impending haboob. The dust storms that rivaled apocalyptic movie special effects sometimes marched across the Valley of the Sun, dropping inches of dirt.

Obviously, the weather warning didn't apply on a damp day in Bath, England.

The offending cell continued to scream while I unbuttoned my jacket pocket and removed it. Once it was off, it told me I had a paper due the next day. I picked the most egregious alarm so I wouldn't forget.

Which I had.

"My Comparative Civilizations paper," I explained sheepishly as Lily stared at me. "I have to write an essay. Last semester, my whole schedule was spent on the internship with Ms. Niven. Now, I keep forgetting I actually have classes."

When I dropped the failing Earth Science class, my overly enthusiastic and helpful student advisor signed me up for this course instead.

"You're dead brilliant. You can write it tonight," Lily said, handing me a box of goodies while she balanced a tray of hot tea.

After rushing back to the Baths, Lily settled me into the lab with my sausage roll and tea and told me to focus.

Which I couldn't.

Luckily, Marcus strolled in right then, tea in hand, and said, "There is a server at the Pump Room who looks—"

"Like me. Lily. We know," I interrupted, then pounced on him for information. "I have a paper due about an aspect of society that spans across different cultures. Any ideas?"

His eyes seemed to cloud over as he sat, thinking. "I've just come from the Discovery Zone, and the field-trippers are playing games."

"Games. Which ones?" I asked. I already knew that the ancient Roman Tabula eventually became backgammon. The biggest difference was that the Romans started with all the pieces off the board, and there were only three dice. Since that game spanned millennia and countries, it was a good start.

"What is there besides tabula?"

Standing to check my morning's work, Marcus answered, "The children are playing dux right now."

"What is it?"

"It's very much like draughts," he said as he flicked through the pictures. "These are excellent."

"Thank you," I said, my face heating at the compliment. I silently thanked my mom for all those years of her telling me that if something was worth doing, do it right. "I incorporated your lighting suggestions." Returning to the original subject, I told him, "We don't have draughts."

"You must. Chess board with flat pieces that jump over one another."

"Oh! Checkers?"

He sort of shrugged and nodded simultaneously.

"Perfect. I'll go down and look when I get off."

"You've done more today than the previous team member covered in a week. Go downstairs and watch the children play. Primary source research."

"Thank you!" I said over-enthusiastically, but I was too excited to pull back. "You're awesome!" I added, grabbed my things, and hurried to the Discovery Zone.

I knew from my professor mother, and Tori that educators loved primary-source research. Tori always asked me to go to the Bath Abbey to confirm something she already researched so she could claim first-level authority.

Downstairs, I explained my research and received permission from the teacher to watch the kids play dux. Kind of like checkers, with aspects of go, I put together an effective outline of comparison in my head.

Once done, I headed to Roger's office at the church to grab a ride home and get the paper written.

Only after I hit submit that evening did I realize that I had missed a vital piece of information about the criminal mastermind.

# Chapter Fourteen: Damning Evidence

Pondering the previous day's activities, I knew Lily had mentioned something important. But my research paper pushed all other thoughts out of my brain, and I couldn't resurrect it.

Unable to jar my memory, I called Edward to tell him about the photo of Parikh that I had taken in Glastonbury. Although the shot was damning against the inspector, Edward needed to know.

After a few minutes of chatting, he said, "You have something you don't want to tell me."

"Oh, come on," I complained. "I get it when you can see my face, but how do you know from just my voice?"

Edward chuckled. "Because you were going to tell me before I got called away from the boat. What is it?"

"Before Lily and I went over the Chalice Well, I held my camera up and took bursts in a circle at the abbey." I took a deep breath, then added, "And Parikh is in one of them."

"Bloody hell," Edward cursed uncharacteristically.

"Yeah, I know."

"There were eyewitnesses, but no one with pictorial evidence until now. Can you bring it to me?" he asked, in a slight breach of protocol.

Grateful that he let boyfriend mode overcome cop mode for the morning, I said, "Sure." Seeing Edward was a million times better than contacting Douglass directly.

Heading down the hill to his boat's current mooring, I gave a shout as I boarded. James stuck his head out the door. "Come on in," he invited. "I'm making smoothies."

Holding the green concoction he handed me, I sipped before committing to drinking. Lemon and apple covered grassy notes that were not unpleasant.

"This is tasty," I told James as Edward and I crowded together at the kitchen table. I mirrored my phone's photos onto Edward's laptop and swiped through them.

Landing on the picture, I pointed at the man.

"Damn," Edward said, examining the tidy figure with the trim beard and wire-frame glasses. "You have to give this to Douglass."

"Ugh," I grumbled, then clapped my jaw shut. Douglass may be a jerk to me, but it didn't make Edward's professional life any easier for me to complain about him. "I guess so."

"Budge up," James said, sitting on the bench beside me. He studied the screen. "What, him?"

Edward and I made depressed sounds of agreement.

"The bloke watching a juggler?" he asked.

To clarify, I enlarged the image, although the pixelation made it blurry.

"That's not DI Parikh," James said.

"Of course it is," I insisted, then thought better of it because I preferred it not be him. "What are you saying?"

"The nose is all wrong," he said.

Edward squinted at the screen. "How can you tell?"

"Look," James said, and turned to a drawer in the saloon area. Extracting a sketchbook, he flipped through some pages, then presented us with a page with "Parikh" written at the top. There were three pencil drawings of the inspector from different perspectives.

"You've been practicing," Edward said excitedly, punching James in the arm.

James blushed, and a babble of Scottish Gaelic erupted from them, which sounded pleased and congratulatory.

Beaming at them, I was happy to admit that James seemed to be turning his life around.

Flipping through the pictures, he showed Edward his progress. The touching moment between brothers didn't last long before they realized how much emotion they were displaying.

"Right," Edward said.

"The sketch," James said, pretending he hadn't just hugged his big brother. "Look at Parikh's nose. It's straight with a little twist at the top, like it might have been broken once."

Acknowledging that his skills captured the detective perfectly, we returned to the photo.

Zooming in and out, we agreed the person I identified as DI Parikh had an impish upturned nose.

"It's not him," Edward said.

"That's great. We can give this to Douglass to prove that all those eyewitnesses were mistaken at Glastonbury."

With a shake of his head, Edward said, "It doesn't prove Parikh wasn't there. Just that someone else was."

"Still," I insisted. "It'll help. Annoying as he is, Douglass can't ignore that it throws some statements into question."

"True," Edward said, sounding doubtful.

"It can't hurt." After considering every interaction I'd had with Douglass, I asked, "Can it?"

Thinking about it for far too long, Edward gave James a questioning look. They mutely communicated something I couldn't read, and then he shook his head. "It can't. Let's go."

"Go?" I asked as Edward covered half the length of his boat in a couple of strides and opened the door.

Turning, he popped back in to discover I hadn't moved.

"Coming?"

James didn't offer any help, so I jammed my phone in my jacket pocket and followed Edward.

"Where?" I asked, hoping against hope it wasn't to see Douglass.

"One Stop Station," he said. His current mooring wasn't far. We climbed the stairwell, crossed the river, and entered the community hub.

I eyed the printers suspiciously, wondering if anyone kept track of who used them. Closed-circuit cameras would help identify who printed the note that got Parikh in so much trouble. As Edward marched to the constables on duty, I canvassed the open space with its kiosks and stands of pamphlets. Spotting a couple of tell-tale dark bubbles that encased CCTV, I caught up to him.

"Did someone scrub the footage from those cameras?" I asked, sounding like a TV show detective.

"Inconclusive," Edward answered before introducing me and the Parikh look-alike picture I had on my phone to the constables. "The pictures on this cell need to be entered into Douglass's files."

I exchanged my phone for a form granting all kinds of permissions that I should have read, but didn't.

As I handed it over, Edward got a call. My attempts at eavesdropping failed, but judging from his expression, it was official.

"Everything okay?" I asked when he hung up.

"Sorry, luv," he said, zipping his jacket. "Must run."

Much as I loved Edward's position at the Major Crimes Unit, there were times when it got in the way. Like when he left me at the mercy of random constables.

"Miss McGuire? Constable Douglass wants to talk to you," one such constable reported, handing me a receiver on a landline.

"Why didn't you tell us about these pictures earlier?" Douglass demanded. No preamble. No 'How are you holding up?' Just the assumption that I was doing something wrong.

Discarding a myriad of retorts, I took a steadying breath, counted to five, and answered, "I only took selfies with Lily at The Chalice Well. These were all from the Glastonbury Abbey, so I thought they weren't important."

A grunt. "Have you shared them with anyone?"

"No," I said, annoyed. It was a valid question, considering I had taken pictures of evidence before and shared them with Tori, but the way he asked it irked me.

Another grunt, and he was gone.

I handed the receiver back and waited for them to return my cell.

Waiting without a cell was boring. It's not that I couldn't be patient, but I could answer emails or chat with someone if I had technology.

Instead, I people-watched—a little creepy but ultimately entertaining. Four people came in, used the printer, and left. Not a single employee paid any attention. King Arthur could have printed the letter Parikh found, and no one would have noticed.

After what seemed like an eternity but was probably only ten minutes, the constable on duty returned my phone.

I tapped my photo library. The Glastonbury pictures were gone. "Hey," I protested after checking the deleted folder, "where did my photos go?"

"Sorry, miss," the constable said without sounding even slightly sorry. "Constable Douglass's orders."

If I didn't have the picture, how would I figure out why the person in the photo looked familiar?

A thought struck me as I climbed the hill to Greenway Lane, and I texted James. 'Do you think you could do a sketch of the person from my photo from memory?'

'Maybe. Trusted the coppers, didn't you?'

Yes, I did, and yes, they took my phone and pictures. Instead of admitting this, I sent, 'You now work for the police.'

Three dots loomed as a response, but no words came through except one. 'Yes.'

Not sure if the 'yes' meant he worked for the police as a sketch artist or if he could do the drawing for me, I stowed my phone and hurried to Ash Tree Cottage. The outcome would be clarified with minimal effort on my part. A portrait would appear, or not.

It turned out that the sketch materialized quicker than I imagined, as James showed up at our door just as Meryl took a roast chicken from the oven.

"I've invited dear James to dinner," Meryl called.

*Dear James*, OMG.

"You can cook," I said by way of greeting James.

"But I can't afford food yet," he whispered with a wink.

My friends here often used the word 'cheeky,' and I couldn't think of an American equivalent. The description suited James perfectly.

"Your ability to know when dinner is on the table is unparalleled."

"A talent when you grow up poor."

As we washed up in the kitchen and helped Meryl and Roger carry food into the dining room, I thought about what he said.

I knew Edward and James's childhood had been rough, but I hadn't considered what it was like not to know where your next meal was coming from. My parents, a college professor and a successful businessman, always provided me with anything I needed. Even when I wanted to prove I could make it on my own, my dad still managed to insert his monetary support into my efforts. A warm hug from either was only a phone call away.

I ached for Edward and James as I thought of my parents. I should probably put those thoughts into communication with mom or dad, but not before dinner.

After eating and helping with dishes, James showed me his sketch.

"I wanted to set it down while it was still fresh. The meal was a bonus."

"Meryl loves it when she can feed the masses. You're always welcome," I said, surprising myself.

For the first time, I understood why the Priestlys invited everyone to their table. Being an only child had many bonuses, but learning to share wasn't one of them. It felt good. Although technically, it wasn't my food.

James pulled a sheet of paper from his jeans pocket and handed it to me.

Unfolded, it revealed what at first glance looked like DI Parikh.

I was about to complain until I saw that the nose was wrong.

"It's almost like he wanted to disguise himself as Parikh, isn't it?" I mused. "I swear that nose is familiar, though."

"Maybe it's someone you know?"

Taking his suggestion into account, I did the math. If my inner circle consisted of fifteen friends, and I factored six degrees of separation, I had to sort through at least ninety people. And that's only if it's someone one of my friends knew.

"Ugh," I said, realizing it was an unattractive phrase that I used too often, and promised to find something new. "Blast." Ninety was a daunting number, and there was no guarantee the person in the back of my mind would be connected. This mystery guy could be a waiter or a random tour guide.

In addition, that ever-present specter of the mastermind being someone close to us haunted me. What if I saw him and didn't recognize him?

"You have an artist's eye," I said, making James blush. "Who do you think it looks like? Anyone you've seen?"

Meryl and Roger came into the living room and asked about what we were doing. Because they knew so many people in the community, I coerced them into helping us identify the man in James's drawing.

"Oh, why, that's DI Parikh," Roger declared with such confidence that I believed him for a minute.

"Of course, yes," Meryl agreed. "James, you are a talent." She cocked her head to the side. "Except, the nose isn't quite right, is it, dear?"

Roger took the sketch and held it under the light. "Hmm. You need to work on that."

"Actually, I have some of the detective that show his nose. You see, this man's is a bit upturned. I tried to shade it."

Before James sidetracked the conversation into artistic technique, I cut over the Priestlys' murmurs of appreciation. "I mistook the real man for Parikh as well. But this man looks familiar, and I can't pinpoint where I've seen him."

Holding his hand across the lower part of the drawing's face, Roger nodded. "Yes, you're right. A familiar face." He handed the drawing to Meryl. "Perhaps the church?"

*The church.* If I added in everyone Edward and I served cinnamon rolls to for Christmas, my list of people I'm vaguely connected to went up to about 300—no wonder the Parikh look-alike seemed familiar.

Giving up on my identification quest for the evening, I sent James on his way before he talked Meryl into making a trifle for dessert.

Once the gate was secure, I fetched Roddy from his hutch and brought him inside for a special dinner of Timothy hay. Roger purchased the treat for his rabbit because the last freeze destroyed the garden clover.

Tentative at first, Roddy soon realized his luck. Shoveling the hay into his cute little face at an alarming rate, his manners abandoned him. Bits and pieces clung to his chin like a sage colored beard.

As we laughed, Roger said, "Roddy's like Sherlock Holmes with one of his disguises."

"All he needs are fake glasses, and he'll be transformed," I added, picturing spectacles on his nose bobbing up and down with every ecstatic chew.

Ending the evening on that delightful note, I headed upstairs, clinging to joy for as long as possible. But something triggered a thought, and it refused to be silenced.

Roddy in disguise, combined with Roger's hand over the beard on the sketch, crystallized into an idea that wouldn't go away. My earlier musing returned. It really was as though the mystery man purposely disguised himself to look like DI Parikh.

When I examined James's drawing, I tried mentally removing the facial hair but couldn't picture it, so I snapped a photo of the sketch with my cell. The camera app let me erase unwanted elements, but when I removed the beard, it got rid of half the face.

As I fumed at technology for not working exactly how I wanted it to, I called James.

"What now?"

I held back a retort as I actually did want something from him. "Can you draw him again without the beard and glasses?"

"I dinnae ken," he said, although his thoughtful tone made me hopeful he'd try. "I'm going off a memory of a single photo."

Scratching sounds came through the phone. Pencil on paper. I held my tongue and twisted my hair around my finger as James hummed.

"Nae, it's no good."

"Why not?"

"I don't have enough to go on. It wound up looking like that bartender chap."

"Which one?"

"Lily's bloke."

"Donny?"

"Aye, he's the one," James answered and disconnected without saying goodbye.

Donny.

When he met us at Ludo's after the Fayre, he had a glop of something on his chin.

Spirit gum, he told me, because he had dressed as a merchant for the event.

Donny with a fake beard.

Donny.

# Chapter Fifteen: A Rat in Our Midst

Thoughts swirled out of control as I plucked moments from the past few days and made tenuous connections.

*Donny as the mastermind?*

It was even more ridiculous than thinking that Lily planned everything. Well, equally absurd. And after the reaction I got from Edward and James when I offered that theory, I wanted to think the idea through more thoroughly.

Nothing made sense until I pieced it together like a floor plan in my mind. Whoever was manipulating us might have been using chess, but my brain liked architecture, so I made a blueprint. Each friend was a room. Donny and Lilly were next to each other, as were Parikh and Edward. I was on Edward's other side, which meant the only way to put Donny next to Parikh was to make a circle. Houses aren't built in circles. There needed to be something in the middle, like a grand hall we could all access.

Donny worked at The Boater, so I used that as the common meeting place. In my mental floor plan, everyone easily accessed it and each other.

Still, it didn't make sense that Donny was a crime boss. No matter how adept an actor was, parts of a person's true self always shone through. Donny lacked ambition. I pondered the correct word to describe him and finally landed on one my mother would use: callow.

Young and inexperienced, just like me. But I was halfway through a university degree and working in a foreign country. I couldn't turn off that drive and couldn't disguise it. People would see it.

When Lily talked about Donny, she never wistfully painted a picture of a fantastic future. In fact, the only thing Donny wanted was to manage The Boater someday.

"Manage The Boater," I said to no one. That was the critical tidbit Lily revealed that I hadn't remembered. Donny had been passed up for promotion when Mac suddenly appeared on the scene.

Donny needed to answer some questions before I went down another rabbit hole.

* * *

After spending the morning photographing in the Roman Baths Museum lab, I speed-walked to The Boater for lunch. With my laptop in hand, I planned to write the first draft of my next assignment while I observed Donny in his natural element.

When I walked into the main room off Pulteney Bridge, the space was empty, so I headed downstairs. The patio was closed due to the chilly, wet weather, but there was a small room I usually ignored. Today, it was warmly lit and inviting. As I ducked my head around the corner to say hello, something whizzed past my ear. The sound conjured the rondel at Sham Castle so vividly that I dropped to the floor.

"Lily, my lover! I'm so sorry," Mac hollered as he rushed to help me. "Not herself then, but Lily's doppelgänger. Maddie, was it?"

Heart pounding, I agreed and moved away from what I now saw was a dartboard, with four projectiles quivering in the bullseye.

Indicating the board with a jerk of his head, Mac explained, "I'm trying to find a place to hang one for games. This is no good, clearly."

"I'm glad your aim is accurate," I said. "Do you participate in the competitions?"

"Me? No. Save that for the patrons."

A blast of cold air preceded Donny in from the patio. "All the benches are chained to tables," he said before seeing me. "Y'alright?"

Still not knowing the proper response to the question, I said, "Hi," in a squeaky voice.

"Why don't you take our patron up for a nice cuppa?" Mac suggested as he removed the dartboard from the wall and scanned the cramped room for another location.

"Right. Come along," Donny said, ushering me gently toward the stairs to the street-level bar. "What happened?"

"I almost got speared with a missile."

"Ah, Mac is a dead shot, he is," Donny said with a grin. "Pot of tea?" he offered, grabbing a thick-walled ceramic cup from below the counter.

"Actually, after that near miss, I think I'll have half a pint of Bath Ale."

Smoothly swapping the cup for a barrel-shaped glass, he said, "You just like it because the rabbit makes you happy."

"Too right," I said, borrowing a phrase from Lily.

Bath Ale's elongated rabbit logo did make me happy. But my smile faltered when I remembered Roddy's hay beard and why I came to The Boater. *Why was Donny disguised as DI Parikh?*

"So, Donny," I said, failing to sound casual, "it sure was nice of you to try and find Lily at the Fayre in Glastonbury."

Deftly sliding the beer across the counter to me, he agreed. "I wish my phone hadn't died when I got there so I could have found you. Particularly when…you know."

After we found the knight, Lily tried multiple times to contact Donny, but every call went straight to his voicemail.

"Yeah." I wondered if the same mysterious dead-battery culprit that drained Parikh's phone had also killed Donny's. "Forget to plug it in?" I asked, fishing.

Shaking his head, he said, "No. I plugged it in, but must have done a bad job of it." He touched a charger behind the bar. "Sometimes I'm so busy that I pull it out of the wall."

"Did anyone recognize your costume?"

"More than I thought would. It was a clever idea," he said, rubbing his chin. "That beard was itchy, though. The man at the fruit stand offered me a job when I juggled oranges."

"Where did you get the spirit gum?"

He tilted his head quizzically, wondering why I cared.

"Uh." Quick on my feet. That's me. Scrambling to come up with a plausible explanation for my curiosity, I blurted out, "Just in case Simon and Dolly decide to have a costume party." Not an impossibility. Although not likely either.

He laughed. "I thought you were going to take up theatre while you were here. I had some from when I did magic at my nephew's birthday. Mac had the embroidered vest and the glasses. Felt like a proper merchant," he added with a grin.

"That sounds like so much fun!" I feigned enthusiasm, wondering what kind of glasses and whether Mac had a pair of wire-rim, non-prescription, clear lenses lying around. "Did you take a ton of pictures?" I asked, sipping my malty ale.

Donny grimaced. "I went to take a selfie in front of the Abbey..."

"And discovered your phone was dead," I finished.

"That's it."

A dead end on pictures. The lack of battery proved remarkably inconvenient for me and advantageous for the mastermind. "It's so great that Mac had everything you needed for your costume," I said, changing directions. "Does Mac cosplay?"

"And when would I have time for that, I ask you?" Mac's voice said from the stairwell.

I jumped, toppling the glass and spilling the last of the beer. For a big guy, he was quiet, and I hoped he hadn't listened too long.

In case he had, I attempted more questions to sound friendly. "I guess this place takes up a lot of your time. What did you do before becoming manager?"

Rather than answering my question, he pointed to my empty glass. "Another?"

The image of someone slipping a pill into a drink popped into my mind, and I shook my head.

"Mac isn't just a bar manager," Donny said with a hint of pride. "He owns a business property. Isn't that right, Mac?"

"Do you want to try a cider?" Mac offered.

Again, I shook my head. "No, no. I'm not used to alcohol this early in the day."

That statement made it weird that I was still in a bar, but I pressed on. "I've been here for Jane Austen Day," I said, hoping to pull Mac into a conversation about costuming. "Have either of you ever dressed in Regency clothes?"

"That's a special day, innit?" Mac said in reference to the festival celebrating the famed author, where fans dress in period clothing. "Everyone looks right at a home in Bath."

"Are you from here?" I asked.

"I'm from all about. You sure I can't get you anything?" he asked, nodding at the glass again.

"No. I should be getting back."

As I zipped my jacket and shuffled outside, Mac barged over to hold the door. Rather than a courtesy, it forced us close together in the small, dark entry. He smelled of stale beer and menace.

I fled onto Pulteney Bridge and bumped into two people before getting the rhythm of walking on the left. Shaking off the unease, I asked the clouds not to rain and cataloged what I had discovered.

Most people liked to talk about themselves, but Mac hadn't answered a single question. Not even the easy ones, like where he was from. "All about" doesn't mean anything.

Donny enjoyed our chat and not only answered questions but added details.

If all roads pointed to The Boater, Mac was the key, not Donny.

Before jumping too deep into this latest theory, I reviewed the list of reasons I had thought Lily was the criminal mastermind, starting with her idea to take me to the Arthurian Fayre.

Since I was aimed toward the Baths and the Pump Room, I stuck my head in to see her. After some idle chit-chat, I asked what made her decide to go to Glastonbury that day.

She shuddered. "I wish he'd never told me about it, if I'm honest."

"Me too. But it was really cool until, you know…I'm glad I got to see it."

"But not the…" she trailed off, and I rubbed her arm. "Bloody awful."

"Who told you about it? Donny?" I asked.

"Nah. Mac talked it up because he used to go as a knight. He said everyone should see it, even foreigners. Not to be missed, he said. Wish I had missed it."

"Mac talked about it?" I sounded like a parrot, repeating everything Lily said.

After spending all that time trying to induce Mac to talk about any subject, it sounded like his recommendation had ulterior motives.

I changed the subject and sent Lily back to work, thinking happier thoughts.

Mac had access to schedules. It was his idea to tempt me, the foreigner that I am, to the Fayre. He owned a property but still took the manager job at a pub—a position that allowed him to suggest and move us the way he wanted.

But why? Before today, he came across as just an affable guy. I could have imagined the threat I perceived as I left. I've misread people in the past. And Donny never mentioned Raibead, the man, or the gang. So why would Mac have it out for Parikh?

The buzzing of my cell interrupted my musings. Edward's name on the screen made my heart skip a beat.

"Hey," I said, casually.

"Ah, lassie," Edward sighed. "It's good to hear your voice. Alas, that's all I get for the next few days."

It was my turn to sigh, although in an entirely different, disappointed way. "Is MCIT sending you out of town on a case?"

"Aye. I'm leaving James with the boat and staying at a B and B. Watch out for him."

Smiling, I agreed. "That's gotten easier now that he is proud of himself for working with the police."

Edward gave me the details of where he would be, but reminded me that I probably couldn't contact him.

"It's okay," I said, even though it was not even a little okay. I changed the subject. "What do you know about Mac?"

"From The Boater? Nothing, really. Is he your latest suspect for the mastermind?"

"I hear you putting air quotes around mastermind. It's a good word!" I laughed at the absurd term. "But yes. You know that picture of Parikh that isn't Parikh? I think it's Donny. And Mac is the one who told Lily to go to the Fayre with me, gave Donny the day off, and provided most of the elements of Donny's costume."

The silence on the other end of the line lasted so long that I thought the call had dropped. "Are you still there?"

"That's actually compelling information. Damn! I wish I were involved in that investigation and not Douglass."

"Mac's also a dead shot with darts. He has the talent to throw that rondel that missed me by inches."

"I'll look into Mac's background before I leave."

"Are you able to tell me what you find without violating anything?"

There was another silence, and then he agreed. He wouldn't do a full background check, as that level of scrutiny raised flags, but he could do some exploring.

* * *

Waiting for Edward to call me back with what he found was torture. The wind whipped across the Avon River and through my jacket, making the rest of my walk home colder. By the time I got to Bear Flats, a smattering of rain started, and when Greenway Lane finally came into view, I was soaked and freezing. Fortunately, a neoprene cover kept my laptop safe in my bag.

Meryl and Roger weren't home, so I took off most of my clothes in the boot room and scampered up the two flights of stairs to my studio, aka my princess tower.

After throwing on an oversized sweatshirt and warm leggings, I dried my hair and waited.

Not one of my strengths.

At all.

I called Edward.

Before I could ask about his progress, he barked, "What else do you know about Mac?"

Since I didn't know anything, I offered the tidbit Donny let drop. "He owns a business property. I don't know what or where."

"Right." Edward hung up.

I proofed my Games Across Cultures essay again before turning it in. The next assignment was a short discussion regarding the change in naming conventions from BC and AD (Before Christ and Anno Domini, the year of our Lord) to BCE and CE (Before Common Era and Common Era).

Because the name change referred to the same years, it seemed like much ado about nothing, as the Bard would say.

Shakespeare always made me think of my mom, and I checked the time. She would think something was wrong if I called this early. I missed her, though.

Just as I opened a puzzle game to kill time, Edward called back.

"What did you find?" I said without waiting for a "hello."

"It's not bad, but it's not good either. I need to do more digging."

I counted to twenty-three by prime numbers, then calmly, coolly, and collectedly asked again, "What did you find?"

"Settle down, lassie, I'm getting to it." He took an audible breath. "I found a warehouse owned by a holding company that Mac's last name is associated with. The property isn't registered in his full name, but might be tied to him. It's a small-scale manufacturer of some sort, producing souvenirs. The interesting thing is that his place is adjacent to the warehouse that burned down over Christmas."

"The warehouse with the drug ring evidence in it?"

"Aye."

"Who owned that? Is it the same holding company?"

"No, not the same."

"Well, who got paid the insurance money from that fire?" I knew they had already checked, but I had to ask.

"No one. It wasn't insured," Edward said.

"Is there any reason to believe Mac owned it, too? Could he be the drug ring leader that Parikh is still looking for?"

The impact of my question hit me like desert wind, so hot it stole my breath. If Mac were the drug leader, he had ample reason to hate DI Parikh, the man who dismantled the distribution network in the South West of England.

"No evidence, no. That's the bad part. A shell company owned the drug warehouse. We never found the person who owned it. Now that I have a name, I can explore from both ends."

Edward paused before adding, "Maddie, my love, you could be on to something big. If Mac is involved, he's more dangerous than you can imagine. Make sure he doesn't know you suspect him."

Unfortunately, it was too late for that.

# Chapter Sixteen: I Know a Guy

Confessing to Edward that I went to The Boater and pumped Donny for information about Mac didn't take long and didn't surprise my constable. It concerned him, though.

"I have to leave, and I doubt asking Douglass to keep an eye out for ye would go over well."

I may have growled.

"For either of you," Edward added.

Unable to control my dislike of Constable Douglass, I said, "I wish we could frame him for something so he would believe it was possible to frame Parikh."

"Maddie," Edward cautioned.

"No, not to hurt him. Just to make him realize it's possible."

"Be careful, will ye love?"

After saying goodbye, my mind spun around planting evidence on Douglass. He needed to understand that Parikh was being set up, and plain old police work wasn't pointing the guy in the right direction.

Yes, he had a supervising detective who understood all that, but taking Douglass down a notch also played into my decision.

Because a decision had formed.

Since Tori was in a time zone closer to mine than my mom, I opened my computer app and called her.

"Hola!" she chimed, followed by something in Spanish I couldn't translate.

"You're beginning to enjoy your DC Embassy internship more, I take it?"

"Sí! The key to avoiding rats is to not go out at night."

"That seems like good advice in any case. So, I need you to talk me out of something."

A Cheshire Cat grin spread across her face. "A fun thing or a bad thing?"

The problem with carrying your childhood best friend into adulthood is that they were there for every bad decision.

"Bad. It's Douglass."

"Ah." Tori employed the stock response I used when the conversation wasn't going well. It was more annoying than I realized.

"Ah, indeed," I responded, using Simon's standard reply, similarly annoying. "I think Mac is the mastermind, but I can't tell Douglass because he won't listen to me."

"And," Tori prompted.

"And, so I want to plant evidence pointing to Mac on Douglass," I finished in a rush.

"And," her expression took on the mischievous aspect she got when she figured something out, "you know a guy."

"Well…"

"You're going to contact Gabriel," she said, referring to the faux French intern I worked with over Christmas at the Chedworth Roman Villa.

"His name is Harold." As I found out, Gabriel was neither French nor an intern, but a thief and a conman.

"Gabriel sounds more romantic."

"Tori," I said, attempting my mother's best warning tone to keep my friend from getting all mushy about Gabriel.

Also, so I wouldn't get taken in. Unfortunately, I thought of him as Gabriel, too, mysterious and oh so charismatic.

"This is an under-the-radar, slightly off-the-reservation job. Nothing more. Not an assignation," I reminded both of us.

"You never told me you had his phone number," she sighed, still sounding wistful.

"I don't. He told me to contact a pub in London and ask for him. I don't know if there is more than one bar with that name, so this may be all for naught."

"You sound like your mom.

"You're doing a crappy job of talking me out of this."

Tori grinned, then opened her large brown eyes wider, aiming for innocent, no doubt. "I think it is a good idea. One, you, personally, are not doing anything illegal."

"Except for contacting a thief whose information should be given to the police."

Ignoring me, she continued. "Two, you will be providing Major Crimes with a vital clue that needs exploring. Three, that clue may not be taken seriously if you bring it up directly."

I sighed. "Fine. I'll try it. Like I said, I might not be able to find the right pub."

"You found ancient coins when no one else did. You can find a boy who wants to be found by you."

Once Tori and I disconnected, I tried to talk myself out of contacting Gabriel since she didn't. "It's a bad idea," I said out loud. "I probably don't remember the name of the pub he told me to call."

*The Captain Kidd,* my subconscious provided more promptly than I wanted to admit.

"Probably not even a real pub," I said, hoping the sound of my voice would somehow convince me to stop searching.

It didn't.

There was one in the East End of London. I called it.

"Hi. I'm looking for Gabriel."

"No Gabriel here," a gruff voice answered without asking if he was an employee or patron.

"Oh, sorry. It's Harold."

"No Harold, either," he said before hanging up.

I might have stuck my tongue out. "Rude."

Without the chance to give my name, there was no way to carry on with this plan.

After double-checking that there wasn't a second pub in London with the name, I gave up and focused on my class's discussion of year conventions.

I dutifully researched the pros and cons, presented a balanced perspective, and added my informed opinion.

As I closed my laptop, my phone dinged. A text message read, 'GWR 9:13-10:44 AM Bath to Paddington. Tomorrow.'

Confused, I texted back. 'I'm afraid you have the wrong person.'

'Number not in use.'

Anyone could type that. I called and got a very official-sounding recording: "This number is not in use."

Official or not, the voice recording could also be fake. I went downstairs and used the Priestlys' landline, thinking an unknown phone might get through. I got the same message.

*Gabriel.* He must want me to meet at the train station at that time.

*Or,* a voice in my head that sounded appallingly like my mother's said, *Mac is setting a trap.*

Only one way to find out.

* * *

The next morning, I relayed my plans to go to London to Meryl and texted the times to Dolly, Simon, and Edward, although he was already out of range for his new case. I didn't tell anyone why I was going, but no one questioned it. For the months I'd been in England, I hadn't spent a day in London yet. Everyone told me to have fun.

Remembering my promise to check on James while Edward was out of town, I strolled to the river to find their blue narrowboat. They were on day three of their mooring, so it was still by the bridge near the rugby pitch.

Not that James needed supervision, in my opinion. He had two respectable employers, the Roman Baths and the police, who were pleased with his artistic skills, and his pride shone whenever he talked about his work. Not to mention how much he enjoyed keeping Edward, and therefore himself, well fed. I finally accepted that his gang-related activities were behind him.

I would ask where he was going to move the boat next and maybe invite him to dinner, but he didn't need to be watched.

"James," I called as I came alongside.

"Bark, bark, bark, bark!"

"Uh." Edward did not own a dog.

"Hush," James's voice commanded, and the barking stopped.

James opened a window. "Oi."

"Where did you get a dog?" I demanded.

"What dog?" His innocent expression was so convincing that I almost bought it.

Almost.

Instead, I stepped aboard and called, "Here, boy!"

A gorgeous black-and-white border collie pushed from behind James and ran to my side, smiling and tail wagging.

"Oh my, aren't you the cutest thing I've ever seen? You match Old Nigel the horse," I told him. "What's his name?" I turned my attention to the boy Edward had entrusted me to control.

"Milo," James said. "Ain't he a beaut?"

"Hello, Milo. Who's a good boy? Hmmm?" While I patted the dog, I glared at James.

"Whose dog is this?"

"Found him, didn't I?"

"Have you looked for his owner?"

"He's a stray. Digging through the trash, the poor fella."

Milo's deep brown eyes gleamed, and his coat almost glimmered in the sunshine. "This dog is not a stray."

James shrugged.

Infuriating.

"Find the owner, or I will," I threatened, but couldn't stay long enough to do anything else, or I'd miss the meeting time at the train.

As I hurried toward the train, my impending adventure kept me from fuming about James and the fact that he almost certainly stole that dog.

I climbed the ornate stairwell and crossed the bridge. When I reached the small, street-level entrance of the station, I stopped and looked for threats. No one watched me, so I headed up the stairs to the tracks where the train to London would depart.

The platform was mostly empty. Certainly no Gabriel. And no one close enough to throw me in front of a rushing locomotive. It seemed odd that there weren't more commuters working in the city, so I checked the timetable. Trains to London departed every half hour.

The 9:13 time in my text would be pretty late for someone going to work. With that little mystery solved, I waited.

Minutes ticked by, and still no Gabriel. Or Harold, as I should call him.

The forest green nose of a Great Western Railway engine sped up the track. Maybe Harold was on that train and would join me in Bath.

Four women, two elderly gentlemen, and one father with two toddlers disembarked.

Was I supposed to get on and go to London? What if I was wrong about Harold and the message had been from Mac, luring me into danger?

But if it was Harold and this was my chance to help Parikh, I should take it.

Figuring that a train was a lousy place to attack someone, I got on moments before the doors slid closed. The Britrail pass my dad purchased for me didn't require a specific ticket or destination. I could hop on anytime and go anywhere, although I preferred to stay around Bath, so I hadn't used it much.

The other great thing about the pass was that Dad spared no expense and got me first-class accommodations. For a brief moment, the spoiled teen in me was disappointed that I didn't have a private compartment. Instead, first-class meant the car looked like the rest of the train, but the seats were bigger. I checked the little lights above each seat and found a green one, meaning it was available for the whole trip. I made a mental note to reserve a spot for my trip back when I got to Paddington.

A trolley came by offering drinks and goodies. I got tea and biscuits, which, of course, were cookies. By now, I should know the difference. Also, who keeps biscuits on a cart? Still, once I accepted what they were, I had one, and it wasn't too sweet and had a peppy zing from the ginger.

An official came by, checked my phone for tickets, and informed a Japanese couple in the car that they didn't have first-class accommodations. They apologized and moved on, and I wondered how easy it would be to ride without paying.

"Ma chèrie, I knew you couldn't stay away," Gabriel said with his silky French accent.

*Thief and con artist*, I reminded myself. "This is strictly a business proposition, Harold," I said firmly, attempting not to be taken in by his fake identity.

He ran a hand over his light brown, spiked hair and grinned. "Can't blame a bloke for trying," he said in his Cockney lilt, looking sidelong through long, thick eyelashes.

Grabbing the second biscuit from my packet, Harold took a bite and asked, "And what do you need from a man with my unique talents?"

I had been so distracted by the thought that I was walking into a trap set up by Mac that my carefully laid-out logic failed me.

"It's not entirely…" I paused, thinking of the right term, and landed on "above board."

"Illegal. The word you're trying so hard not to say is 'illegal.'" Stuffing the last piece of cookie into his mouth, he said, "Ginger. My favorite. Got any more?"

"No," I said, ignoring the second packet deep in my pocket. Not a lie since they were Golden Oat Biscuits, not Stem Ginger.

It didn't matter, as the trolley returned, and Harold asked for three packs of biscuits with his tea.

"Do you even have a first-class ticket?" I whispered.

The grin returned.

We stopped talking as the train pulled into Reading, commuters disembarked, and new riders found their seats.

After taking the time to formulate my argument for why he should help me, I used the last leg of the journey to convince him.

"It's not exactly illegal. I'm not asking you to steal anything, just to leave something where a constable can find it."

"Our friend Douglass, is it?"

"Yes." I started at the beginning of finding the knight and the fact that DI Parikh had been framed.

"I don't want to get Douglass in trouble," I said, surprising myself at the truth of the statement.

"You say this as if you just realized something important," Harold commented.

Emotions tended to display across my face like neon signs. I was getting better at masking it, but I had to concentrate.

Rather than denying it, I decided talking it through would help me to understand. "It's true. I had wanted to frame Douglass so he would know what it felt like. Now, I just want to point him to the right suspect."

"Are you sure it's the right suspect?"

"Well, no." Mac could be exactly what he appeared. I sighed, doubting everything I'd been so sure of. "But he's a better prospect than the detective inspector, and he should be looked into."

Harold's eyes flickered almost imperceptibly, and he stood. Taking my hand, he kissed it and said he'd return shortly.

While he was gone, the ticket inspector rechecked my pass. Once he cleared the car, Harold returned and resumed his seat.

"How did you know he was coming?"

"What is it you Americans say? Not my first rodeo." His Texan drawl was pitch-perfect.

"You have a facility for accents," I said, impressed.

"I have a facility for a great many things, ma chèrie." Gabriel's persona took over Harold, changing posture and intimacy, willing me toward him with his whole being.

Heat rising to my cheeks, I deflected. "That's creepy. It's like you have split personalities."

Laughing, Harold said, "Well played, darlin'." Eyes dancing, he leaned forward. "Back to business. Point one: Planting evidence on a police officer is highly illegal. Just so you know. Point two—"

"Stop saying 'point,'" I said sharply because I was sure he was going to turn me down.

"Two, it is very dangerous for the fella pulling it off. Three, breaking in is breaking in, whether you're leaving something or taking it. Four—"

"Fine," I interrupted. "I get it. It's too dangerous." Deflated, I tried to see his perspective. "I'm sorry. I shouldn't have asked."

"I didn't say 'no,' darlin'. But there are consequences. Compensation, for one."

I hadn't considered that I would have to pay him. And relying on charm to get what I wanted sometimes took me down a road I wasn't willing to travel.

# Chapter Seventeen: Egypt is Here

Resisting the urge to bat my eyes at Harold, I strove for a neutral expression and asked, "How much to plant a rondel in Douglass's path without implicating him or making him look bad that would point him toward Mac at The Boater?"

Frankly, I couldn't believe I was so concerned for the man I called Constable Meany not too long ago. Edward's influence was rubbing off on me. Too illegal was too far.

Harold's devilish grin rivaled Tori's. That smile that says they know how far to push me was unnerving. "That, my darlin', depends on what you're willing to do for me."

A slight flutter of excitement but also panic flared in my chest. Pulling into Paddington Station saved me from having to respond.

The light, airy, transparent ceiling welcomed visitors with its elegance. The barrel-vaulted spans, originally glass, were replaced with polycarbonate glazing in the 1990s.

"Have you not seen it before?" Harold asked, apparently reading my awed expression.

I shook my head. "No. My dad had me take a coach from Heathrow to Reading, where I caught the train to Bath. I haven't been to London since."

With a smile, he guided me to a bench, stopped, and drew his hand through the air in a 'Ta-da' motion.

Paddington Bear in bronze, reclining with a curious expression on his adorable features.

"Oh!" I squeaked, getting teary at seeing a childhood dream.

Eyes shining, I followed Harold deeper into the station before realizing I had no idea where we were going.

"Whoa, whoa, whoa. We still need to talk. And where are we?" I halted our downward progress, much to the grumbling of those behind me.

"It's time for your compensations, ducks."

"Could you stop calling me pet names? I couldn't stop you from saying Madeline and using Maddie at Chedworth, and now you refuse to use real names at all."

Leaning so that I caught a gentle whiff of spicy cologne, he whispered, "Safer."

Paranoia kicked back in, and I scanned the crowd, looking for I didn't know what. Mac following me, I guess. *But he would send a pawn*, I reminded myself.

"Do you sense danger?" I asked as he pulled me further down the tunnel.

Which sounded like a character in a kid's spy movie, so I stopped, yanked my arm free of his grasp, and turned on my heel. Fighting to the left side of the walkway, I marched back toward trains and daylight.

"Ma puce, don't be like that." Harold's French accent purred in my ear.

"What does that even mean?" I said, refusing to be sucked in again.

He faltered momentarily, then recalled, "Flea, I think—my flea. That's a weird one."

A smile crept across my face without my permission, but I kept walking.

"Hold on, Maddie."

"What? Where are you taking me? People are expecting me back in Bath, just so you know."

Speaking of which, I texted my friends to tell them I arrived in London without incident.

"Your payment—"

"I'm not going to walk blindly into something I might not be willing to do," I said, then wished I hadn't added the 'might' into my declaration. "I mean, won't do. That's what I meant. I don't know what kind of girl you think I—"

His guffaw stopped me.

"What?" I snapped.

"You called me, remember? Come on."

"Oh." Cheeks burning, I hung my head and followed him to a tube station. "I've never been on a subway," I said, then remembered that term meant a pedestrian tunnel under a street in the UK. "Underground," I amended.

Chicago, where I went to university, had a light rail system, but it was named the L because it was elevated. I never rode that either.

The brightly colored maps of different lines were obvious enough for me to read despite my being cartographically challenged. We hopped on the Elizabeth Line.

Harold still hadn't told me where we were going, so I memorized each station in case something happened, and I had to return to Paddington on my own.

After only one other stop, we screeched to a halt at Tottenham Station, and Harold guided me off the train, through the turnstiles, and into daylight. Pretty straightforward. At least he wasn't taking me to the middle of nowhere.

Swiveling my head in every direction, I continued to note landmarks so I could reach the station in a hurry if needed. After five minutes of walking, we approached a massive Greek Revival structure I recognized from textbooks.

"The British Museum," I said in awe. I might have gaped.

Harold had tickets for both of us. Hardly a payment on my part, but I was too filled with wonder to say anything.

The Great Court's tessellated glass ceiling linked the four wings of the museum, flowing around the cylindrical Reading Room at its center. The white walls and Balzac limestone floor gleamed in the overcast weather. I'd seen so many pictures that it welcomed me like an old friend.

Ancient Greece, Roman statues, Egyptian mummies.

Overwhelmed, I turned to Harold. "Where do we start?"

"I know how you feel about the Romans, but we start this way."

He led me to a hall and stopped before a large rectangular slab with a sloping top as if its corner had cracked off. I would have recognized it anywhere.

"The Rosetta Stone," I whispered, so overcome with emotion that tears welled in the corners of my eyes. The stone was a pillar of archaeology and language, with the same text written in hieroglyphics, Demotic text, and Ancient Greek. A discovery of this magnitude inspired every archaeologist, including me.

Hiding my snuffling in a stray tissue from my jacket, I pulled myself together. "Thank you," I said and hugged Harold on impulse.

To his credit, he didn't take advantage of the moment, allowing my joy to flow.

"This is awesome in the truest sense of the word," I said, turning in a circle to take it all in.

"Stay in Egypt or go to Rome?" Harold asked.

"Are those lamassu?" I asked, instinctively drawn toward the winged lions with human heads flanking an entrance.

"Egypt it is," Harold said, chuckling.

"Assyrian," I corrected without thinking before reciting the details I learned from my first archaeology course. "They protected the goddess Lama. Some have lions' bodies, others bulls'."

"They're unsettling."

"Five legs," I pointed out while examining every inch of the precise carving. "From the front they stand, but their legs are depicted in motion from the side."

Skipping from display to display like a little kid, I spewed a stream of facts that Harold didn't ask for.

The faience shabti of sixth-century BC kings and queens engrossed me for so long that a German tourist asked if I was a researcher. Instead of answering, my inner tour guide popped out, and I launched into more unasked-for information.

The signs explained that shabti were treasured items placed in tombs to guide or assist in the afterlife. They were carved with formulas and the deceased's name.

Rather than repeating the display, I elaborated on the material faience used to create the blue or green statues. Made from ground quartz and minerals that added color, faience mimicked the semi-precious stone turquoise, which Egyptians associated with the sun's brilliance. Fakes were cheaply reproduced in Egypt for decades, and tourists in search of a deal were often taken in by painted plaster.

The German nodded politely, and I marched to the next room. Unable to contain my excitement, I continued to lecture. My fervor reached its height at the mummy exhibit, where a papyrus of Anubis weighing a heart was displayed.

"Anubis was the god of the scales. What people did in life affected their hearts. Anubis weighed the heart against a feather, and if the heart weighed more, Ammit there," I pointed to the crocodile-headed beauty waiting in anticipation, "would devour it. Along with your soul."

"A whole new meaning to 'feeling light as a feather,' innit?" Harold looked around the room. "I never noticed how many mummies there were."

"There would be more if the Victorians hadn't eaten them."

Harold stumbled.

I grinned. It was hard to surprise the conman.

"To be fair," I added, "the practice had been in place for centuries. And the Victorians also put mummies on display for scientific study, which we are quite grateful for."

My hands started to shake, and I suddenly felt faint. "Speaking of eating," I said.

Harold picked up on my hint and guided me back to the Great Court and food. At a grab-and-go cafe, I ordered tea and scones, which I stuffed inelegantly into my face. Not yet satisfied, I returned for a ham, tomato, and cheese toastie.

While eating at a more stately pace, I pictured what I wanted to see next. So many images came into my mind that I gave up and stared at the glass ceiling.

"Your brain is full," Harold said.

"Huh? Oh. Yeah. I think you're right."

"There's nothing for it but to come back another day. Let's get you back to Paddington."

Much as I wanted to argue, I had to give in. My mind was reeling with information. Now that my belly was full, I needed sleep.

We retraced our steps back to the Underground, which had grown far busier in the late afternoon. Grateful to Harold for guiding the way and keeping me from getting trampled, I relaxed with the gentle rocking of the subway car.

Once we reached Paddington and were at street level, we stood by the coffee shop just outside the train gates.

I needed to thank Harold properly for our adventure. My sleepy mind came up with a few different forms of what that might be, and I attempted to shake myself into thinking clearly. No need to swoon just because a boy intuited how much I would love a museum.

To be honest, I felt like Belle when Beast showed her the library.

And Harold wasn't nearly so beastly.

"Thank you for today," I said, standing close to him. "It meant more than you can imagine." I touched his arm and squeezed it lightly, his sinewy muscles taut under his light jacket.

My phone dinged.

Ignoring it, I melted a little as Harold stepped one leg closer, almost encasing me in his presence. The spicy scent caught my attention, and I leaned in.

My cell dinged again.

Electricity crackled between us so brightly I could feel the hair on the back of my neck tingle. The anticipation, like an insistent undulating drumroll, kept me riveted to the spot.

A small voice in my mind told me that the expectation was the best part. If acted on, the attraction would fade.

*Maybe*, I thought, silencing my inner voice.

Harold tucked a stray wave of hair behind my ear, then dragged his fingers along my chin. A frisson shot through me, and I tilted my face closer to his.

The ding of another text interrupted.

And another.

Then another.

"I should check that," I said, my voice thick and low.

Eyes boring into mine, Harold nodded, although in that moment, he was Gabriel, the unattainable fantasy.

I broke contact and retrieved my phone, which rang in my hand.

Dolly insistently requiring attention. "You absolutely must come to the spa tomorrow. Horseback riding. And a facial, obviously."

"Obviously," I responded, relief flooding through me from the distraction. "Of course! I'd love to."

We worked out details, including when Gilbert, the spa's driver, would pick me up.

"See you tomorrow!" I said, taking a deep, cleansing breath, bringing common sense to every part of my being.

Relieved at the interruption, I steeled my nerves for another onslaught of magnetism, but when I turned, Harold was gone.

I searched the station but didn't see his lanky form anywhere. As I approached the exit to find him, I heard a train screech. My ride to Bath pulled up, and I changed directions to catch it.

Displaying the ticketing app on my phone, I scanned it at the gate and speed-walked to the first-class car. Closer to rush hour, most of the seats were reserved, a step I forgot to take when I arrived.

At the end of the second car, I found an open seat at a table with an elderly couple. It turned out they were also at the museum that day, and like me, they were exhausted.

After a brief chat, they fell asleep, leaving me to ponder my day, my actions, and my feelings.

Almost allowing Harold to kiss me was an issue. *Allowing*, my inner voice scoffed, putting the word in air quotes. True. If he had made the first move, I would have followed.

On the bright side, for my growing level of understanding of what being in a relationship meant, I didn't initiate a kiss. Which, given my track record in high school and my freshman year of college, was a kind of big deal.

My phone dinged again, and the eye roll at Dolly escaped before I could stop.

But it was from Edward. The smile that spread when I saw his name warmed my entire body.

'Surfacing from the cell dead zone for a couple of minutes. Enough to say I miss you. Home in two days.'

Two days. Sooner than he anticipated.

"Good news?" The woman across from me had awoken and must have read my expression.

"Yes," I confirmed. "My boyfriend will be home soon."

"Well, you hold onto him. Any boy who can make a girl smile like you is worth keeping." She patted her husband's arm. "Just like my Johnny."

Flitting arguments about not wanting to settle down, or make mistakes that my parents made by settling too soon, bounced around my brain, but couldn't find purchase. The excuses I'd used to distance myself from other boyfriends didn't hold up now.

My companion had drifted off again, her head on her husband's shoulder.

Wishing Edward were with me right then, I jerked when I realized I had not confirmed any details with Harold about what I wanted. We had been discussing hypotheticals, and I was so astonished by the grandeur of the British Museum that I never returned to my original purpose.

Instead, all I accomplished was to have a date with a boy I shouldn't have. A conman that I shouldn't know how to contact.

*Excellent.*

Pulling up my class's website on my phone, I checked the next assignment. With some creative wording, I could use my experience at the museum to fit the topic. So, not a total loss of a day.

My Games paper got a ninety-seven percent without explaining why it wasn't perfect.

Still, I didn't manage to help DI Parikh in any way, which had been the plan. Tomorrow, I'd be at the enchanting DeValence Medispa, which meant another day of no progress.

If Mac was the criminal mastermind behind the knight's murder, he was safe from any level of investigation.

Terrifying news, considering my ill-advised questioning at The Boater.

# Chapter Eighteen: Off with the Fairies

The weather couldn't have been more beautiful when Gilbert, a boy from a quaint village and Dolly's driver, picked me up from Ash Tree Cottage.

"Nice day for it," Gilbert said as I exited the gate. He stood tall by Dolly's electric car with the De Valence Medispa logo emblazoned on the door. The logo, an adaptation of her family crest, sported red bars across a field of white, each with a small bird, the Medispa name intertwined with sprigs of flowers.

Despite the fact that someone there tried to kill me once, I had a great fondness for the spa.

"Thanks for picking me up," I said as he held the door open and bowed. Gilbert took his position as chauffeur seriously, so I wasn't about to tell him not to bother with formalities.

Unlike other drivers I'd experienced, Gilbert cultivated a relaxed pace, and I enjoyed the sparkling blue winter sky as we headed to Gloucestershire.

As we pulled into the medispa's circular drive, Dolly, the lady of the house, greeted us. *She is an actual lady*, I thought, struck by the number of times I'd used the phrase to describe my friends' moms. No matter how often I thought I was getting the hang of living in a different country, something always reminded me of my foreignness.

Eying her, I asked, "How did you know we were here?"

"I removed all of Uncle and Winter's cameras except for the one by the front gate. Absolutely lovely to see you," she trilled, throwing her arms around me.

"Thank you, Gilbert," we called in unison as he returned to the car.

"Of course, miss, my lady," he responded and pulled away.

"Do you want to go for a ride? The weather has been so beastly it's been a chore, but we have respite today."

I grinned. "Yes, please."

We bypassed the main entry and looped over to the stables. As I opened my mouth to ask if they had gotten a new groom, Rupert appeared.

"Rupert! Aren't you needed at Comer Manor?" I asked.

"No horses there," he answered. The precocious lad was Hawthorne's nephew. Simon and Lady Vivian often gave him odd jobs for spending money, but his most recent passion was caring for the stables. "Besides, everyone's here."

The cryptic statement led me to believe that Lady Vivian was visiting the spa, maybe with Simon.

Riding boots that once belonged to Dolly's mother gleamed by the entry, and I exchanged them for my hiking shoes before entering the building.

I paused as my eyes adjusted to the dim light inside before I beelined for Old Nigel. The enormous black and white draft horse had a place of honor in the stable, and a bag of apples hung nearby.

"Hey, big fella," I greeted him, and he reached his head over his gate. Patting his long, white blaze, I cooed at him.

Rupert beamed, and I said, "You've done a fantastic job caring for him. His coat is so shiny."

"I got him off his sugar kick," Rupert informed me, and fed the horse an apple to prove his point.

When I first met Old Nigel, the horse was too spoiled by sugar cubes to consider fruit.

"He looks much happier for it."

Old Nigel's black-and-white markings reminded me of Milo, the border collie James acquired. "Dolly? How much do sheep herding dogs cost?"

"If they're trained, as high as £20,000. Why?"

Eyes flat, I said, "James said he found one." I put air quotes around found. "Conveniently, while Edward is not only out of town but also out of cell range."

"Could he have?" Dolly's voice pitched higher on every word, doubt escalating.

"James told me the dog was a stray, but he's gorgeous and healthy, so I don't think so."

"That's a dangerous business. I imagine it is as big a crime as your cattle rustling."

The image of wide swatches of chaparral covered with herds of cattle triggered a pang of homesickness.

"Any ideas about what I should do with him?"

"James or the dog?"

"Both, I guess."

A stomp, stomp, and neigh of complaint came from the yard, and I turned to see a striking chestnut bay. "Are you jealous, Lancelot?"

Another stomp accompanied by a commanding gaze.

"Okay, okay, I'm coming."

I strode to the horse and stared at the tiny saddle. "Oh, yeah," I said, remembering Dolly didn't own Western-style saddles.

While Rupert gave Dolly a leg up onto Merlin, I led Lancelot to a hay bale and used that to boost myself. Lancelot sighed as if suffering a great indignity, but I found it the easiest way to get into an English saddle.

"Two hands for the reins," Dolly reminded me, as I reverted to holding both in my left hand, a habit after training in breakaway roping.

"Right. Geez. It's only been a couple of months, and I've forgotten everything about riding this way."

"It'll come back to you. Tally-ho," she said before flying away at a gallop.

"You're not going to put up with that, are you, Lance?" I whispered in the bay's ear as we gained on Merlin.

Once on the trail, we slowed to a walk, and I resumed our conversation. "Edward tasked me with keeping an eye on James. What do I do about Milo?"

"Milo is the dog in question?"

I nodded.

"Try checking pet finding sites for lost dogs that meet his description. If a farmer is missing a trained herder, it would be a police matter."

"Is there a police log that shows local calls?" The Tempe paper back home listed weekly police incidents, most of which dealt with frat parties getting out of control, although the occasional drug bust came up, too. And once, the police were called out to corral a bull that had escaped and was terrorizing traffic.

"If it were local to here, the council offices might post something. I don't know about Bath."

Unfortunately, the only constable I knew who could tell me was out of town, and the last person I wanted to know about the situation.

As we rode in silence, the scritch-scratching of the tree branches rubbing in the breeze set me on edge, reminding me of the trouble I was trying to help with.

"Why did you name your horses Merlin and Lancelot?" The link to King Arthur, the knight in the Chalice Well, and the mastermind who framed DI Parikh intrigued me.

"Merlin, because when Uncle and I first saw him as a colt, he sparkled in the sunshine like magic. Lancelot, well, you've seen him."

Patting the horse on his neck, I smiled. "Gorgeous and full of charisma."

Dolly turned Merlin as if sensing my heart wasn't in riding, and I gratefully followed.

"You're with the fairies today," she commented.

I took the statement to mean that I was off in la-la land. "Sorry. It's the detective inspector. I found a suspect but..."

"But Edward isn't on the case, and Douglass won't listen," Dolly finished for me.

"When you're with the fairies, do they help you think?"

"Oh no. They are quite mischievous. If you stay too long, you'll go batty." Disturbing.

"My suspect," I began, unsure if I wanted to distract Dolly with my woes.

"Is it someone I know?"

Her excited voice urged me forward. "I think it might be Mac, the manager at The Boater."

I explained my reasoning from access to schedules to my suspicion that he was also the drug lord.

"Of course, I'm wrong about people. A lot," I confessed. "I even thought you were orchestrating murders for a while."

She laughed. "Quite. But the lovely thing about you is that you'll admit when you're mistaken."

Reflecting on the ridiculous tactics I used to avoid apologizing to Edward for taking pictures of evidence, I took Dolly's statement as a huge compliment. I'd come a long way in the months I'd been in England.

"I didn't use to," I admitted. "I think Edward's rule-following nature is rubbing off on me."

"What's the difference between means and opportunity?"

Glad that she hadn't dismissed my logic, or flat out laughed at me like James, I said, "Means is that they could do the crime. Like, Mac is a great dart player, so he could have thrown the rondel at me. Opportunity is, was he available to set everything up?"

"Someone threw an ancient dagger at you?"

I shrugged. "Trouble finds me."

"I see."

Dolly's comment sounded like my mom when I was making excuses.

"Fine. I sought out trouble."

"A refreshing quality that has helped innumerable times," she said with a smile that faded as she thought. "The way you describe him, Mac is a bit like the fairies. Hidden, but always there, bending our wills to his desire."

"I've been calling him the mastermind, manipulating us like we're pawns in a chess game."

"The dead knight was his opening move."

We walked the horses to the stalls where Rupert awaited. "I'll give them a good brushing, my lady."

"You sure?" I asked, wondering how he would reach all of Lancelot. "I can help."

"Oh no, miss."

Rupert's horrified expression indicated I shouldn't press. The staff here at the spa and at Simon's manor were dedicated.

After swapping shoes, Dolly sent me upstairs for a refreshing mini-facial and manicure. Presentable, I donned the spa's robe and fluffy slippers to meet Dolly in the drawing room.

"Better?" she asked.

I hugged her. "Much."

Lady Vivian entered and stopped before me. "I suppose it's because of you that I am now in charge of flowers and invitations?" she asked, her intense, velvet blue eyes boring into me.

"Uh." Once again, the stunning and vast vocabulary my mother endowed me with failed.

"I don't know what my nephew was thinking, not bringing me in earlier. Although his talents are many, horticulture is not one of them."

"There is the saffron," I said, referring to the crop in the massive greenhouses he had constructed at Comer Manor to offset the cost of running the place. Saffron, almost as pricey as gold, already brought in enough to repair the roof on the main house.

"And the lavender," Dolly added, indicating the spray of purple flowers in a vase by the window. She purchased much of the lavender crop for sachets and scented oils used at the spa, and available in their gift shop. "But of course, that's all you, isn't it, Viv?"

Lady Vivian indulged us with a smile for a moment. "Hawthorne is the true master of our secret fertilizer recipe," she said, referring to the butler's carefully guarded basement workshop at Comer Manor. "But yes, I do not believe Simon would have gotten far in his plan without my help." She turned her unsettling gaze on me. "Thank you for steering him in the correct direction."

Unsure if Lady Vivian meant my suggestion to utilize Comer Manor's land to make money, or that Simon needed to ask his aunt for assistance with wedding plans, I said, "Your orchids are spectacular. Who better to select flowers for the wedding?"

"Now," she said, turning her gaze to Dolly, "how are you going to make Maddie fit into the wedding party?"

"With lavender, of course. The maid of honor and the flower girl have silk dresses in a gorgeous pastel purple. On the other side of the aisle, Maddie will wear a silk, double-breasted trouser suit out of the same material." She eyed me. "The style will emphasize your long legs, but I am hoping to convince you to wear ballet flats so you don't tower over the entire wedding party."

Simon was only an inch taller than me, and Dolly barely reached my chin.

"Ballet flats are my favorite." A small lie. I loved my three-and-a-half-inch heels when dancing at a bar that I shouldn't have been in. Bouncers are less likely to check a fake ID too closely if a girl is looking down at them.

Trying to appear excited about a trouser suit and flat shoes while Dolly and Lady Vivian discussed flower arrangements proved too much. I crossed the room to a chess set nestled within a globe to keep my expression from bringing down the gathering.

The pieces were arranged mid-match, and I wondered whose turn it was.

"Maddie, child," Lady Vivian's voice cut through my musings, "come and try on your outfit."

Positive I would look like a 1970s grandmother in a tracksuit, I attempted a pleasant appearance and headed back to the fireplace.

"And do stop looking so dour," Lady Vivian added as I ducked behind the dressing screen placed by a wall.

Removing the slacks from the hangar, I had to admit that the luxurious material was a gorgeous color. As I slipped them on, I was amazed at how well they fit.

A cream shell tucked in seamlessly, and when I shrugged into the double-breasted jacket, I looked ready for the red carpet.

"How does it fit?" Dolly asked.

"Exquisitely," I said, stepping from behind the screen. "How did you get it to fit so right without having my measurements?"

"Do you like it?"

She and Lady Vivian lifted my arms and moved me around like a mannequin until they were satisfied.

"Well done, Dolly," Lady Vivian said stiffly, the equivalent of screaming praises from the rooftops.

"I love it," I said, hugging Dolly.

"You'll wrinkle," Lady Vivian commented at my display of affection.

"Changing," I replied, returning to the screen and switching back to my spa robe.

A polite knock on the door, followed by Simon entering. "Progress?" he inquired.

"Quite," his aunt answered without elaborating.

"Did you tell her?"

"I thought I'd leave it to you."

"I'll just need to borrow Maddie for a moment, then," Simon said, his expression stoic.

My stomach dipped. Even though I still don't get a lot of subtext in Simon's conversations, I knew he and Lady Vivian had bad news for me.

# Chapter Nineteen: Players on the Board

A dark cloud covered the sun, bringing a chill that settled over the drawing room. Grey and gloomy, the weather mirrored everyone's mood.

Simon beckoned me to follow him out, but I hesitated to leave the warmth of the fire. "Can we stay?"

Dolly stood and came next to me for support, which I wasn't aware I needed.

"A representative from DI Parikh's lawyer informed me that he has been called in for more questioning," Lady Vivian informed us.

Plopping onto the hearth, I groaned. "I'm tired of whoever this criminal is always being one step ahead of us."

After a moment, I asked, "How come they called you? Aren't there client confidentiality laws?"

Lady Vivian glanced at me, then at Simon.

"Aunt Viv is paying for the fees," he reminded me.

Heat rose to my cheeks, and I hoped I would one day act with the proper level of English decorum.

"Maddie thinks she knows who this mastermind is," Dolly said, covering for my faux pas.

The excited clamor of this news presented itself as Simon raising an eyebrow in my direction.

"Hear me out," I began in an attempt to ward off interruptions.

"I will leave you to it," Lady Vivian interrupted, smoothing her pink jacquard jacket as she exited the room. She never looked out of place, despite being the only spa visitor not wearing a robe.

"Mac," Dolly said. "From The Boater."

"Way to steal my thunder," I complained. Rather than continuing, I said, "That's a theater term."

They stared blankly.

"The first theater to use a sheet of metal to create a realistic thunder clap got rave reviews, so another theater company sent someone to steal it, which turned their show into the bigger hit."

"Is that apropos of anything?"

"No, not really." I sighed. "I miss my mom." As soon as the statement left my mouth, I regretted it. Both Simon and Dolly had been orphaned and raised by a relative. "I'm sorry," I muttered.

"Don't be," Dolly said with a quick hug. "Why don't you call her?"

Checking the time, I nodded and wandered into the quiet hallway.

"Beautiful child!" My mother's voice sang, simultaneously wonderful and annoying.

"I'm not a child, Mother," I whined, sounding very much like a child.

"You don't know anyone taking Adderall, do you? Tori's not using it for concentration? It's not as harmless as people think."

Talk about random. "No, Mom, what?"

"One of my students is experiencing tribulations, and I worry. You're so far away."

A rare break for my mom. Her complaints usually centered on my degree, not my lifestyle choices. Of course, that's because I edited the information I shared. "My boyfriend just broke up a drug ring."

"Did he? Stupendous." She sounded relieved.

"Are you okay?"

Rallying, she said, "Categorically capital, now that I hear your dulcet tones. What are you up to?"

"I'm at the spa for my fitting. Dolly picked a gorgeous design."

"Oh, I can't wait to see. Are you wearing pants or a skirt?"

"Trousers, mom, geez, not pants."

"What?"

"Not all words have a direct translation," I said, feeling smug.

After two seconds, during which I pictured her patiently suppressing a retort, she asked, "Did you need something?"

"No," I said, not wanting to confide how lucky I was to have a mom when so many of my friends here didn't. Just hearing her voice gave me the boost I needed. "Love you, Mom."

When I returned to the drawing room, Dolly and Simon had pulled the chess set globe to the couches by the fire.

"We are white, and Mac is black. Walk us through his moves," Simon directed.

"A pawn to print the letter at the community center. A pawn to plant it. A knight to add a sleeping draft to DI Parikh's tea. A bishop to lift his keys and leave them for Edward. And a knight to get his personal email address and grant time off to Edward.

"All that, before we even knew a game was going on," I finished.

"Our opponent is a cheater," Dolly said. "That's good information to know."

"Stacking the deck in his favor," I said, nodding.

"You are mixing your metaphors," Simon pointed out.

"It's my metaphor, I can mix it if I want to." Although now that he said it, I couldn't. "They're both games," I added, getting in the last word.

Simon arranged the board. "Since we didn't know what was happening, we will move only our pawns. All in all, a poorly played game." He moved a black knight forward, setting it to be sacrificed.

"Here's where my analogy falls to the ground," I said. "Our side didn't take the knight."

"No, but we're not getting anywhere by not playing his game," Simon commented as he updated the pieces. Using our king's pawn to remove the knight from the board opened a vertical column, making our side vulnerable.

"Now what? We're all behind a line of pawns except our king," Dolly noted. "But I don't play."

"Neither do I," I admitted.

Surprised, Dolly said, "But why on earth not? You love maths."

"That's the problem. Three moves in, there are nine million possible ways to go. I get muddled."

"That sounds like you think too much," Dolly commented.

"Not something I get accused of too often."

A knock followed by one of the spa cafe staff with a tea cart halted Simon's remark, for which I was grateful.

Simon moved a bishop to threaten our white king.

"Beggin' your pardon, my lady, but Lady Vivian thought you might like some tea."

"Perfect," Dolly said. "Thank you, Francine."

Francine glanced at the chess set and cocked her head. "White doesn't know how to play," she said, then flushed crimson and snapped her mouth shut.

As the server backed toward the door in horror of her comment, Dolly uncurled and approached her, offering words of comfort and instruction.

"Village girl?" Simon asked, although he knew the answer. Dolly hired all her employees locally to help the town's economy.

"She's quite brilliant," Dolly responded without answering. "I might set up a scholarship for villagers who wish to attend university. She could use it to cover housing fees."

As she passed his side, Simon lifted Dolly's hand and kissed it.

Embarrassed at the intimate moment, I studied the chess set. "Francine's not wrong. Even with the black knight gone, the board is unbalanced, and our king, DI Parikh, is threatened. The problem is, all our players are acting like pawns. Whether Mac is behind this murder or not, we need to recast ourselves."

I picked up pieces and replaced them as I spoke. "I think Lily and Simon can become bishops to sideswipe the mastermind from a direction he's not anticipating."

"Lily?" Simon asked, and I figured he wanted to be closer to royalty.

"Whoever set this all in motion already used her as a pawn. He won't be expecting the change. And you always come from odd directions."

The white knight reminded me of Edward, but I thought better of it. "We need to keep Edward out of this. James too. He's already in trouble because of that dog."

"Dog?" Simon asked.

"Milo," Dolly said. "I'll explain later." Her ability to remember names and details from any situation was unrivaled.

"Dolly, I don't want to involve you either. You have enough going on."

"Rubbish."

Grinning, I said, "Good. You're the queen, able to go anywhere and do anything."

Returning my smile, she asked, "Who else?"

"I tried to have someone… well, never mind what I tried," I said, picturing Harold's face inches from mine in the train station. We never confirmed details of what I wanted, and I don't think my relief at being interrupted in that moment helped my cause of getting him to do something for nothing. "We'll need Douglass," I said, changing tactics.

"Good Lord, why?" Simon looked appalled.

"A rook as a feint. We need him to barrel straight toward the solution, so our bishops can make a pincer move."

"I thought you couldn't play," Simon observed.

"Well, I can, but I'm bad at it."

"You'll do okay with this," he said in a rare moment of encouragement. Dolly must be rubbing off on him.

I sighed. "What if I'm wrong? I've been wrong about a lot of dangerous people." All the confidence I had when I applied for an internship fled my being. Now I questioned my conclusions when I should be bold. My mother would call it maturity, but that's not how I saw it.

"Perhaps, but you come to it in the end."

While I stared at Simon and he patently ignored me, Lady Vivian returned. We focused on her.

"Ah, tea," she said, and we waited while she poured a cup, splashed in a bit of milk, and then perched on a winged back chair. "Yes?"

Simon and Dolly affected bored expressions.

I attempted patience and failed. "Did you hear from DI Parikh?"

She eyed me, nibbled a petite scone, and sipped the rest of her tea as if I hadn't spoken.

Tension expanded in me, taking over one muscle group at a time until I was a bundle of knots. I would never get the hang of England.

"DCI Bray called," she finally said, and it seemed like she would not continue.

I avoided screaming in frustration.

"How is he faring?" Simon asked, while Dolly said she needed to invite him to the spa.

The DCI with the Avon and Somerset Constabulary had been a kind source of support the first time I stumbled over a body. His cousin used to hunt with Lady Vivian, so he was connected to the aristocracy in some way I didn't understand. However, those connections helped get things done.

Sturdy, with iron gray hair, Bray demanded respect but never raised his voice. Without his vouching for Edward, my constable would never have been accepted into the police force. The DCI also recommended that Parikh and Edward be transferred to the Major Crimes Investigation Team. All in all, a lovely man and a great resource.

In theory, he should have news for us if everyone would stop chatting about trivialities.

I ground my teeth and sat on my hands to keep from flying across the room to strangle information out of someone.

After making eye contact with me, Simon smirked.

My mother would tell me that patience indicated intelligence and self-control, so I took the high road and didn't stick my tongue out.

One eternity later, Lady Vivian said, "DCI Bray is, of course, staying on the periphery of this unfortunate business."

The phrase "unfortunate business" was used for everything from a picnic spoiled by rain to murder.

"However, interesting news came to light today. A rondel was discovered inside a locked patrol car."

A gasp escaped my mouth before I could stifle it. Recounting my conversation with Harold about planting evidence, I asked about the cost of the deed, but I didn't say what he should plant. *Did I?*

Turning toward me, Simon said, "Almost as if a thief planted it there, wouldn't you say, Maddie?"

The lie that formed about not knowing what he meant was overridden when Lady Vivian said, "There were two different fingerprints on the dagger."

Holding my breath, I prayed that Harold's weren't one of them. The last thing I wanted was for my harebrained scheme to cause him trouble.

Lady Vivian picked up her teacup, examined its lack of tea, sighed dramatically, and replaced it on the side table.

Simon studied his fingernails.

Dolly looked out the window.

I blurted out, "Whose are they? Did they identify either? Are they sure the prints don't belong to the same person? Was Douglass certain his car was locked? How do they know it's related to DI Parikh?"

In a sudden flash of fear that the rondel made things worse for the inspector, I asked more quietly, "Are they blaming him?"

Magnanimously taking pity on my need for answers, Lady Vivian said, "Luckily, the DI happened to be in a police interview during the timeframe in which the rondel appeared. CCTV shows Douglass locking his car. It goes blank for five minutes." She sighed again. "Really, I shouldn't be sharing this. DCI Bray swore me to secrecy."

"We understand, Aunt Viv," Simon said, seeming to close the matter entirely.

Meanwhile, my stomach churned and twisted, worrying over the fingerprints on the Celtic dagger.

# Chapter Twenty: An Unexpected Development

Back in Bath, I fumed about Simon's refusal to extract more information about the rondel from his aunt. What is the point of having aristocratic connections if you weren't going to use them?

Unable to concentrate on my homework, I texted Simon. 'What did you find out after I left?'

'I will see you tomorrow at the Baths.'

Did that mean he had news and would share it? Or that he wanted me to drop it? Enigmatic as a cat, that man.

Since writing a coherent essay was out of the question, I pulled up a chess app on my computer and recreated the board Simon had set up earlier. Our king's vulnerability practically shouted from the screen. How could I protect him without sacrificing any of the pieces on my side?

No clue.

Considering how often I had been wrong about British people and their motivations, I decided to stop thinking of Mac as the bad guy until I had real evidence. It could be anyone, including someone on the periphery. The only evidence I had was circumstantial, and there wasn't much of it. The mastermind would remain anonymous to keep leaps of logic at bay.

"Mordred," I said to the empty room. "The mastermind will from henceforward be dubbed Mordred."

Since the debacle started at Glastonbury with an Arthurian knight, logic dictated that the bad guy be a villain from King Arthur's legend. "History,"

I corrected myself. Mordred was reportedly the bastard son of Arthur's half-sister, Morgause.

From movies, I thought Morgause and Morgan Le Fae were the same person, but Morgan was the Fairy Queen, and Morgause was Uther Pendragon's daughter.

Either way, Mordred had it out for Arthur and everyone good, so he made the perfect foe.

The decision not to think of Mac made me happier. No one likes to picture their friendly neighborhood publican as evil.

Focusing on the chessboard, I planned the next set of moves to save our side from being pummeled. No inspiration came. Rather than wasting more time with it, I flicked through my photos—at least the ones I still had after Douglass erased my Glastonbury Fayre pictures. Those had provided a clue, so when I looked at these, I cleared my mind and let the images speak for themselves.

A bad shot of a magpie taking off before the camera focused reminded me of Sham Castle. Something poked at my imagination, but nothing solid enough to grab hold of.

I still marveled at everyone's reaction to the magpie. I thought it was beautiful, but it spelled bad luck to the locals. Even Edward reacted to it, and he was as stalwart as they come.

The next shot showed the rondel embedded in the tree with the facade in the background. "Sham Castle," I said out loud, which triggered why it was important.

"Castle in chess. Duh."

Looking back at the board, I used my turn to swap a rook with the king. The legitimate move that always felt like cheating to me because it moved two pieces at once. Castling protected the king behind a line of pawns and moved the rook out to threaten the middle of the board.

Since my competitor made several moves before I even knew I was in a game, I thought it only fair to take two turns in a row. Moving the second pawn from the edge opened up my bishop to speed across the board.

I slumped, sensing the pointlessness of the exercise and my metaphor.

Much as it empowered me to cast my friends as chess pieces, I wouldn't send any of them into danger. Or me, for that matter. If the mastermind sacrificed one of his own, he wouldn't hesitate to take out one of us.

A nagging sensation accompanied this realization. Instead of playing around, I should involve the police.

I called Edward, but it went straight to voicemail.

Next on my list, I opened my app and called Tori.

"How was Gabriel?" she asked.

My eyes narrowed. "Whatever happened to 'Hello?' It's a friendly and socially acceptable way to start a conversation."

"Hello. Did he kiss you? Did you kiss him? Was it worth it?"

"Hello, no, no, and what is the real question?"

Wide-eyed innocence. "What do you mean?"

While Tori read me like a picture book, she had more guile. Not that she kept things from me, but she usually held her emotions in check. However, since she had been at her internship, she'd been more open.

Tori and Scott, her sometimes overbearing high school and now college boyfriend, had ups and downs, but she never got sad or giddy around him. She'd been both lately.

And she had a particular obsession with me running off with Harold.

While my detective skills failed at proving DI Parikh not guilty, years of experience with my best friend told me she was hiding something.

"Have you met a boy?" I asked. "Is there a tall, dark, handsome fellow intern at the embassy?"

A series of expressions played across her face from terror to joy and everything in between.

"We haven't done anything yet. I mean, I don't know if he likes me for sure."

"Of course he does! Everyone does." Not an exaggeration. "Tell me."

She did. Nicolas, a recent graduate hired by the embassy for his translation skills, had captured Tori's eye. Not once did she mention Scott.

Which figures. I mean, I finally got around to accepting the guy, and now she's forgotten all about him. For years, I warned her about his controlling nature, but would she listen? No. Not to me, not to anyone.

Now I wasn't sure if I should feel sorry for him. Tori looked and sounded happier than she had in years.

"He sounds perfect," I told her. "Any red flags?" Like, not letting her see her friends, thank you, Scott.

"I think I'm the red flag."

"What do you mean?"

"I'm only here for one semester. Then back to Arizona. Is it worth getting involved?"

She still hadn't mentioned the Scott-shaped elephant in the room.

"It is," I answered confidently, even though I questioned my relationship with Edward every step of the way. "You can't predict what will happen, so let yourself live a little."

"Yeah, well, like I said, I'm not sure it's going to develop. But still, I'm breaking up with Scott tomorrow."

Fear that I steered my friend into dark waters that I couldn't pull her out of, I said, "Wait, what? Tori, don't do something you can't take back."

"You've never liked him," she said flatly.

True, and she had accused me of it before. But after my mom went after him for trying to isolate Tori from me, he'd been a lot nicer to both of us.

"But he's been supportive in the last few months," I said, despite wanting her to dump him for years.

"I appreciate your advice, even though you don't mean it. But it's not just Nicolas. It's that I don't miss Scott. At all. Even a little. When he calls, I find myself scowling at my phone instead of leaping to answer it."

"Did this happen before or after you met your new friend?"

Putting her chin on her hand, she thought for a moment before answering. "Before, actually. When I got here, I was lonely, but free, you know? No abuela, no Scott, no neighborhood friends assuming I was still like I'd always been. You know?"

I did know. When I arrived in England, despite the uncertainties of being alone in a strange country, I felt like an adult for the first time. Even though I went to Chicago from Tempe for my freshman year of college, I basically moved from my mom's house to my dad's realm. Bath was the first place I was on my own.

"You're sure? What if he flies out to win you back?"

"If he does that, it will be one more stunning example of not listening to me."

We talked for the next hour, and as I was about to hang up, Tori asked why I'd called.

"It's not important." She had enough going on without my issues.

"Come on. I told you mine."

It was my turn to sigh. "If I continue down this path, one of my friends will get hurt or dead."

"Including you."

"Aye, lassie, as Edward would say."

"I bet it sounds better when he says it," Tori pointed out.

"It does."

"So you're going to let Edward handle it?"

Another sigh. "He's on another case."

"So…"

"I think I need to go to Douglass," I said.

"OMG, Maddie. You are desperate."

* * *

I woke to a single text from Tori. 'It's done.'

No emojis or extraneous punctuation to let me know how she was doing since breaking up with Scott. I braved peeking at social media. Rather than having an account, I searched for the person I wanted to see and got general info.

The weather cleared enough for me to walk to the Baths instead of catching a ride with Roger. The exercise provided much needed thinking time.

In one of his worst moments, Scott insisted Tori delete all her accounts so that her friends couldn't tell her what a toad he was. Maybe she resurrected them.

I found one entry from her, posted yesterday, her time. 'It's a beautiful day here in D.C.'

Checking the weather app, I scrolled through Washington's forecast of just slightly above freezing rain. So the post was about her, not nature.

"Good for you," I said aloud, sending my friend thoughts of strength and support.

Strange how our paths crossed. Edward was my first serious boyfriend, and we were just getting started, while Tori's first just ended.

Still, the situation unsettled me a little, which provided me with an excellent distraction from my decision to talk with Douglass.

In the light of day, it sounded ill-advised. After all, at what point since I met him has Constable Douglass ever been anything but impossible?

Never. The answer was never. What made me think this visit would be any different?

By the time my musing hit this roadblock, I was at the Baths and relieved not to think about anything but ancient Romans for a while.

Except, there stood Fred.

Sighing, I strode to his side.

"What news?"

My unlikely chess metaphor, the news about evidence being planted, and my suspicion of Mac were too much to relate. Instead, I said, "I found a witness from the morning in question and turned it over to the police."

Fred positively beamed. "I knew you could do it." With that assertion, he left, and I entered the museum.

Marcus met me upstairs in the lab, where I set up to photograph more relics. Since everything else in my world was in turmoil, I plucked up my courage and asked Marcus about my position.

"Has Dr. Daniels said anything about letting me on the dig site?"

"I say," Marcus responded.

Two words told me many things: first, that I was being too forward; second, that my chances were slim; and third, that I needed to keep my head down and prove my worth before asking for favors.

"Sorry," I muttered.

"We thought you were happy photographing." He sounded wounded.

"No, I am. I love it!" I said too loudly. "It's fantastic. Just an amazing opportunity. I wouldn't change it for the world." Clamping my jaw shut, I stopped babbling.

"Your assembly and visual skills are excellent."

"Thank you. I appreciate any job you can give me. And your guidance and training have been invaluable." I grinned, a bit manically.

"Right. Well."

We both stood there for a beat.

"I'll see what I can do. It might be rather nice to have you downstairs," Marcus finally said with an encouraging smile.

"Uh, thank you," I said as he left me to task.

Even with a British boyfriend to study, I still couldn't read the locals. I blamed Simon. He never said what he meant. At least, I didn't think so.

Since that conversation went better than expected, and with Fred's unwavering faith in me to solve the crime, I felt encouraged enough to pull out my cell and punch in Douglass's number.

"Ms. McGuire," Douglass answered my call with disdain dripping from every letter of my name.

"Constable Douglass," I said, striving for friendly. "I have a theory about DI Parikh that I'd like to share with you. It probably won't amount to much."

"Probably not."

I rolled my eyes but held my tongue. If he wanted to hear it, he would need to be civil. If he didn't, hey, I tried.

Waiting for a couple more beats before I gave up, I finally said. "Okay, well, thanks anyway."

"Ms. McGuire," he said again. "I was simply checking my calendar for availability. I will be in Bath later this afternoon. I could meet you at 17:00."

"Right-o," I said, shocked into using one of Simon's phrases. "In the Abbey Square?"

"Fine," he said and disconnected.

Now I had to figure out what to say to him without sounding guilty, blaming anyone, or wasting official police time.

As I considered how to approach him, I returned to my job. Taking pictures and thinking of piecing artifacts together created a zen-like state, and I completely lost track of time. Somehow, Lily skipped her daily check-in for tea and lunch for the team. Without the reminder, I hadn't eaten.

When I came out of my work trance, I was late for my appointment.

And starving.

Not a great combination.

Downstairs, I ran across the square, gave Douglass a "one sec" sort of gesture, and bolted into the drinking chocolate shop. Picking the darkest, most decadent blend on the menu, I wavered on my feet, waiting. Lack of food made me weak and angry, like a wet kitten in a bag.

I ordered one, downed it, and asked for two more, in case Douglass liked chocolate, and then sprinted out to meet him.

Amazingly, Lily sat next to him, and he appeared far less annoyed than the first time I ran by.

"I apologize," I said, "I was hungry."

"Well, no wonder. I knocked on your window, and you didn't look up. Twice." Lily said.

"You're kidding. Was I that focused?" I asked, handing her the spare hot chocolate I'd purchased for Douglass.

"Too right. Next time, I'll bring you scones no matter what. Ta," she added, lifting the paper cup in my direction, which was when I realized I had given it to the wrong person.

"Chocolate?" I asked, offering my second cup to Douglass, who, thankfully, shook his head no. I slurped it before he changed his mind.

No longer starving, just jittery, I looked from one to the other, waiting for an invitation to sit.

"Constable Douglass here has been telling me about Mac. Did you know he has a forge here in town? He makes Roman-looking things to sell to tourists."

"How can you have a forge in a city like Bath? They seem so, I don't know, loud and dangerous." I sat on the far side of Lily, so I didn't have to touch Douglass.

"It's in a warehouse on Locksbrook Road, ain't that right, Constable?" Lily answered, much to Douglass's annoyance.

"Lily, please. I did mention discretion."

To Douglass, I'm "Ms. McGuire," but Lily gets a personal first name. I don't know what I did to make him so mistrustful of me, but his opinion hadn't grown kinder. If anything, now that I saw how nice he was to other people, I felt even more picked on.

"Yeah, but not to Maddie. She's in on everything."

"That, Lily," Douglass said, "is exactly the problem."

# Chapter Twenty-One: The Problem with Douglass

Achill settled over the Abbey Square as the sun set. The busker packed up her violin, taking the lovely strains of Vivaldi with her. Sitting on a bench with Lily and Constable Douglass, I contemplated what he meant by my involvement being a problem. So far, I hadn't done anything except find a body. With Lily, I might add.

"Ms. McGuire. Are you denying that you have kept important information from the police in general and me specifically?"

The hand that was not holding the drinking chocolate went to my face.

Lily found this the perfect moment to take our empty cups to the trash can and abandon me.

"You can't ask questions that make a person sound guilty, no matter how they answer." I'd mentioned this before, so I'm sure he did it now to bug me.

It did.

"You know what? I don't even know why I called you. Mistake on my part. Big one. Talk to you later." The last I added as I stalked away.

"Ms. McGuire," he said in a commanding tone that annoyed me further.

"Maddie," I said. "Everyone calls me Maddie." I wished I had my mom's standard response, which was, "Dr. McGuire, actually," but I didn't have my bachelor's degree yet, let alone a PhD. "I thought I could help. Obviously, you don't want me to, so I'll go."

At this point, as I stood over a seated constable squawking, Lily returned and patted my arm.

I deflated.

Nothing like a gesture from my childhood to settle me down.

Turning, I plopped on the bench.

"What is it you wanted to ask Maddie, Constable Douglass?" Lily asked politely.

The question seemed out of place as I had been the one to instigate our meeting. I watched him curiously.

With exaggerated slowness, Douglass pulled out his phone and showed me pictures of a rondel. "Do these look familiar to you?"

"Well, yeah. It's the rondel someone threw at me by the Sham Castle. Did the SOCO team find it?"

He shook his head no but didn't say anything more.

"Is it real or a knock-off?" I asked.

"It's my job to ask the questions."

"I answered yours." It came out more petulant than I wanted. I forced my jaws together.

Lily gave Douglass a look, and with an effort, he asked, "What information do you have for me, Ms. McGuire, er, Maddie?"

"My theory, and I know it is just a theory, is that…" I paused, reconsidering my approach as I didn't want to implicate myself, and started again. "Since I don't have evidence," I said instead, hoping that if I pointed it out, he wouldn't, "I'm going off what I have seen. I think DI Parikh was framed, which you may or may not agree with, but I know in my heart that he wouldn't kill anyone. Based on that assumption, the person with the biggest motivation for ruining him and his career is the leader of the drug ring that Parikh dismantled. That person must be someone we all know."

Douglass's face remained impassive, which, for him, was an improvement over perpetual disgust.

"That all?"

*No, of course not,* I thought, considering the piles of ill-advised theories I'd devised and discarded. But it was all I was willing to share with him.

I shrugged.

Douglass stood and stomped off without a backward glance.

In a stunning display of maturity, I didn't sneer.

"A drug kingpin," Lily said with a wistful tone. "Is that what they call them? That's wicked smart. Ruins my guess."

Surprised, I said, "You have a guess? Do you think Parikh was framed, too?"

"Aye, yeah, such a nice man. If I had to guess, Constable Douglass doesn't really think DI Parikh did it, but not enough to admit it out loud. The constable has been ever so kind once he realized I wasn't you."

I sighed, crumpling under the weight of Douglass's suspicion.

"He thinks all these bodies are my fault," I complained.

"You do have a knack for finding them," Lily said.

*Great.* Even Lily thought I was a death magnet. To circumvent the epic pout I felt coming on, I asked Lily about her theory. "You haven't spent a lot of time with DI Parikh. Why do you think he was framed?"

She thought for a moment and then said, "He came to see me after my accident with the bus."

Surprised, I said, "Wait, what? I didn't know that." Lily had been struck by a bus when I first met her, and I thought a crazy person had shoved her, mistaking her for me.

"He was worried about you, I think. He wanted to make sure I hadn't been pushed." With a shudder, she added, "Dead clumsy, more like."

She continued, "Well, the person who framed the detective knows the city, so my choice is Thomas."

"Who is Thomas?" I asked, not recognizing the name.

"At the farmer's market."

"The farmer's market," I repeated doubtfully. "The one over by Southgate?" Just to be clear.

"Aye, he sells tomatoes, and if you mention the quality isn't top-notch, he'll come after you with a pitchfork."

It sounded like a bit of an exaggeration. "But, why would he frame DI Parikh?"

Lily's hand made a waffling motion. "Don't know, do I? Why did that crazy lady attack you?"

"Good point," I said. The crazy lady in question had not only sent me a severed human ear, but also entombed me. "But…" I trailed off again, this time because Lily's villain was only vaguely less absurd than me thinking she was the mastermind. Lily hated excitement in most forms, and yet she found a body with me. No one understood better than me how processing the atrocity turned into investigating and theories.

After pondering the possibility, I conceded that it was plausible. "A farmer's market would be a good place to cover up selling drugs. You could hide baggies at the bottom of fruit trays."

Preening, Lily said, "I never thought of that, but you're right." She grinned. "Still, I don't think he's the one. I just didn't like getting yelled at the other morning."

I laughed, tension releasing from my knotted shoulders. After all, the conversation with Douglass could have gone worse. Most have. This time, he didn't try to incarcerate me or ask me to stay out of it. All in all, a step in the right direction.

"Thank you for helping me talk to Douglass," I said to Lily. "It goes better when there is a buffer between us."

"He's not so bad." She leaned in, conspiratorially. "That rondel he showed you, they found it in his car."

Shocked, I asked, "He told you that?"

"Not really. I overheard him yelling over the phone and asked if he was okay."

"Whoa." That bit of information explained why Douglass didn't scoff when I said I thought Parikh had been framed. Maybe we could count on him in this investigation as the rook to barge forward.

Hopeful for the first time in a while, I stood, wobbled, and plunked back on the bench. The drinking chocolate sugar high came crashing down. As I sat shivering in the chilly wind, my teeth chattered. No way I'd make it home like this.

"I wonder if Roger has left the church yet," I muttered, texting him.

"Do you need something?" Lily asked, falling into her role as server.

"He's coming."

Within moments, Roger circled in front of The Huntsman and beeped the horn, texting his arrival. It sounded like a beacon of warmth with a promise of food.

"Come on," Lily said, tugging me to my feet.

"Are you okay to get home?" I asked. "Roger would be happy to drive."

"Nah, I'm close."

As I shakily stumbled toward my pickup point, my confidence in the situation grew. Talking to Douglass proved to be, if not pleasant, somewhat useful. He could turn this thing around for us.

I wanted to ask Lily more about what she overheard about the rondel, but it would have to wait.

"Text me later with everything you can remember about the conversation you overheard, okay?" I asked.

"There's not much more. You know my brain, full of holes."

Hugging her as we approached the car, I said, "Thanks again."

"Thank you so much," I said, slumping into Roger's car. With shaky hands, I clipped the seatbelt, then pawed at the buttons to raise the window. After locking and unlocking the door, the window whirred up, cutting off the cold wind and with it, a scream.

"Did you hear that?" I asked, hoping it had been my imagination.

Roger's head cocked to one side, and he lowered both windows.

Another scream.

We bolted out of the car, which beeped unhappily as it stalled. Roger went back and turned off the engine.

"This way," a stranger shouted, running past me toward the back of the Abbey.

We followed him to the nook where a resurrection statue watched the scene. The statue depicted Christ bursting from his burial wrappings, looking oddly like a mummy in the fading light.

Mimicking the statue's open-handed stance, Lily stood over Constable Douglass, pale as a sheet, offering his prone form to the crowd. Pointing to the blood oozing from Douglass's head, she opened her mouth to let loose another wail.

Swooping in, Roger enveloped Lily, shielding her from the sight. He bustled her away.

With great care, I stepped nearer Douglass. His chest rose and fell, but quickly and in an irregular pattern.

"Call nine, one, one!" I shouted, stunned at seeing Douglass in such a state.

"What?" someone asked, pointing out my error without saying as much.

"Nine, nine, nine!" I corrected, sounding like an unhappy German.

Several reports happened at once, and it didn't take long for a response.

The screech of a siren got louder as it approached, then cut out as EMTs took over the scene. The local PCs, police constables, appeared, and I shrank back.

I hadn't seen what happened, discovered him, or called emergency services, so there was no reason to get involved. And it would be better if I wasn't found on the scene of another bloody incident.

Circling to the main street, I almost fainted from hunger as the scent of Indian food wafted down on me from the second-story window.

Not sure if I could make it up the hill to Greenway Lane without the benefit of sustenance, I turned around to see if the bread shop on the other side of the Baths was still open.

The Abbey clock said 6:23 p.m., and I turned again, remembering that everything closed at six.

As I trudged up Manvers Street, I cursed the number of shops that only sold fudge and not real food. Of course, if I'd eaten lunch, I would be charmed by the displays. But I hadn't, so now everything mocked me.

A Tibetan restaurant below street level called to me. I went down the steps, only to have a server flip the sign to 'closed.'

"Sorry, love. Private party tonight."

A couple of steps later, a car almost plowed me over on the sidewalk.

"Eek!" I shouted.

"Maddie, there you are," Roger said, pushing the passenger door open for me. "I thought I'd lost you."

Grateful to the point of tears, I eased into the seat and pulled the door closed.

"Thank you."

"Here." He handed me a square granola bar, which I would never get used to calling a flapjack.

The cellophane wrapper proved too much for my trembling fingers, so I tore it open with my teeth, scattering crumbs all over me. The sticky, sweet oats and dried fruit tasted like heaven, and I chomped through the little bars like a freight train.

Restored to somewhat human, I checked the state of my surroundings and found oats pretty much everywhere. I started eating them one at a time, picking each delicately, then placing it in my mouth in a fair imitation of a monkey.

"Where did you go?" I asked between nibbles.

"Lily was in bad shape. I got her to Meryl, and then rushed back to find you, but you'd disappeared."

Not wanting to admit that I was hiding from the officials, I said, "I tried to find food."

He glanced at me and the state of his formerly clean interior.

"I failed," I added.

As we sped to Ash Tree Cottage, I frantically contemplated exactly what had happened in the town square.

Douglass had been attacked. It didn't look like a moped ran him over, but rather that someone had used a blunt object to crack his skull.

A whole different kind of trembling took over me. Mordred, my name for the evil mastermind, was getting desperate. Attacking an officer in a crowded tourist area was a rash, ill-conceived move.

The problem was that it took out our side's rook.

In my strained metaphor of a chess match, Mordred the Mastermind still controlled the board.

# Chapter Twenty-Two: What Lily Saw

The car raced up to Greenway Lane. Roger took corners at an alarming speed and sailed into the garage while the door rose.

After unclenching my fingers from the armrest, I hustled inside after Roger. We found Lily with Meryl. My friend's pallor hadn't improved, despite the tea Meryl pressed into Lily's hands.

"Drink up," I said, buying into the English mythos that a cuppa would fix anything.

"Was he…?" She couldn't finish the question.

"The EMTs talked to him as they placed him in the ambulance," I said, opting to use calming language. "I'm sure he'll be fine." I hoped he would be fine.

Her reaction, while understandable, was more intense than I expected. Somehow, she seemed to take the attack on Douglass personally.

The couch fit one more, so I settled in next to Lily.

Surveying the three of us, Roger went to the kitchen.

"He'll be okay. Really." I assured her, hoping it was true.

Lily nodded, her eyes vacant.

A loud bang caused us to jump.

"Not to worry," Roger called from the kitchen. "Everything is under control."

The interruption broke the tension, and Lily smiled a little.

"Do you want me to call Donny?" I asked.

Somehow, more blood drained from her face.

"Or not. You can stay here," I added, looking at Meryl, who firmly nodded.

Bustling in with fresh tea and biscuits, Roger said, "Garibaldis to lighten the mood. Works every time."

Confused, as I often was when it came to England English, I looked at the snacks he brought. Flat, rectangular cookies filled with something purplish-brown.

Before my parents divorced, we went to Catalina Island off the coast of Southern California. Dad took me snorkeling to see Garibaldi, the bright orange state fish of California.

Lily gobbled one, with a faint, "Ta."

Glad that they distracted her, I took one and sniffed. Not orange flavored. Or fish, for that matter.

I took a small bite. Then another. "Yum."

"Have you not had one before?" Roger asked.

Shaking my head, I confessed, "No. Jaffa cakes are as exotic as I've gotten." The chocolate and orange over a sugar cookie base were utterly delicious.

Meryl stood, collected a garibaldi, and she and Roger left the room, presumably so I could talk to my friend.

I didn't know what to say, so I ate another cookie.

Lily looked so upset when I mentioned Donny that I suspected him of being the mastermind again. Could he have fooled us with an affable act?

It was hard to believe. In a movie, he would never be cast as Modred. More like a random townsperson.

Still, something had shaken Lily so badly that she wouldn't talk and didn't want me to call him.

The only situation that made sense was that she saw something she shouldn't have.

"I should go," she said as she stood.

"No, you should have more tea," I insisted, tugging her back to the sofa. "You can tell me, you know. I've seen a lot of stuff."

After a steadying gulp of sugary tea, she said, "I think I saw someone." She shook her head. "No. No. It couldn't be."

Before I pressed her for more information, the Priestlys returned, full of forced good cheer.

"The room is all set up," Roger declared.

"I laid out some pajamas for you," Meryl added.

Roger continued to fill in both sides of the conversation since Lily remained mute.

I took Meryl aside. "Are you sure? I've brought problems to your door and never want you to have to experience that again. We could call someone to keep her safe."

"She needs love and comfort to keep the shock at bay. Perhaps we can drive her to Manchester in the morning to stay with her parents for a few days."

Sometimes, a situation calls for a mom. Meryl's wisdom now and Lily's mom's presence at her home would fix anything.

While Meryl got Lily settled upstairs, I texted in my aristocratic connections, aka Simon. 'Can you ask your aunt to contact DCI Bray for me? It's about the attack on Douglass. Lily might have seen something.'

No response for way too long.

'She's here at the Priestlys' house.'

Still nothing.

Roger, who must have seen me engrossed with my phone, asked, "Have you had any luck contacting your police friend?"

Probably meaning Edward, I gave him the full rundown on everyone. "Edward's on assignment and not in cell range, and of course, DI Parikh is out of commission. I'm trying to reach Simon to get in contact with his connections." I rechecked my phone as I followed Roger into the kitchen. "But naturally, he's ignoring me."

"That bread you and Edward made," Roger said, as he checked the roast chicken in the oven, "was rather quite tasty."

"Thank you. We used Meryl's recipe. The process is therapeutic for Edward. He's very upset by the accusations against his boss."

"He can do therapy here anytime, if that's the result. It's nice for Meryl to have a break. Puts her heart and soul into caring for everyone." Pride and concern mingled in his voice.

So true. Meryl's capacity for caring for others was unrivaled. What she needed was a weekend at the De Valence Medispa. Dolly would comp it for me, but I didn't want to be presumptuous. Not to her anyway. I'd ask my dad to pay for it.

When Meryl rejoined us, all my gracious thoughts flew out of my head, and I pounced. "Did Lily say anything? What did she see?"

Instead of answering, Meryl reported on our guest's condition: "I gave her chamomile tea to help her relax, but I don't know if it will help. Do you know her parents' phone number?"

I did, but I hesitated to call them. Lily lived in Bath because it was so much quieter than Manchester. Would sending her home be more chaotic?

She needed to go somewhere safe, though.

Again, Dolly's place came to mind, but she had a business to run and a wedding to plan. The last thing she needed was a catatonic client who might or might not be a magnet for danger.

I checked my phone to see if Simon responded.

He hadn't.

I typed in, 'Dude!' but erased it. With me up in the lab and him down at the dig, I hadn't seen as much of him as usual. He might be drowning under a pile of Baths-related issues and/or wedding work, and I was distracting him.

A polite knock on the boot room door interrupted my fuming-fueled musing.

Roger answered and welcomed Simon and DCI Bray.

Sending a silent thank you to the patience gods, I punched Simon lightly on the shoulder and said, "Thanks, buddy."

His expression remained aloof as he exhaled in exasperation.

"Hello, sir," I said to the detective chief inspector and introduced him to the Priestlys since I couldn't remember whether they had met him.

Polite murmurings all around, followed by an offer of dinner.

"Quite nice, but I'm afraid it's going to be a long night for me. One of our own was attacked," DCI Bray answered.

"I'll just fetch Lily, shall I?" Meryl said, moving through the opening toward the stairs.

When she arrived, still clutching her teacup, Lily did not look any better.

"Does she need food?" I whispered to Meryl.

"She won't take a thing, poor dear."

DCI Bray shook Lily's hand and led her to the couch by the fireplace. "You carry on with your dinner," he said, indicating we should leave the room. "It smells delicious."

Before serving ourselves, Meryl made a to-go, or take-away plate, as they say here, for the inspector and set aside a small portion of nibbles for Lily.

I laid the table in the dining room, straining to overhear the interview in the living room. Tiptoeing across the hall, I paused, listening. The murmuring was too low, so I went back to the kitchen.

"Could you hear anything?" Simon asked through a clenched jaw, making him sound, if possible, even more pompous, but also quiet.

I shook my head. "She's terrified of something."

"Indeed." He offered to take the platter of roast chicken from the kitchen to the table. After setting it down, we both snuck across the hall.

Lily's voice, suddenly full volume, "No, I don't know for certain. But what if it is him? And what if he saw me? How am I supposed to trust my boyfriend?"

Wide-eyed, I turned to Simon. "Donny?" I mouthed.

"Ms. McGuire," DCI Bray intoned.

Caught like I'd been passing notes in class, I affected an innocent expression and entered the room. "Mrs. Priestly just wanted me to tell you that she made up a take-away container for your dinner when you're finished," I said, smiling too big.

Simon had abandoned me at the first sign of trouble, so I backed out of the room and fled to dinner. "Coward," I muttered at Simon as I sat.

Eating took second place to listening for news from the other room, so much so that we all jumped when the DCI appeared in the doorway.

"I'll just be on my way. Thank you for the meal, Mrs. Priestly."

As he showed no signs of filling us in before he left, I asked, "What did she say? Who did she see? Is she going to be safe here?"

DCI Bray closed his eyes and called Roger and Simon out to discuss. Not that I felt slighted by my exclusion, but no way was I going to let a bunch of males talk about next steps without me.

"What's going on?" I said, one step behind Simon.

To his credit, DCI Bray continued without commenting on my presence, which he should have included in the first place.

"She'll need a safe place for a few nights. I'm afraid Ms. McGuire's residence is too well known."

"She can stay at the manor for a few days. Mrs. H. will be happy to fuss over her. I'll send Rivers in the morning."

The thought of care and feeding by Mrs. Hawthorne, the delightful cook at Comer Manor, filled me with warmth. Rivers, Lady Vivian's driver, was another story. The stout, mild-mannered-looking man treated the streets of Bath like a Le Mans race course.

"Right. Well, that's sorted." DCI Bray said and took me to one side. "Leave this to the professionals, Ms. McGuire. This is dangerous business."

"I will," I said, wanting to mean it.

After the DCI and Simon left, I trudged upstairs to do homework.

Since I'd spent a lot of time thinking about forges, I used the experience to write a paper on how the Iron Age moved weaponry from bronze to sharper, sturdier, and deadlier swords. Ignoring armor and chainmail, I focused on the evolution of daggers between the Classical Period and the withdrawal of Roman influence in England.

The Medieval Period highlighted the importance of good blacksmiths. Iron, while an excellent material for swords, was a fickle mistress due to its impurities. Heating and cooling temperatures had to be carefully monitored, and it's not like they were sitting around with laser pointer thermometers.

Throughout my research, I couldn't help but ponder Lily's comment that Mac owned a drop forge. I wanted to go downstairs and ask her more. However, after talking with the police, she had settled, and I didn't want to rile her up again.

Taking a cue from her, I brewed a cup of chamomile tea and attempted relaxation. The first sip was grassy. The next more so. A childhood memory of reading Peter Rabbit came back to me. Peter's mother gave him chamomile, which he clearly considered medicinal.

I had to agree, preferring his siblings' dinner of milk, bread, and blackberries.

* * *

The next morning, Lily's face held color again. We chatted about nothing, except her excitement about staying in an actual manor house.

Roger hurried in, saying, "I must be off. Do you want a ride to the Baths, Maddie?"

"No, I can walk. I'll wait with Lily for Rivers," I said to Roger's retreating back after double-checking the time.

I could also warn her about Rivers' driving speeds. Although she might not think flying down a country lane at rollercoaster speed was out of the ordinary. A lot of English drivers went faster than I would.

Roger returned inside and called, "Your driver is here!" before ducking out again.

"Do you have everything?" I asked Lily uselessly, since she borrowed everything for the night from Meryl and me.

"Aye, yeah. See you," she said, and rushed out after a quick hug.

My shoulders dropped, tension releasing that I didn't know I'd been holding. With a deep cleansing breath, I picked up the knife to slice more bread and noticed the scones Meryl wrapped for Lily still sitting on the counter.

Snatching them, I bolted sock-footed into the cold, misty morning after Lily. The gate closed, and I raced up the stepping stones, my feet growing colder with each leap.

"Lily!" I called, tumbling out of the gate to see her sitting in the back seat of a car.

Not Rivers' car.

Not Rivers behind the wheel.

183

# Chapter Twenty-Three: The Wrong Car

The prickling chill that traveled from my damp socks up my spine was only half due to the cold. Lily was about to get into a car with a stranger. A dangerous stranger.

"Lily!" I shouted again.

The driver pulled his cap lower, obscuring more of his face except for the malicious sneer directed at me. That expression removed any lingering doubt I had about the driver's motivation.

Lily opened the door wider and put one foot on the ground.

Maybe if I didn't let on that I knew it was the wrong car, the driver might let her out. "You forgot your scones!" I called, sounding ultra-cheery and weirdly like Shirley Temple. "Meryl would just be ever so heartbroken if you ran off without them."

Swinging her other foot onto the pavement, Lily attempted to stand, and the car lurched forward.

"Hold on," she said, slapping the car's roof.

Focusing all my will on the driver to stay put, I called, "Would you care for any scones for your drive? I'm sure we have plenty to spare!"

The car lunged again, but I grabbed Lily's arm and tugged her onto the narrow sidewalk.

Confusion slowed her movements, and I was afraid that if I told her what was going on, she would freeze completely. Kind of like my feet.

"We'll just head back inside and pack some up for you, won't we, Lily? Come along!"

"What's happening?" she asked, stopping our retreat.

The driver and aspiring kidnapper caught on faster than my friend and put the car in reverse. The open door swung toward us, leaving little room between it and the stone wall. We could try to run behind the sedan and over to the park, but if he got out and chased us, we wouldn't stand a chance.

The only option was to get Lily back into the gate, but she wasn't responding to my urgings.

"Please, Lily, just hurry."

Wondering how much force it would take to remove a car door by ramming it into two girls, I flattened against the wall as the car picked up speed. The edge of the door caught the smooth stone surface, creating a hideous screech and leaving us no room for escape.

I nudged Lily toward the gate, but she stumbled.

"Get ready to jump," I yelled, intending to leap onto the vehicle's trunk before it smashed into us. Edward did it once to great effect.

We were saved from gymnastic heroics by the arrival of Rivers. Never had I been so happy to see his car speeding down tranquil Greenway Lane.

The kidnapper must have seen the car approaching at terminal velocity as he slammed the gears and took off, the door swinging shut from the momentum.

Tires squealing, Rivers halted, jumped out, and gave a little bow. "Sorry, I'm late, miss. This must be your friend. Lily, is it?"

"Yeah?" she answered, confused.

"Did you happen to catch the license plate of that car?" I panted between panicked breaths.

"What car?" Rivers said.

Instead of answering, I asked, "Do you want some scones to take with you?"

"No, thank you very much indeed, but Mrs. H. would be most put out if I came home with foreign scones." He rubbed his hands together in anticipation. "It's a treat to go to the manor during the week."

Rivers' boss was Lady Vivian. During the week, she used an apartment at the famous Royal Crescent, residing in the manor only on weekends.

Rivers bundled Lily into his back seat, exclaiming about the joys of seat warmers. Once she was belted in, he waved and took off. Lily's hand wobbled my way as well.

Looking at the scones, a little worse for wear after our adventure, I shrugged, opened the packet, and stuffed one into my mouth.

The tips of my socks had gotten so wet that they plopped like a giant frog with each step.

Splurch, splurch. Splurch, splurch.

Entering the boot room, although 'mudroom' made more sense at this particular moment, I peeled off my dirt-soaked socks and went to the fire to warm my toes.

While waiting for the shock to set in, I texted Simon.

'Lily is safely with Rivers. Tell Marcus I'm going to be late. Also, tell DCI Bray that someone tried to take Lily.'

'Right.'

The detective chief called after that bombshell. I told him the make and model of the car and what I thought was the license plate.

"Yes, well, probably stolen," he said, although I wasn't sure if he meant the car or the plate. Maybe both.

"Why did she enter the car?" Bray asked, referring to Lily.

"Roger told us her ride was here." The car must have been trolling the street waiting for her to come out, and Roger mistook it for Rivers.

"Well, no harm done," he said and hung up.

"Tell that to my socks," I muttered.

"Maddie, dear. You're going to be late. Do you need a ride?" Meryl asked.

I nodded, my mouth full of a second scone.

More than my feet were numb at this point. The kindness from my landlord should have triggered tears, but nothing. Maybe I was getting better at handling random attacks.

* * *

By greeting, Marcus said, "You're not late." He sounded pleased.

"I got a ride," I said without further explanation. Nonchalant, that's me.

With a flicker of a smile, he left.

Experience taught me that bottling up emotions never ended well, so I said to the empty lab, "Someone tried to kidnap my friend this morning and run me over."

DCI Bray's voice came back to me. *Well, no harm done.*

"I guess I'm fine," I said, and got to work.

Since I hadn't checked on James, I used my lunch hour to go to the boat.

Mist continued to engulf the city, creating shadowy menace around every corner and soaking my hair. I pulled the ponytail into a ballerina bun to keep wet tresses from leaking down my neck.

The boat, which should have been moved, wasn't. This was lucky, since James hadn't offered a location for his next mooring.

"Bark, bark, bark!" Milo, the border collie's, greeting pierced through the closed windows of the narrow boat.

No one calmed him or opened the door to see why the dog kept fussing.

Hanging onto the rail, I stepped on board. "One hand for you, one for the boat," Edward had told me when I almost tumbled off the side carrying two beers.

"James?" I knocked on the door.

"Bark, bark!"

"Hi Milo! Who's a good boy?"

There was no way James slept through this ruckus, so he must be gone.

Poor Milo, trapped inside. Ire rising, I couldn't believe how James just left him locked up.

Having been raised in Tempe, where it was illegal to leave a dog in a car because the sun raised temperatures to deadly in less than ten minutes, I was appalled that Milo couldn't leave to do his business.

"It's only forty degrees," I reminded myself to keep from flying off the handle when I found James. "Fahrenheit.

"Still, you need a break, don't you?" The last I directed a Milo.

"Bark!"

I tried the door. Locked as one would expect. Tiptoeing along the gunwales, I checked the windows and portholes. All locked but one.

My fingers dug underneath the sliding sash, and I tugged up. It slid smoothly, but I figured the dimension was about twenty by thirty-six inches, which I couldn't fit through.

Milo jumped on the built-in couch and let me pat his head. His white blaze practically glowed against the rest of his dark fur. Bright eyes, full of intelligence, regarded me, probably wondering if I would figure out how to enter.

Scratching his ears, I discovered a collar with a tag. 'Milo,' one side of a dog bone pendant read.

"Let's see who you really belong to," I said, flipping it over. 'James' and the owner's phone number. I checked, and the number belonged to Edward's brother.

Well, even if he stole the dog, he claimed it as his own.

A paw came up on the windowsill, demanding attention.

"You're right," I said to the dog. "I can't fit, but you can."

Backing up along the tiny walkway at the side of the boat, I made enough room for Milo. I grabbed his collar and said, "Come on out, boy."

Deftly, he exited the window like a pro and waited for me to reach the deck where the front door stood. He whined, looking longingly at the grassy park in the distance.

"Okay," I said. "I'll take you for a bio break, but no playing."

His full fan tail wagged.

A leash hung by a hook near the door. I attached it, and we hopped off. Tugging me hard, I trotted behind him, unsure of the proper command to get him to slow down because repeatedly shouting "Heel!" got me nowhere.

At the first patch of grass we got to, he relieved himself for an extraordinarily long time. Then he pooed, and I panicked because I didn't have anything to clean up with.

"There's a dog waste station over there," a random person walking by said.

I considered it helpful, but the tone was of someone telling me what to do. "Thank you!" I attempted to keep the sarcasm from my call.

We trotted over. Milo was much calmer now, and I grabbed a bag. He went again before we got two steps.

"Really? How long were you in there?" I asked him, grabbing another bag.

After cleaning his impressive deposits and throwing them in the proper bin, we headed back to the boat.

On the deck, I said, "Go back inside." I pointed to his exit path.

He did.

"Who's the best doggie ever?"I asked as he gazed out the window and waited for me.

I pushed as far into the window as possible. A fog of dog food scent filled the interior cabin. Twisting, I saw a cupboard open and a bag of food knocked over.

"Did you break into your kibble?" I asked.

He turned his head to the side, ears up, as if to say, "Well, yeah. What was I supposed to do?"

The bag was almost full, as if he had only eaten the amount he required for his breakfast. But if he wasn't the kind of dog to eat everything in front of him, what caused him to open the food in the first place?

"How long have you been alone?" I asked, searching for a water bowl. He had one, dangerously close to empty. "Do you have water?"

In answer, Milo paced to the end of the couch, went to the galley sink, which was full of water, and drank. Content, he hopped into an easy chair and curled into a ball.

It was possible that James left for Bristol for the day to do witness sketches, but he would have taken Milo out before he left. Had James been gone all night?

I texted him again and tried calling, but it went straight to voicemail.

"Look," I told Milo, "I need to go back to work. You stay here, and I'll come back after my shift. Okay?"

Milo lifted his head, made eye contact, then rested his muzzle on his front paws.

Securing the window so he wouldn't follow me, I walked to the Abbey Square, grabbed a pasty at the corner shop, and then was off to the lab for the afternoon.

* * *

James still hadn't made it home when I returned the narrow boat. Every time I got close to trusting him, he disappointed me.

"Milo?"

"Bark!"

"Hold on," I said, and clinging tightly in the dark, I made my way to the unlatched window.

If possible, the dog exhibited even more grace when I let him out this time.

When we got to the little deck, I took my eyes off him, and he flashed off the boat.

"Milo, stay!"

Good dog that he was, he did.

I jumped off after him, and he stood, ready to run.

"Stay!" I commanded. "I've had a long day, and you are not helping right now. Come."

Again, he did.

"On board." I pointed.

Milo leaped and waited, whining.

"I will take you in a minute, but you need to wait."

Clipping the leash onto his collar, I patted his head.

"You're a very good dog," I said, sitting on the dew-covered stool by the door at eye level with him.

He cocked his head to the side again, inviting me to continue.

"I'm sorry I yelled. I was afraid you would run off, but you're far too well-trained for that. Not a stray. Also, it's not good if James disappears and leaves you alone."

At the mention of James's name, Milo whined and looked at the park.

"Do you miss him? I miss Edward. And my mom." A little tear formed at the corner of my eye. "And my dad, and Tori, and someone tried to take Lily this morning, and if Rivers hadn't shown up, I don't know what would have happened. They might have taken me too or run us down, and I don't know how they found Greenway Lane, and everything I touch here ends badly."

With every word, my voice grew more shaky. By the end, I was full-on sobbing, the trauma of the morning taking hold.

Milo put his paw on my leg, and when I reached for him, he launched his body into my lap. The stool wobbled, and we both collapsed onto the deck.

He stood on me, licking my face.

"Okay, okay," I laughed. "Geez, how much do you weigh? Let me up."

The dog stepped to the side, allowing me to sit.

"Thank you," I said, hugging him.

With my breakdown completed, Milo changed gears and put his paws on the step to the exit. He didn't leap off this time, but he swiveled his head toward me, then at the park, then back at me, then back at the park.

"Fine, we'll go."

Milo did his business, and we went for a short walk.

As I turned us back, a large, scary man with a threatening voice yelled, "Oi! Where'd you get that mutt?"

# Chapter Twenty-Four: Not a Mutt

The park had very few people at this time of year. Bare trees lurked starkly along the path, obscuring the hulking figure that uttered the question.

Surprising me, Milo growled as the man neared us, confirming he was talking to me.

"Mutt?" Offended at the slur to Milo's breeding and disposition, I went on the defensive. Ignoring the fact that this might be the very farmer who owned and trained Milo in the first place, I said, "None of your business."

Far from heeding my ill-advised response, the man became more aggressive.

Only then did I realize how much I had misjudged the situation. This man might not have anything to do with Milo and everything to do with the attack on Douglass.

When this bit of information sank into my brain, the man bore down on me, huffing.

Milo moved between us, protecting me, barking wildly.

I pulled him toward me, ready to run, but Milo stood his ground, teeth bared.

Rather than coming after me, though, the man lifted his heavy-clad boot to kick Milo.

"I'll take care of those teeth, I will!" he yelled while I leaned down, grabbed Milo by the scruff of the neck, and shouted, "Up!"

Milo launched into my arms, his head connecting with my jaw and causing black dots to dance before my eyes.

Our attacker went full on Charlie-Brown-trying-to-kick-the-football-at-Thanksgiving and landed flat on his back.

"This is my dog," I shouted at the prone figure. Blinking rapidly to clear my vision, I shifted Milo to balance his weight and stood tall. "Don't you dare come looking for him again. Ever!"

Sitting and rubbing his head, the man muttered, "Good riddance to you both. Stupid mutt."

So, Milo, not Douglass. Relieved, I struggled away from the farmer. Milo was small for his breed but still heavy. I carried him around a bend before collapsing to the ground.

"Did James rescue you from that man?" I asked him.

Tail wag.

Since my assumptions pinballed all over the place, I wouldn't carve the thought in stone, but my estimation of Edward's brother went up a bit.

With the realization, concern replaced annoyance. *Where was James?* If he were the kind of guy to rescue a dog from an abusive owner, he wouldn't leave Milo alone like he did.

Pulling out my phone, I hit Tori's number.

"You're calling from an actual phone," she observed.

"Why don't you say 'hello' anymore?"

Ignoring me, she asked, "What's up?

As Milo led me, I said, "Are you at work? I don't want to bother you."

"I can take a break." She shouted something, switching to Spanish without a hint of accent coloring her English.

"You're amazing."

"Granted. Again, what's up?"

While Milo marked everything in sight, I told Tori, "In order of least importance, I need to eat dinner, figure out how to tell Edward about Milo, and find James."

"Who is Milo?"

"The border collie."

"K."

"I think James stole him. But I also think James did so because the owner was abusive." I explained our previous encounter.

Tori whistled, which I couldn't ever remember her doing before, and I wondered if it was a newfound relief at not dating Scott.

"How did the breakup go?"

"Very well for me, and I don't have to worry about my former other half, so great all around."

"I'm happy for you," I said, meaning it.

"You tried to warn me about him. Everyone did."

"Yeah, but it's different on the inside."

We got all mushy about friendship, and then Tori said, "Why don't you walk the dog over to The Boater?"

"I'm still not sure who Mordred is, so I'm staying away for a while." There was, however, a little Thai restaurant on the stairway landing from Pulteney Bridge to the Avon.  Close enough to The Boater for me to keep an eye out, but not directly in harm's way. If they complained about Milo coming inside, I could order to-go.

"Is Mordred your new name for the mastermind? I like it. Very in keeping with the dead Arthurian knight."

"I thought so," I said, relating the latest developments.

"Whoa, wait. Someone attacked a constable in public? That's crazy."

"I know, right?  And Lily never told me who or what she saw, so I don't know what I might be walking into."  I paused for a moment, remembering something I overheard. "Not that I was eavesdropping, but I heard something about not trusting her boyfriend."

"So, Donny could be Mordred the Mastermind, nice alliteration, BTW. Why did you discount him?"

I shrugged even though Tori couldn't see me. "He does magic? I don't know. He just seems so darned nice."

"You know, in every movie ever, it's the nice guy who did it."

"Sometimes the butler did it."

"Point. But yeah, he could be Kaiser Souza-ing us," I said.

"I don't think you can turn a character name from an old movie into a verb."

Laughing, I agreed, as Milo pulled me up the steps to Pulteney Bridge.

"I'm at the restaurant. Thanks for being you!"

Unfortunately, the Thai restaurant was closed. I went up to street level, discovered a little Indian place, ordered a takeaway, and aimed to go back down to river level.

Milo kept tugging, wanting to cross the bridge.

"Look, dog. I'm in charge," I said.

Zero improvement in my companion's behavior.

A large tree protected a bench by the tourist boat, and I hoped it wouldn't be as wet as an exposed seating area."Come," I said with a tug, "with," grunt, "me."

He relented, and we went down to the river.

Cold, dark, and not the best place for dinner, I shoveled spicy vindaloo into my face. Spicy didn't cover half of it, so I opened the raita and frantically spooned the cooling yogurt mixture into my mouth using naan bread for a utensil.

And this was how the reporter Jeffery Dailey found me—on a chilly bench, container balanced on my lap, and yogurt dribbling down my chin.

"Blrph," I said as he sat next to me. Uninvited, I might add.

Handing me a bottle of water, he said, "Down the sink. Looks like you need it."

Most of the time, when Jeffrey leaned into his cockney roots, I swear he made up rhymes to annoy me. This time, he at least made a little sense for "drink."

"Thanks," I said, then downed half the bottle. "I forgot to order liquid."

I wanted to ask what he wanted and why he was there, but it seemed rude after he gave me water. However, the reporter made his living by drumming up the worst angle of any story and exaggerating it, so I kept my guard up.

After our team's discovery at Chedworth Roman Villa near Gloucester, I gave Jeffery an exclusive. I did it to keep him off the trail of Gabriel, but the gesture made our relationship less adversarial.

Not that I trusted him. Oh no. But at least I didn't feel the need to call the police the second he sat down.

"What's your name, my cherry hogg?" Jeffery asked Milo who had put his paw on the reporter's knee. So much for being a good judge of character.

Cherry hogg definitely sounded made up, but I wouldn't give him the satisfaction of asking how three syllables made sense for 'dog.'

"Milo," I said. Brief answers were better when dealing with the press.

Now, I know that both police and reporters use silence to make people talk and tell secrets. I know this. And I try to resist, but sometimes it is just too much.

"What story are you working on?"

Rubbing his hands together like a B-movie villain, he said, "I'm glad you asked me that, Miss Maddie."

That statement made me regret asking.

"When I needed a source for Roman archaeology, my favorite intern at the Roman Baths popped into my head."

"I work for the dig team now. I'm not just an intern."

"Are you now? All the better."

Sometimes, pride in my position backfires. "But really, I'm just a student. Not an expert," I said, hoping he'd leave me alone.

"You're the one for me, you are." Pulling out his phone, he showed me the screen. "What do you know about this?"

The picture of the rondel had several simultaneous effects.  My curry/yogurt-filled naan tumbled to my lap, Milo lunged at a squirrel spilling my open water, and I yelped in shock at the sight of the dagger.

"Nothing, really," I tried, but Jeffery was having none of it.

"Stuck a nerve, I think. What do you know?"

Wiping bright orange goo from my khakis with one hand while rescuing the bottle with the other, I gave up on any pretense of innocence and went on the offensive.

"A lot," I claimed. "And if you want to hear any of it, you need to offer me a deal. What have you got? Don't newspapers pay for information?"

Jeffery's features collapsed, and his cockney accent became more pronounced. "I'm just a poor working lad, I am, trying to make a living."

"You would be more believable if you didn't get the cunning look in your eye," I told him, not falling for the wounded weasel act.

He straightened and regarded me. "You're getting smarter, you are."

Considering I hadn't fallen for his fake detective act on first encounter, I saw this bit of flattery for what it was—another con.

"If you don't want to know, hey, that's fine by me. The police wouldn't want me talking to you anyway."

I stood, deposited my trash in a nearby bin, and tugged Milo toward Edward's mooring.

He sat.

"Milo's making sure you mind your manners, he is. Not polite walking out in the middle of a convo."

"Milo," I whispered, "you're ruining my exit."

His eyes cut to me, then to the stairway to the Pulteney Bridge.

"No. Come." Up to this point, he obeyed my commands without question, but now I didn't know what to do. Carrying forty-five pounds of squirming dog for half a mile wasn't an option.

"Come here," Jeffery called, and Milo, the traitor, pulled toward him.

"Fine," I conceded to the dog. To Jeffery, I said, "No more acts. What have you got?"

"Forgery operation, innit?"

"Why would anyone forge rondels when you can pick up a replica for fifty bucks?" I asked, but then realized that a forgery sold as authentic with accompanying provenance would be worth a lot more. A real rondel fetched well over $1,000. Not as lucrative as drugs or counterfeit coins, but once the initial cost was covered, a few items made a lot of money.

"Now she's got it," Jeffery said, apparently reading my expression.

"It's safe, because you also make cheap knock-offs for tourists to cover the fact that you're making forgeries," I said, continuing my line of logic. No one would look into why a company making fake daggers bought supplies. "The only risk would be the document forger," I added. "Who's providing the fake provenance?"

"That's what I'm coming to you for."

Made sense, I supposed, but I was disappointed he didn't have more information.

"Do you have the paperwork for that dagger?" I asked, indicating the picture on his phone.

Another photo, which I had to zoom in on. Nose inches from his screen, I saw that the bill of sale came from a well-known, legitimate gallery in Corsham.

"I've heard of this place. How do you know it's fake?"

"Asked them, didn't I?"

"Don't sound so offended," I said. "It's not like you've never cut corners to land a story. What did they say?"

"The email is their name, but instead of an 'o' it has an umlaut in the domain name."

I zoomed further and nodded. "I wouldn't have known that wasn't legit. Good con. Is the site active?"

Jeffery shook his head no.

Clever on the forger's part. Set up the domain, probably with a provider in a different country, then cancel it before anyone comes after them. Of course, outsmarting everyone is the mastermind's forte.

Swiping back to the image of the rondel, I pouted a little. Somehow, it felt worse to be threatened by a fake dagger instead of a real one.

"Alright, your turn," he insisted.

After telling him about the knife-throwing incident at Sham Castle, I shrugged. "I don't have a lot. But I know DI Parikh is innocent and being elaborately framed. He collects ancient weapons, so the attack on me landed him under more suspicion."

Instead of being annoyed at my lack of participation in our little game, he nodded. "You're not wrong there."

"Really?" I was right, no doubt, but I wasn't expecting support from the reporter.

The unexpected encouragement unlocked a piece of information in my brain, buried by the attack on Douglass. "I have heard," I said, not naming the constable as my source, "that there is a forge in the warehouse district."

"Is there, now? News to me it is."

I couldn't tell if it was actually news or if he was just saying that to keep me talking.

Since I didn't know much more, I stood. "Thanks for the info on the fake daggers," I said. "Time to take my buddy here home."

Milo, however, still stared at the stairwell up to the street level of the bridge.

"Come on," I said, tugging.

Steadfastly, he refused to budge, and his collar started to slip toward his ears. The term "doggedly" must have been invented for a border collie.

"He's on the scent of something. Can't ignore it when that happens," Jeffery said, taking the dog's side.

Giving up, I let him tug me toward the bridge, Jeffery following along.

"He's not a bloodhound," I pointed out.

"Need to find a sheep, don't they? Smart," he said.

Could Milo be treating James like a little lost lamb? It was worth exploring.

At street level, Milo crossed to the middle of the street, went in circles, and sat, looking expectantly at me.

I looked at Jeffery. "I grew up with cats," I said.

"Come on, boy, which way?" he said to Milo, extending his arm.

The dog circled wider, nose checking the ground and air, but he found nothing.

"Looks to me like whatever scent he's following got put into a car," Jeffery commented.

Such a devious scenario wouldn't have crossed my mind, but it made sense when I pictured Milo's route.

Had James been taken from his narrowboat, marched to the bridge, and forced into a car?

# Chapter Twenty-Five: Forges and Forgeries

With no scent for Milo to follow, he whined, then sniffed the spilled food on my slacks.

"You'll need to soak those," Jeffery advised, uncharacteristically domestic. "For the stench, if nothing else."

This bit of advice annoyed me, as I didn't have many sets of work clothes, so I ignored him and ruffled Milo's ears instead.

"Sorry, boy. Let's go home."

Jeffery didn't join me and took off in the opposite direction from my route.

"What's that way?" I asked.

"Locksbrook Road," he said without glancing back.

Tugging on Milo's leash, I got him back to the river and the narrowboat.

We stepped aboard together, and I checked for signs of life. None.

Milo came to the same conclusion, pranced down the gunwale, checked the window, returned to me, and pricked his ears.

His look of distress would have been comical if it hadn't echoed my misgivings about James.

"Go inside, and we will form a search party in the morning."

Milo gave every appearance of having understood everything I said, and didn't like it. Not one bit.

He bolted off the boat and returned to the bridge at full speed.

"Milo!"

Good boy that he was, he sat, waiting for me to catch up.

I did, retrieving his leash and giving in to his demands. "Okay, we'll have one last look."

Back at the bridge, Milo investigated The Boater's storefront.

While he sniffed, I texted Edward. He wouldn't receive it anytime soon, but I had been cowardly in not telling him about Milo. At the last moment, I added Simon to form a group chat.

'James hasn't been home for two da—'

Milo lunged, and I accidentally hit send.

'Sorry. The dog lunged. Two days. Also—'

Before I could explain further, the border collie gave a mighty charge, knocking the phone out of my hand.  I watched with horror as my cell tumbled into the road and beneath the tires of a speeding motorcycle.

"Seriously?" It was like he aimed for it.

I retrieved the crushed device. The screen was smashed and stayed on for moments before shutting down.

When I turned to admonish Milo for causing the mishap, I couldn't find him.

"Milo?"

Nothing.

"Milo!"

A single bark drew my attention to a black-and-white streak a block away.

"Be that way," I said, bitterness tinging my words.  I thought we were friends. "Run away. James shouldn't have gotten you anyway."

Turning my back on him, I headed toward the opposite side of the bridge and my way home.

Three sharp barks caused me to turn around. *Did he want me to follow?*

Two barks answered by thoughts. Two for yes, one for no?

Even if I wanted to, Milo was too far ahead, and I didn't have a phone to call for a ride.

He waited, then barked again.

I jogged a few steps, but he took off, maintaining the distance between us. "Milo, sit!" He did. "Stay."

Running this time, I tried to gain ground, but after a few yards, he took off and went faster.

Then he stopped and waited for me.

I dithered, not wanting to be dragged into the night by an insistent border collie, but also not wanting to miss the chance to find James. What if Milo really caught James' scent and knew where he was going, and I ignored him?

"Come on, Milo," I muttered. "Give me a better clue."

As if summoned by the dog, a cab pulled slowly up the street.

I stuck my hand out, hailing it, which I'd never done before. Arizona didn't have taxis rolling around the suburbs. I hadn't seen many in Bath, and had once been told that I couldn't just call a taxi and expect it to come.

"Thank you for stopping. I didn't think taxis did that here."

"I normally don't, if I'm honest," she said. "I dropped off a bunch of lads at a stag do and forgot to turn my sign off.

"I appreciate it."

Much as I wanted to say, "Follow that dog," I didn't think it would go over well. Instead, I picked the only location that fit all my puzzle pieces. The picture, far from complete, offered vague glimpses. But the property that kept coming up from the warehouse fire last Christmas was the only place in the city that would allow a forge on Locksbrook Road. "The warehouse district on Locksbrook Road. That way," I pointed at Milo's retreating form.

I didn't know if I was out to retrieve the dog, find James, or uncover the forger, but I couldn't sit and do nothing. Milo needed me—and James.

"Two miles," she informed me. "Easy."

The car heater worked wonders on my vaguely damp clothing, and I allowed myself to close my eyes and enjoy warmth for a moment.

"Pardon me for asking, but what is that smell?" the driver asked, rolling down all the windows, cold wind whipping through the backseat.

"Vindaloo," I said, fighting a shiver. "And maybe yogurt that's starting to sour. I'm so sorry. My takeaway fell on me."

"I've had worse," she said, and I was grateful she didn't kick me out.

Turns out, she didn't need to, as we pulled to a stop on the street. "You're sure this is the spot?"

Looking around, I wasn't sure.

Dark and quiet, the street exuded all the charm of a zombie apocalypse.

No sign of the dog, but he couldn't have run faster than we drove, so that wasn't a surprise. Unless I totally misread everything and came to the wrong place.

"Can I take your card and call you if this isn't the right place?"

She nodded.

As I took it, I remembered my cell landing in the street. "Never mind. My phone got run over."

"If you don't mind my asking, why this street?"

I sighed. "A wild goose chase. My friend is missing, and his dog seemed to want to come this way, and I think there is a forge making fake antiques here." The last bit didn't fit in with the other things I said, but it sort of tumbled out of my mouth.

With a nod, she said, "Yeah, there's a forge right over there. Me mum had a fit over it going in, even though she never comes this way."

That information sealed the deal for me. "Okay, thanks again for stopping, and sorry for the odor."

My taxi friend drove away, leaving me in the moonless night. Rather than dwelling on the absurdity of the decision to leave the car, I gave a tentative whistle for Milo.

Nothing. No answering bark to reassure me I was on the right track.

I turned around to study landmarks so I could walk home later, then I headed toward the building my driver had indicated.

As I got closer, I heard thumping sounds. The windows were covered, so I couldn't see what was going on, but raised voices carried to me.

Nothing for it but to try and break in.

*Or you could find a phone and call the police,* the voice in the back of my mind that sounded way too much like my mom said. Bad timing on the voice's part. I could have asked the taxi driver for her cell.

Ignoring the turmoil in my brain, I turned the handle on the front gate. It opened.

"Okay," I whispered, setting my purse near a decorative pot, "that's a good sign." Not sure if I said it because I believed it, or to convince myself, I slipped in.

Not much better lit than the street outside, I examined the little office. It had a desk I could hide under if needed, a coat rack, and a display case with a fake, shiny rondel. "Step into History," a sign proclaimed.

Near the desk, a wall of hammers, like I'd seen at the blacksmith's, served as decor. Unlike the dagger, these looked real, able to handle the fiery forges.

I was in the right building, but no landline presented itself. Not that I had a single English phone number memorized.

Behind the desk, a simple door seemed to be the exit to deeper parts of the building. I crept toward it, watching every step to avoid noise.

I needn't have bothered. The closer I got to the door, the louder the thumping got. Peeking through the gap between the doorframe, I saw another poorly lit room, with a large square piece of machinery, almost as big as the office, working away.

Scrape, crash, scrape, crash, it's rhythmic cacophony echoed through the warehouse. The forge.

Shifting my view, the backs of two t-shirt-clad men blocked a third sitting in a chair. Their voices didn't carry my way, so I took a chance that they wouldn't hear the door open.

After grabbing a heavy hammer for protection, I waited for a crash and slipped through, checking the handle to make sure it didn't lock automatically.

No one looked my way as I scanned the cement floor for a hiding place. Luckily, rows of supplies, metal blocks from the looks of it, were stacked in two rows on either side of the door, stretching to the corners. Stacked about five and a half feet high, I had to duckwalk around the room's perimeter so my head wouldn't be seen over the rows. The added weight of the hammer made the movement extra awkward.

I was near the men now, but the supplies were packed so tightly I couldn't see through them to check on the seated person.

The room was warmer here, close to the pounding forge. Wishing I'd left my jacket outside, I inventoried my surroundings. The artificial aisle I stood in was open at both ends. If two people came after me from each side, there were enough toeholds in the supply wall to climb up and over.

Checking my pockets, I found a disinfecting herbal spray that Dolly formulated for me, a hair scrunchie, and a used spork from dinner. I'd abandoned it there in favor of using naan to eat. A mistake I wouldn't repeat, I vowed as a whiff of stale curry hit my nose.

A loud thunk accompanied a sudden, unnerving quiet. The forge's master switch had been turned off, leaving hissing heat and ticking metal in its wake.

Surprised, I fumbled the spork from my fingers, but caught it before it reached the floor. Wishing I'd set the hammer down before the noise stopped, I looked for a soft spot to leave it.

"Oi, I thought you threw out that food. You know I hate that foreign crap," a rough voice complained.

About me.

Setting the hammer on my foot, I pulled out the spray and squirted the stain a few times, hoping to mask the odor. The last thing I needed was for the men to come looking for the source of the smell.

"Had fish and chips, didn't I?" a second voice, equally menacing, responded.

"Maybe it's just him. You should chuck him in the bin with the rest of the trash," a third, alarmingly familiar voice said.

*James.*

James at his most obnoxious.

The disturbing sound of a fist hitting flesh made me wince. Someone shutting James up.

I sank to the floor, thought better of it, and stood, readying myself for flight or fight, gripping the hammer.

Now that I found him, I didn't have a plan. Should I escape and send help, or figure out a way to free James?

Having been in dangerous situations before, I knew my limitations. I couldn't even run with all the abuse my knees had taken in the past few days. My best bet was sneaking back to the office and out to find a phone.

Besides, the herb spray only made the stale vindaloo more intense.

As I snuck along, quads burning from the funny squat position I'd chosen to walk in, I overheard a case-specific question: "What do the police know about the forgeries, Bailey?"

They referred to James as "Bailey," which made sense because it's his last name, but it sounded like they thought he was Edward.

And James wasn't correcting them.

These two thugs must have thought James was Edward, because he was on Edward's boat. Kind of like me assuming the Thai restaurant would be open because it always had been.

While I admired James's tenacity for not letting them beat information out of him, I was afraid he was digging a hole he couldn't escape. If they discovered he wasn't the real deal, they might dispose of him.

Not releasing him might be the case no matter what. What is it they say? If the victim sees the kidnapper's face, they're already dead.

All the more reason to retreat now and send help for James before it's too late.

# Chapter Twenty-Six: Too Late

Much as I wanted to bash my way to James, I listened to my inner wisdom for once and continued to sneak toward the office door. It hadn't made noise when I came through it before, but the forge had been on.

Now, in the relative quiet, I hoped the hinges didn't squeak. Bracing for the worst, I pulled on the handle. Amazingly, the door swung open silently.

I hurried through, then closed it with hardly a click of sound.

The breath I was holding whooshed out, followed by a deep inhale I immediately regretted. The odor coming from my clothes amplified in the small space.

Not one to stick around, I sought the night's fresh air. Cracking the outside entry, I scanned to confirm the parking lot and street were still empty.

After replacing the hammer in its display, I escaped into the night. Cool air wicked away my fear and the decaying food odor on my clothes.

Looking from side to side, I spotted my landmark for the direction home, and as I took a step, I heard gravel shifting behind me.

I spun around and collided with a muscular man.

"Hello, my lover," Mac said, his icy voice making the familiar greeting a threat.

"Mordred," I said. However, just because he was forging antiquities, it didn't mean he also framed DI Parikh. I needed more information.

All of which was interesting, but I spent too much time thinking instead of getting out of there.

Too late. I ran only a few steps before Mac knocked me over.

Picking me up like a bag of flour, he threw me over his shoulder despite my kicking and screaming.

The advantage of having a fit was that I made plenty of noise in case someone was about and could call in a complaint. Once inside, I knocked several hammers off the wall as we went through the cramped office. In the chaos, I grabbed a small one from the set.

About seven inches long, I calculated that it would fit within the length of my forearm. I slipped it up my jacket sleeve while landing a pretty good knee to Mac's stomach.

The downside was that when he got into the forge area, he dumped me onto the hard floor and aimed a kick at my gut. I rolled into a ball quickly enough to have the force of the blow impact my shin instead, but it sounded like he cracked the bone. Every movement shot pinpricks of fire through my leg.

I might have whimpered a little.

"Oi!" James shouted in my defense, which, as he probably expected, drew Mac's attention to him.

"Bloody hell," Mac said when he took in James's face. "You eejit. You got the wrong Bailey."

The word Bailey was punctuated by Mac backhanding the closest thug. I wanted to identify each minion with a characteristic, but their wife-beater shirts, muscled arms, and crew cuts were identical.

Rebuffed, the thug took his wrath out on James with a similar punch. "Liar," he accused, as though that was worse than kidnapping and murder.

Rubbing his face where the blow landed, the thug said to the other, "Take him out back. We can use the forge later."

*Oh crap, oh crap, oh crap!* They're going to kill James and dispose of his body in the forge.

"Hold up," Mac instructed. "We can still use him. This one likes to draw pictures for the police, I've heard tell. Isn't that right?"

The string of swearing that erupted from James rivaled any gangster movie I'd ever seen.

Mac merely smiled and said, "Get me the end nipper."

Cute sounding though the name was, my whimpering intensified. The blacksmith had several nippers used to remove excess metal from a finished but still-hot piece.

"You," he said, suddenly furious at my presence, "how would a scar across that pretty face do for you?"

I curled tighter into a fetal position and attempted to whine more quietly.

While Mac and his terrifying minions focused on finding implements of torture, I moved like a roly-poly bug to see if I could untie James. My painful moans were not faked, but I stayed quiet enough not to draw attention to myself.

James's foot nudged my head, and I glanced up at him.

He shook his head no.

Unsure if he didn't want me to put myself in danger or if he had a plan, I instead worked on freeing the hammer I'd secreted away.

Removing a piece of wood with a metal head from a tight jacket sleeve required standing and straightening my arms, neither of which was possible at the moment. I uncurled my fists, but kept my knees close to my chest to hide movement.

The further the hammer emerged, the more unnatural my position became, but it had to be done. What good was a weapon if I couldn't reach it?

After their fiendish conference, the three forgers came back to James and me. Mac held the handles of a giant nipper, which he opened and snapped closed like an angry alligator.

I stopped moving and surveyed the room, looking for anything that would help. The forge itself occupied a larger-than-necessary part of the room.

My interest in the machine halted when Mac said, "Grab his hands. We'll see how well he draws without a thumb."

What sounded like a swarm of bees doing a tango filled my head, and I had to fight not to faint. Mac was going to destroy James's hand with one snip.

One of the thugs walked behind the chair James was tied to. "What the hell?" he managed to ask before James, with border collie-like agility, stood, grabbed the chair, and swiped it at the guard.

The chair, metal but lightweight, rang with a single note as it struck the thug's head.

The dazed man stumbled but did not go down.

James swung again in an uppercut, knocking the thug out.

"Yeah!" I shouted, but my celebration was cut short when thug number two grabbed the chair and tossed it across the warehouse. I understood now why he didn't want me to draw attention to the chair. He'd already untied himself.

When the clatter stopped, the snap, snap of Mac opening and shutting the nippers filled the space. Both kidnappers kept a wide berth around James, treating him like a rattlesnake that was ready to strike.

Subtlety not available as an option, I uncurled, straightened my arm, and removed the little hammer.

"James!" I called and tossed the hammer to him.

His hand flashed out, and he caught it without his eyes leaving his two assailants. Picking thug two as his target, he pirouetted, ducked a haymaker punch, and whacked the man in the head.

I marveled at the grace and violence of the act. Again, I wondered what kind of neighborhood gang had taken Edward, James, and their older brother. What else were they capable of?

However, now was not the time to daydream about my boyfriend's past, as evidenced by the fact that I hadn't noticed Mac switch his attention to me.

Relief when I saw the nippers by the forge turned to terror when Mac approached me with a hot poker. Why a modern drop forge needed such a thing was beyond my ability to care. Maybe he had it to extract information from people. Right then and there, I decided I would tell him anything he wanted to hear.

Pulling me upright caused lightning bolts of pain to shoot up my legs. Shin splits times a million.

Gasping, I collapsed, but he held me tight, red-hot metal poised menacingly before my face.

Ignoring the pain, I got my feet under me so that I wouldn't accidentally stumble into the poker.

"Settle down, lad," he said to James. Mac didn't need to make any threats about what would happen if James didn't obey.

My eye would be the first thing to go.

I might have whimpered again.

James threw away the little hammer, hitting an unconscious thug in the process. The man didn't react.

We waited.

Technically, James could have left me to my fate. After all, we hadn't known each other all that long, and he and Edward were only recently reconciled. But a boy who saved a dog from a violent master wouldn't leave me.

"What's your next move, Mac? You've had everything planned up to this point," James said.

"And a good plan it was, too," Mac responded.

I hoped James could trick him into reciting a villain monologue to buy us time.

Time for what? I had no idea since no one knew we were here. All I knew was that being alive was better than the alternative.

But Mac didn't give in to the temptation and wax poetic about his evil genius.

James did it for him. "You have quite an investment here that you wouldn't want to lose. I could disappear, and no one would care, but she," James pointed at me, "has a lot of people who would look for her. A crime-solving American intern would be missed."

Mac adjusted his hold on me, listening to James's logic.

"You can't stay. You know that. Go now while you still can. I'll come with you. Your guards could use some training."

The poker wavered for a moment, then dropped away from my face. Mac pushed me roughly to the cement, a position I was more than happy to be in.

As James spoke, I inched sideways, distancing myself from Mac and his vicious weapon.

Rather than being taken in by James' offer, Mac surprised us both by bolting at James, holding the poker like a lance.

# Chapter Twenty-Seven: Ramming Speed

I watched in horror as Mac approached James at ramming speed. For a big man, he was fast. His weapon had cooled, but still glowed like a demon eye aimed at James's chest.

It would take a lot of force to penetrate a ribcage into a man's heart, but Mac had the strength, and the heated metal would help clear the way.

Scrabbling to my knees, I launched my skinny frame at Mac's legs, but didn't slow him down. I took off my shoe and threw it.

There was no way I could fight the man, but maybe I could distract him. The other shoe followed the first.

It was enough for James to deflect the blow to his arm. He howled in pain as the burning metal connected with his bicep.

Grinning manically and panting from exertion, Mac laughed, adjusted his aim, and went in for the kill.

Screaming like a banshee, I ignored my leg and kicked the back of Mac's knee with all my might.

Mac's stagger, and my unholy scream, got James moving. Holding his charred arm, he ran to the chair and brandished it, keeping Mac at a distance.

An ashen pallor covered James's face. He wouldn't stay upright much longer, and I didn't know what to do.

Mac circled like a predator, making occasional exploratory swipes at James with the poker.

The chair countered every thrust, but with less force each time. James wouldn't last another minute of this game.

"Bark!"

The incongruous sound stopped us all.

"Bark! Bark!" Milo's voice came in loud and clear from outside the window. He had managed to follow the trail and find James. *Good dog.*

Now, a sudden fear that Mac would do something to Milo gripped me so hard I wretched, throwing up vindaloo in a disgusting orange heap.

Which, apparently, was Mac's kryptonite. "Clean that up! Now! Get it out of here this instant!" he screamed.

"Geez, don't you run a pub?" I said, wiping my face. "People throw up all the time in bars."

Flippancy is not welcome in many situations. Honestly, in most situations, but it's particularly bad when someone wants to kill you and dispose of your body in a fiery tomb. Too much adrenaline had come and gone, and my ability to think abandoned me.

Mac's wild look kick-started my brain. "Sorry. Where are the cleaning supplies?" I asked as sweetly as possible.

Mac ignored James to come after me again.

Backpedalling, I stepped in the pile of sick, slipped, and fell, landing in the mess and scattering bits of used food.

The situation was too much for Mac. Changing his grip on the poker to hold it like a javelin, he cocked his arm to throw.

Which is when Lord Pacock and Lady Gwendolyn entered the warehouse.

Ignoring the tableau before them, Dolly said, "Oh, good, you're here. I'm sure you've seen the announcement of our upcoming nuptials. We decided we absolutely had to have some of your sweet little daggers as a guest gift at the reception. Isn't that right, Simon?"

"Indeed," Simon added, looking bored.

My mouth dropped open, gaping in shock.

"Of course, we expect a discount for a batch order," Dolly continued, outwardly oblivious to Mac's threatening pose and James's tottering form.

Mac lowered his weapon to stare at the beautiful couple in disbelief.

"We're expecting 200 at the reception, and we will want something for the children as well. Do you have any replicas suitable for toddlers? Or are they all weapons? No matter, really, we can dull the points so they're not dangerous. A burbolt, as it were."

Sobbing, I began to fear that help wasn't on the way and that Simon and Dolly had unknowingly walked into danger.

That's when Milo danced in, licked my face, sniffed my repulsive clothing, wagged his tail, and leapt toward James.

Finally, James dropped in a heap, the chair clanging to the ground with him. He wrapped his arms around his dog and kept a bleary eye on Mac.

The bright flash of a camera went off, spurring Mac to move. Appearing in slow motion, he spun and stumbled toward the back of the warehouse.

Something about the word "warehouse" sounded warning bells, and my sobbing abruptly stopped.

"We have to leave," I said, clear-headed. "Simon, help James. He has a third degree burn on his arm."

Without comment, Simon and, surprisingly, Jeffery Dailey, the reporter, strode to James's position, helped him up, and half-carried him out of the forge room. Dolly followed, while Milo and I brought up the rear.

"Keep going, Dolly," I said when everyone stopped in the office. "And, we should get those men out, too."

This statement got James's attention enough for him to ask, "Do we have to?"

"I think so, yes," I said, shooing with my hands to keep Dolly moving. And distance her from me, as I could not be any grosser. She, James, Milo, and I moved into the car park and the street.

Simon and Jeffery went back in and pulled the two thugs, still unconscious from James's fighting skills, and dragged them to the front gate. Leaving the henchmen in a heap, Simon and Jeffery joined us.

"You take pen and ink to a new level, you do," Jeffery said, which I surmised meant stink.

I couldn't argue. "Why are you here?" I asked instead. "Or more importantly, how did you find us?"

"Was walking this way when Milo ran past. Followed him, didn't I?"

At this, Milo perked his ears and tilted his head, tail held high.

"I thought he lost the scent," I said. "What was he following?"

"Treats," James croaked. He needed a doctor.

Milo's tail wagged excitedly at the word.

"I keep them in my pocket, and started dropping them out a crack in the flatbed they pushed me on."

"Good boy," I said to Milo. I wanted to ask James how and where he was forced onto a truck, but it wasn't the time. Neither of us was in great shape. Instead, I asked Simon, "Are the police coming? James needs treatment."

Simon turned his head at the approaching sound of sirens, then looked back at me and nodded.

"Thanks, buddy," I said.

The corner of his mouth twitched in a smile.

EMTs loaded James into an ambulance despite Milo's persistent insistence that he be allowed to accompany his master.

Handing me treats from the gurney, James said, "Take care of him."

"Key to the boat?" I asked, feeling that his mental faculties weren't firing on all cylinders, as that would have been more helpful than dog biscuits.

"Under the welcome mat," he whispered before the emergency technicians took him.

*Honestly?* After all those gymnastics I did getting to the window, the key was by the door the whole time. Note to self: Look around next time I need to take a dog out.

As the ambulance pulled away, more sirens approached.  DCI Bray emerged exuding a quiet calm.

Tears threatened again, my relief at relinquishing control palpable. But I channeled my inner British stiff upper lip and pulled it together. It simply wouldn't do, as Simon would say. That, and for me to be quiet. *I'd save him the trouble,* I thought.

But now that help had arrived, I wasn't sure I could hold on. It seemed like such a perfect time to collapse.

"Everybody is out," I reported, noting the quaver in my voice. "Mac went the other direction, but I assume there's a back way."

"Miss Madeline, how nice to see you. Why did you feel it necessary to pull out the unconscious men? And should I ask how they got in that condition?"

Questions I should have prepared answers for, but hadn't. I couldn't tell him I'd been trying to clear DI Parikh's name and decided to investigate in the dark night, or that Edward looked up information on Mac and the warehouse district fire for me, or that James was a closet ninja.

Staring at him, my connection to reality wavered, the black dots from earlier returning.

"Miss Madeline, are you quite all right?" DCI Bray took a step toward me, and Milo got between us.

The border collie didn't growl or bark. His tail swished slowly.

"That's a good dog," Bray said, and Milo's wagging picked up speed.

I dug my fingers into the dog's thick fur. "He kicked me," I muttered, more dark spots swirling in my vision.

"Jones!" Bray called, and the large figure of a constable appeared by his side. A constable who had once fainted on me, trapping me under his bulk.

Avoiding eye contact with me, he said, "Sir?"

"Ms. McGuire needs attention. She's going into shock."

"Nrmf," I said, attempting, "No, I'm fine," and failing miserably.

I was helped to the back of a car and covered with a blanket. Milo jumped in with me. Seemingly out of thin air, a paper cup of hot, sweet tea appeared.

After half a cup, I started to comprehend words again. The Brits were onto something with this tea thing.

Dolly was explaining why they were there. "You see, the reporter explained that James and Maddie needed help. Simon called you and picked me up, and we rushed to town."

She continued, recounting her plan of pretending to order a large number of souvenir daggers.

"Do British people give out favors at weddings?" I asked, testing my voice.

"No," Simon spoke for the first time. "Ridiculous American tradition."

"Better now, Miss McGuire?" DCI Bray asked.

Nodding, I said, "Thank you."

"Now, can you tell me why you felt the need to empty the building?"

A boom, followed by a rumble and a wave of heat, drowned out my response. The warehouse burst into flames.

Everyone on foot retreated away from the building as fire burst through the windows one at a time. Since the answer to Bray's question blazed before us, I didn't speak.

"An accelerant was used," DCI Bray surmised. "That, along with the forge, will make for a very hot fire that won't leave evidence behind."

"Will this help?" Dolly held up the poker Mac had been threatening us with, using one of Simon's silk handkerchiefs to keep her fingerprints from it.

"How did you get that?" I asked.

"It did seem important."

The roar of a motorcycle joined the racket of approaching fire trucks.

Swerving into the area at a dangerous speed, the biker barely braked before setting the stand, leaping off, and running toward me.

Kneeling by the side of the car, he pulled off his helmet, hair tousled, concern etched in his intense brown eyes. Edward, back from assignment, rushed to my side.

At which point I remembered that I was covered in spoiled food, revolting vomit, and puffy from crying.

*Excellent.*

# Chapter Twenty-Eight: What is That Smell?

"Lassie," Edward said, in an uncustomary public display of his native Scottish accent. He leaned in close, looking deeply into my eyes. "What is that smell?"

"I'm gross," I responded needlessly as the stench encompassing me increased at every moment.

Jones, not my biggest fan already, would be furious if the odor lingered in his car.

"I need to change," I said, also obvious.

Nodding, Edward said, "Right." Slapping on his official cop face and posh accent, he approached Bray and asked permission to take me home.

"We can't close her in a car." When Bray raised his eyebrows inquisitively, Edward added, "It would have to be burned."

Feeling the last part was unnecessary, I took a breath, ready to launch a defense on my behalf. The scent, which I had grown somewhat used to, asserted itself, and I gagged, more bile threatening.

"Burned," I repeated, agreeing with Edward's analysis.

"Another emergency vehicle is on the way to check on her," Bray informed us. The first one had focused on James and the two unconscious men.

Edward shook his head. "She's spent too much time at Comb Park as it is. Her landlords will ease her through the shock."

The Royal United Hospital was off Comb Park Road, a little over a mile from the Baths and Abbey, and not a destination most visitors sought.

DCI Bray took way too long to agree, but he finally did with the insistence that Edward stay with me.

A strong insistence. Very strong.

This is when it struck me that Mac escaped out the back door and was now on the loose.

And no way would I bring trouble to the Priestlys' door. Not again.

"Dolly!" I called, but it came out wispy and made my head spin.

Jones, happy to leave my company, I imagine, trotted to her and pointed at me. She responded immediately.

"Besides a hot shower, new clothes, and a commendation for bravery, what do you need?" she asked.

"Do you have an open room at the medispa?"

"Absolutely. You could stay with me, if not."

I shook my head. "Not for me. For the Priestlys. If Mac comes after me, I want them safely away."

Looking around, I wondered where my purse wound up. My shoes were in flames, no doubt, as I had thrown them at Mac. I couldn't remember where I put anything else.

Dolly handed it to me. "This?" she answered my unasked question. "You left it outside. Lucky, really, as we knew we arrived at the correct warehouse."

Numerous questions formed, including how she knew the purse was mine, but none were important.

Unzipping an inner pouch of the bag, I retrieved the credit card my dad had pressed on me before I came to England. "For emergencies," he said with a wink. My arguments of independence fell on jovial, deaf ears as he slipped the card into my purse.

I'd never used it, determined to rely on myself, but I figured this counted as an emergency. He'd been to De Valence Medispa, so he would understand when he saw the charge.

Handing Dolly the card, I said, "Swear you'll let my dad pay for this." She wouldn't have believed the funds came from me despite the name on the card. "He can afford it, and you and your staff deserve the booking."

"Leave everything to me. I'll send Gilbert to pick them up so they won't be followed."

Grateful, I smiled at her. "You're amazing."

As Dolly made arrangements, I searched for Edward.

At his bike, he arranged blankets, the better to keep my clothing from touching his motorcycle or him.

He returned, wrapped me tighter, and supported me to his chrome and leather chariot. My mom would forgive me for riding without a helmet under the circumstances.

By its side sat a pair of enormous wellies. The iconic British rain boots looked as though they could fit a grizzly bear.

"Stop staring and put them on. It's not safe to ride barefoot."

Since my feet were close to freezing, I didn't argue. Slipping them on, I felt like a little kid playing dress up.

Hoisting my leg over the seat, the boot flew off my foot and landed in front of the bike.

Edward dismounted, saying, "Allow me," and retrieved the boot. Replacing it on my foot, he then arranged me before snaking his leg over the seat again. "Don't move," he added.

Before he could start the bike, I said, "We can't leave Milo."

"Milo's the dog?"

I nodded.

"Why does my brother have a dog?" he asked through clenched teeth, followed by something that sounded like, "The great numpty."

"Count to ten," I advised instead of answering.

By my pacing, he only got to five before he bellowed an order.

"Jones!" Edward shouted. Not too long ago, he and Jones held the same rank, and technically still did as Edward was on probation at MCIT. However, Jones responded quickly and with deference. "Take the dog," Edward ordered, giving detailed instructions that I couldn't hear.

The engine kicked to life, drowning out any more conversation.

The blanket provided some warmth, but it wasn't enough after the bone-chilling drive to Ash Tree Cottage.

Teeth chattering, I stumbled through the gate as Edward secured his bike, the oversized boots flopping like clown shoes.

Roger and Meryl were in the dark garden, coaxing Roddy out of his hut.

"Maddie, dear," she said, as she lured Roddy with Timothy hay and placed him in a wire cage. "Thank you."

"Wonderful surprise," Roger called over his shoulder. "Just what Meryl needs."

"And you," Meryl said to her husband. "You work too hard."

Once the cage door was closed, Meryl explained, "Dolly's testing a pet policy. She wanted us to bring Roddy. There's a corgi at the property now."

When a crazed loony came after me just after Christmas, he threatened Roderick the Rabbit as a form of torture for me. It was unbelievably effective.

Tonight, I'd been so concerned for Milo that I forgot the bunny might need protection, too. Dolly, as usual, thought of everything.

Smiling, Meryl approached, arms out for a hug.

She stopped abruptly. "What is that smell?"

"A trash bag and old robe, if you have one, Mrs. Priestly," Edward suggested.

Without questioning the request, Meryl rushed into the house and returned with multiple items, including disinfecting wipes.

Accepting the bundle with a weak smile, I left Edward to explain my condition. In the boot room, I hid between windows, peeled off my stiff, disgusting clothing one piece at a time, and stuffed them into the trash bag. Shrugging into the robe, I instantly felt better.

After tying the top of a bag with a knot, I set it outside.

Edward, whose back had been toward the door, turned around. "Y'al-right?" he asked.

"Better. Please throw these away. Far, far away."

"You don't want to clean them?"

Horrified, I said, "I don't ever want to see them again. Nor should anyone else." I decided a new outfit counted as another emergency for my dad's credit card. "Did the Priestlys go?"

Sweeping the empty garden with his eyes, Edward nodded. "I confirmed

Gilbert's identification before letting them in the car. They know something is going on, but are too excited to ask about it."

"Good. I'm going to soak. Maybe forever."

* * *

My bath didn't last an eternity, but I did refresh the hot water twice. When I emerged, several things had become clear: something had to be done about my swelling shin, and Edward's boat wasn't safe for anyone.

"Milo should have police protection, too," I said to Edward as I towel-dried my hair.

"I thought of that," Edward agreed. "The dog is with Jones."

Edward's sour impression telegraphed his opinion of the border collie.

"He saved us, you know. My phone got run over, but Milo led Jeffery to us." Thanks to James's bread crumb trail of treats.

A grunt.

"We can't stay here or on the boat. I gave my dad's credit card to Dolly so we can't check into a hotel."

I had a card of my own, but the limit was so low that it wouldn't cover a hold deposit and room charge simultaneously.

"Also, who is guarding the hospital?" I asked, remembering Jones's regrettable attempt to keep me safe.

"Local police constables. Mac's identity is public now. Jeffery snapped several pictures of Mac threatening you before he turned on the flash to distract him."

Much as I was grateful that the camera kept Mac from skewering me, it was annoying that Jeffery made sure he got his story before ensuring my safety.

"Never fully on anyone's side but his own," Edward said, echoing my thoughts about the reporter.

"I was thinking something similar. Still, better the devil you know than the one you don't."

"We should stay at my place," Edward said, changing the subject.

I blinked at him.

"On a boat." I intended the statement to convey my distaste for the idea.

"We can move it."

"It can sink." Considering Mac's penchant for arson, I added, "Or burst into flames and sink."

His arm gestured to take in the Priestlys' living room with its numerous windows. "This place is too difficult to defend. Too many entry points. Plus, it could also burst into flames."

Grinning, I shook my head.

"What?" he asked, sitting next to me.

"Remember the first time you came here?  We went to the basement together."

"Looking for severed human ears, as I recall."

I shuddered.  "Yeah, well, that part was weird.  But remember the architecture?" The cellar was framed on top of solid limestone. "This house is built into the side of the hill. It is only approachable from two and a half sides, whereas your boat is vulnerable from six."

"Six?" It took him only a moment to remember my point about sinking. "Below, or someone coming through the top hatch." He kissed my forehead. "We'll stay here."

* * *

After a fitful night dreaming about fire and floods, I awoke to a throbbing shin and the scent of something baking.

I threw on jeans, a long-sleeved tee, and an oversized sweater before hobbling downstairs.

As I entered the kitchen, Edward pulled scones out of the oven.

"I'm beginning to think I've found the perfect man," I said.

"Coffee or tea?" he asked, smiling.

At first, I craved coffee, strong and rich, the way my dad taught me to drink it my freshman year of college. But eyeing the scones and jam that Edward plated, nothing but tea would do.

"Hot Earl Grey, please. Did you check the perimeter?" I asked as I slathered my scone with clotted cream and strawberry jam.

He snorted. "Have ye been watching detective shows again?"

"That phrase would be from action movies, thank you very much."

His crooked grin appeared, but he responded thoughtfully. "Three times."

Crumbly baked good, creamy spread, and sweet fruit mingled, creating an explosion of comforting flavor.

"Do you think we're safe?" My question went further than no one lurking around the house. I wanted to know that our friends wouldn't be threatened, our property put at risk, and our lives put in danger.

Instead of answering, he added milk to our teas and said, "We need to get you checked out by a doctor."

"Can I use an online one?" Telemedicine was a genius invention, as far as I was concerned, but Edward was shaking his head no.

"We'll go to the National Health Service on James Street. Someone needs to poke at your shin."

"Avoidance of poking is exactly why I want to do it over the phone."

"I promised Simon you would go in person."

Touched, I got misty-eyed at the thought of Simon thinking of me.

"He said Sam wants you to mirror Yvette on tours for the next couple of days, and you need to be able to walk."

I imagined punching Simon in the arm. I knew he was worried about me, but he would never let me get too comfortable. "I don't work for Simon or Sam anymore, and I'm not a volunteer, so he can't boss me around," I pointed out. Followed by, "When do we go?"

Edward checked the time on his phone and said, "Ten minutes."

My intention to run upstairs to finish dressing turned into an arduous climb, pain flaring in a watery explosion with every footstep. "Ow," step, "ow," step, "ow," step.

Fifteen minutes later, we arrived at the medical clinic. A competent and friendly doctor examined my shin and gave me a thorough once-over.

"Where did you get this?" she asked, indicating my bruised leg.

"Someone kicked me." Realizing that I sounded like a battered wife, I added, "He was aiming for a dog that I rescued." An amalgam of events, so not untrue.

"Good for you." Prodding my injury, she said, "It's not broken, but I recommend the RICE method of recovery. Do you know what that is?"

Unfortunately, I had far too much experience with leg mishaps. "Rest, ice, compression, and elevation. I have a compression brace." I didn't add, "From the time a different crazy man wrenched my knee."

The doctor put a poultice on my broken skin and wrapped the area snugly when I told her I had to conduct tours before getting home.

"This will hold you. Rest tonight."

When I emerged from the examination room, Edward was waiting outside, talking on the phone.

His face was grim.

# Chapter Twenty-Nine: Back on Tours

Rain began outside the clinic on James Street, cold and accompanied by an insistent wind. Edward's back hunched against the weather, his hand protecting the cell as he listened.

Maybe it wasn't bad, and he only looked like the world was coming to an end because he was cold.

I snugged the Scottish wool scarf he'd given me for Christmas around my neck and waited.

"I cannae stay," he said once he hung up. "Let's get you over to the Baths. How's your leg?"

"No fractures. The doctor wrapped me up and gave me the okay." A slight exaggeration, but it looked like he didn't need any extra cause to worry this morning.

We walked at a pretty good clip to the museum without me limping. Energized, I kissed Edward quickly and asked him to keep me informed.

Not that I was worried. Not really. More like, concern born from the experience of being hunted by a madman. Or two.

I gave the Bath Abbey a finger wave, missing its calming atmosphere, and bypassed the tourist line to enter the Roman Baths. The soaring white, plastered dome ceiling reminded visitors that Georgian architecture held appeal, as did that of ancient Rome.

Since Simon mentioned that he wanted me to shadow Yvette on tours, I went to the Oversight office to confirm with Sam.

Knocking as I opened the door, I found Sam and Yvette going over the schedule.

"Maddie, me girl!" Sam grinned at me. "Sure, you'll have a cup of tea."

Without waiting for confirmation, she poured water from the kettle into a mug, dropped in a bag, and added a golden dollop of honey from the filigree hip flask Simon bought her. A joke from Simon about her Irish roots, the flask contained honey from a local apiary instead of the traditional whiskey.

The office always maintained a hot tea setup, but Sam's level of solicitousness was out of character.

"Thank you," I said, unable to keep a hint of suspicion out of my tone.

"Let's just get stuck in and get on with it," Yvette said to Sam while pointing to me.

"What?"

"The thing is, Yvette here isn't getting the stellar reviews for her tours that we'd like."

Since I already knew the ask to this prelude, I jumped ahead. "I'll be happy to shadow her, if you'd like. As long as Dr. Daniels clears it and Marcus knows."

"Brilliant," Yvette said, smiling.

"Grand," Sam agreed. "We'll see how we get on."

Somehow, Sam seemed to be more Irish since Yvette's arrival. Her accent thickened, and her word choice, which was always peppered with phrases from her homeland, now dominated her conversation.

I wondered if anyone could tell when I was homesick. Did I use different words? Sound more American? I would listen for it.

"When is the first tour?" I asked.

"One hour."

"Great. Did Simon give you his magic notes?"

Yvette nodded.

"The biggest thing I worried about when I started conducting tours was that people would react poorly to me being American."

I didn't know if other Europeans would care that Yvette was Irish, but the English would. I gave her tips like slowing down to make the accent easier to understand.

"And have some quick responses for every stop in case people ask questions. Like, I tended to answer questions about the water temperature in Fahrenheit, which earned me blank stares. Now I give both, doing the conversion."

"What's the conversion?"

"To convert to Fahrenheit from Celsius, multiply by one point eight and add thirty-two."

She stared blankly, much like a tour group whose attention wandered.

"Double the temperature and add thirty," I amended, using the "close enough" formula.

Brightening, she said, "I ask to wait until the end for questions so I don't lose my train of thought. I never get many."

Gently, I explained that delaying questions meant the person lost interest. "Let them interrupt. If you're lost, look at your notes."

We went through the important parts of the cheat sheet, then I stood at the back of the assembled group and watched her go through it. The advantage was that I could keep a lookout for anyone trying to sneak up and attack me under Mac's orders. No one did.

When Yvette started to get off track, I raised my hand and asked questions to guide her back to the script.

During the second tour, I only had to intervene once, and during the third, not at all.

"She's perfect," I told Sam, back in the Oversight office.

"You did a fine job on that," Sam responded, congratulating Yvette. "There is one more thing," she added, turning her bright green eyes on me.

"Anything," I said, meaning it. Sam welcomed me to the Baths when I first arrived and made sure I succeeded. I would do almost anything she asked.

"Can you make me a training manual. Incorporate Simon's notes on facts, Cliff's jokes, and your presentation tips?"

Beaming, I said, "I'd be honored." Maddie McGuire makes her mark on the Roman Baths. I saw another aspect of my future opening up, opportunities for me to spread my wings.

My musing was cut short when Yvette said, "We heard you were at the fire last night."

Not wanting to relive the trauma, I nodded and attempted to change the subject. "When will you need the manual? And in what format?"

"That can wait," Sam said. "Are ye all right?"

As soon as she asked, my shin began to throb. "I'm supposed to keep my leg elevated," I admitted.

Yvette jumped out of her chair and scooted it toward me. "Set your wee foot up here. What happened?"

If I hadn't been so ill-prepared, a lot of tragedy could have been avoided. Unlike this conversation, which was inevitable, apparently. I wasn't going to be able to avoid recounting the evening, but I didn't need to admit all my mistakes. With select editing, I walked them through the events at the forge.

"Christ on a bike," Yvette whispered when I told her about kicking Mac in the back of the knee to save James. "That's class."

I assumed the phrase meant something impressive. Encouraged, I finished my tale with dramatic flair, embellishing only a little about getting everyone out, the police arriving, and the building exploding.

"Best be getting to your next tour," Sam reminded Yvette.

Swinging my leg down with the intention of helping, she touched my arm. "You stay here. Rest that leg."

As Yvette left, Simon entered, took in my reclined form and cup of tea, and snorted. "Comfortable, are we?"

Ignoring the sarcasm, I said, "Thanks for coming to the rescue last night."

He nodded graciously. "It wouldn't be a month with Maddie if something harrowing didn't happen." He handed me a small bag with a box inside.

"Perfect. That's how I want people to think of me. Seriously, though, you cannot, under any circumstances, put yourself in danger like that again. Your aunt would kill me herself." I unwrapped the package and discovered a cell phone. *How did he know?*

"Quite probably."

Good confirmation to have. "What's this?" I asked, holding up the phone.

Casting his eye heavenward, he shook his head as if I were a particularly thick-headed dog, and said, "Especially as she's set the flower arrangements for the wedding. From Aunt Viv, by the way," he threw in, gesturing to the phone. "Shouldn't you be upstairs?" This, even though he was the one who told Edward about Sam's tour request.

"Sam needed me," I reminded him.

"To test the comfort level of her furniture?"

I nodded my head toward the kettle. "Tea?" I offered to deflect further criticism. "How did she know?"

"People talk."

By "people," he meant the glorious group of friends I was lucky enough to have. I couldn't remember who I'd told about my phone being crushed, but one of them noted it and sent up a distress call.

"Ms. Niven," Simon addressed Sam formally whenever he wanted to remind me of my position in the hierarchy. "Lady Vivian is hoping for a meeting this afternoon, if you're available. She wants to see if any of the Romans are free for the Easter fundraiser this spring."

The Romans in question worked at the Baths to add authenticity. Dressed in period clothing, they interacted with the exhibits and chatted with the tourists. Including them at the fundraiser would delight the donors.

Sam shooed us out of her office to finish scheduling before the meeting, and I wondered whether it would stretch her budget to include them or if she would ask for volunteers.

I decided to see if my dad would provide a stipend for each Roman actor to support the evening. Dad had caused me a lot of conflict by donating to the Baths in the past. This time, he could do it with my knowledge.

As Simon and I walked up to the lab, I downloaded my phone backup. Within minutes, my wallpaper appeared.

Marcus hadn't expected me today, so no instructions were given for which bins and layers to photograph.

After sitting and propping my leg up, I asked, "Are you going down to the dig?"

Simon nodded.

"Ask Marcus if he has anything specific he wants me to do."

Simon nodded again, but didn't leave. For him, this action equalled a complete and total breakdown.

Something had to be done, but not by asking directly. Ticking through the things going on in his world, from stopping a murder the night before, to overseeing volunteers to clear a new room at the Baths, to his upcoming marriage, the wedding seemed most likely to throw him off his groove.

"Speaking of flowers," I said, "how is your list coming along?"

The wedding chores took a backseat to uncovering the plot against DI Parikh for me. We hadn't talked about them since Simon took me to the Glastonbury Tor.

"You don't think," he began, and stopped.

I waited.

Nothing more.

"Surprisingly, I do sometimes."

Ignoring this, he said, "Dolly is extraordinary." A statement, not a question.

"Absolutely," I agreed, using her favorite word.

Pulling out a chair, he sat next to me, but looked at the ceiling. "You don't think I'm doing her a disservice, do you?"

Simon's natural tendencies toward an ideal partner lay in a different direction, but he would do his duty.

I shook my head. "No."

He finally looked at me. "Why not?"

"I asked her about it."

At this point, he sat taller and looked down his nose at me. "You what?"

"I wanted to make sure she knew what she was getting into."

The weight of centuries of aristocratic breeding focused on me as if to say, "How dare you?" But that's not what he said. What he did say was, "You asked her before me?"

His question crashed into me like an Arizona summer monsoon—gale force winds at a hundred and five degree temperatures, full of electricity that stood hair on end. Simon Pacock cared about our friendship. I mean, yes, he asked me to stand up for him at his wedding, but that's different from valuing my opinion as a confidant. I wanted to cry or spring at him and envelop him in a bear hug.

Instead, I said, "Sisterhood."

He smiled.

"We bonded after I dropped her out of a third-story window," I continued. "Second."

"Zero doesn't count," I said, referring to the Brits' annoying reference to the ground floor of a building.

"It is a number," he pointed out.

True. Not that I would admit it to him. "Anyway, she said she would rather have you, with your," I paused, thinking of a delicate way to put it, and came up with, "other interests, than a hundred rich lads who wouldn't treat her nearly as well. You're in, dude." I added the last to disperse any lingering gushy feelings that might get displayed.

"Right, well, that's quite all right then."

Looking pleased, he stood and left the room.

Dolly and Simon's relationship was an interesting one, but they shared a strong mutual respect and genuine fondness for each other. Since I didn't have an assignment in front of me, I spent time comparing them to Tori and Scott.

Mathematically, they never had balance. Scott was a year older in high school, so Tori always felt privileged to be included in his plans, even when she didn't want to do something. Once she graduated, that pattern continued, Scott controlling her social life.

He had some moments, like when he flew her to England after my entombment, but that departure was partially due to my mom going Lady Macbeth on him when he tried to isolate Tori from me. They might have overcome it, but Tori deserved better. Always did.

So, what did that say about Edward and me?

I was smitten with him, that was certain, but he was my first serious boyfriend. Did that mean I would make the same mistakes that Tori and my parents had made? Settling too soon was what had kept me from allowing any boy to get too close until now. I didn't want to push Edward aside if he really was the one, though.

On the other hand—

"Ahem," a voice rang out in the quiet room, interrupting my doodling and pondering.

"Nothing!" I said too loudly, reverting to my stock response whenever my mom caught me doing something I wasn't supposed to. "Uh, hi, Marcus! How are you? Having a nice day?"

"Lord Pacock mentioned you were done with tours?" Marcus asked doubtfully.

"Yes, I am. Done. Thought I would pop back up here to the good old lab and get to photographing, if that's what you needed." My babble adopted a Texan accent.

I took a deep inhale, counting to five. "Or whatever you need."

"Actually, we weren't expecting you, so if you'd like to leave now, that would be fine. We heard you had a spot of trouble last evening."

"A bit, yeah." I didn't elaborate.

"Bright and early," he said as he left, indicating the time I should arrive tomorrow.

Roger would be traveling from the medispa, so I couldn't ride home with him. I sent Edward a text, hoping he wasn't embroiled in police work.

'Meet outside in ten.'

The text lacked detail, but made its point.

I went out the tourist entrance and shuffled to the Pump Room to wait.

In his jeans and leather jacket, Edward walked across the courtyard looking irresistible in a bad-boy way.

My heart fluttered.

"Hey," I said.

"Hey, yourself," he answered, and kissed my cheek.

"What was the call you got this morning about? You didn't look happy."

To emphasize my observation, he scowled. "There's not a sign of Mac anywhere."

# Chapter Thirty: Mordred or Moriarty

The cobblestone walkway formed by the Bath Abbey, Roman Baths, and a string of restaurants and souvenir shops was crowded with people. Accents and foreign languages peppered snatches of overheard conversation.

I ignored them all.

"What?" I didn't mean for it to come out as a demand, but it did.

"Mac's warehouse property is burned, his flat is empty, there's nothing left for him here. There's nothing to worry about now."

*Nothing to worry about?* That sounded like an aphorism someone said when they were sure of the opposite.

"What you're saying then, is that Mac the Mastermind, aka Mordred, is now Moriarty? A nemesis who never gets caught and is always out there? An evil force that can wreak havoc on our lives wherever he wants? No. No flippin' way. This needs to end. He almost ruined Parikh's career, and he would have gone after you next. And let's not forget that he threatened to cut off James's thumb and burn my face! No! I refuse to live in a world where that man is out there. The whole, entire force needs to be after him, and if they won't, I will. I'll go out there myself—"

"I quite agree, Miss McGuire," a familiar, clipped voice said, cutting my rant short.

DI Parikh, looking trim and neat, strolled to us.

My mouth dropped open. Stuffing down my urge to barrage him with questions about his health, his current status with the Major Crimes Investigation Team, and his plan for apprehending said evil nemesis, I instead beamed, taking in his features. Dark circles were only partially hidden by his wire-rimmed glasses. He looked like he could do with a giant packet of garibaldis to pack on some weight. But his eyes sparked with intensity and intelligence, indicating he was up for any challenge.

"Although," he added, "not about you going after him yourself."

"It's so nice to see you, detective inspector. And I'd much rather you go after him. He's scary."

"Agreed. If I may borrow Constable Bailey?"

They moved off together, heads bent in conversation, and disappeared.

After about five minutes of standing there, I realized I should have asked how long Edward would be needed. As my ride home, the information was pertinent, especially as my compression bandage was beginning to itch.

I paced for a minute, decided movement was a bad idea following the tours I'd been on earlier, and limped over to the Bath Abbey. Edward would either assume I was there or text me when he was done.

As always, my first reaction whenever entering the abbey was to tilt my face to the fan vaulted ceiling. The graceful arches calmed me a little. The fact that Mac escaped rankled, and I needed the solace of the space.

I sat in one of the chairs that had replaced most of the intricately carved pews and surreptitiously slipped my phone out of my jacket pocket.

Four messages from Tori, plus a missed call that just appeared on my cell.

'Can I call?'

'You didn't answer.'

'You're probably at work.'

The time these came in my time equalled 4:37 a.m. Eastern Time. What was going on that she called that early?

The fourth message came in an hour later. 'Call when you're off.'

She should be at work herself by now, but this didn't seem like it could wait.

Hauling my aching leg back outside, I huddled against the wall and called Tori.

"Hi," she answered.

"Hi? After all the times you've answered by bombarding me with questions, all I get today is "Hi?" What is going on? Why were you up at 4:00 am?" Some of the angst over my situation bled into my tone, and I apologized. "Sorry. Rough night. You okay?"

"More than okay. Do you know how long it's been since I kissed another boy?"

All worries about my situation fled as the implications of Tori's statement hit me. I wanted to insist on all the details, but instead, dug up her dating history. "Let's see, Austin in third grade, Lucas on the playground over the summer, Will after stealing him from Lexie in sixth grade, Garrett in—"

"Geez, I didn't ask for a list, just the last time."

"Go back. Did you and Nicolas…" I let the question linger.

"Nothing too intense, but we went to the Mall after work and walked the length of it. Twice."

It took me a moment to realize she meant the National Mall, which stretches from the US Capitol past the Washington Monument to the Lincoln Memorial. Based on my middle school trip there, it was a long walk. Not so long, though, as to take all night.

"And?"

"And we talked about, I don't know, everything." Tori's words got faster as she got more excited. "I didn't even realize when he took my hand. Or maybe I took his. I don't know, but it felt so right."

Throughout our friendship, one of us always stayed firmly grounded, providing a base for the other to get carried away. When it came to boys, Tori had always been the voice of reason, while I rated them on how quickly I could chew them up and spit them out on the Chiclets to caramel scale.

Unused to my new position as advisor, I attempted a word of caution. "Not too long ago, you were sure of your future with Scott."

"Not sure. Brainwashed."

I wanted to argue, but I'd used that very phrase to describe their relationship. "Okay, granted. But you can't jump whole hog into the first new guy who comes along."

"I know," she admitted. "That's why I called you. He wants me to stay on for the summer internship program."

"Whoa."

"Whoa plus whoa and whoa on top."

"Wouldn't you have to apply or something?  Give someone else the opportunity?"

There was a slight pause, and I wished we were talking on our computers so I could see her face.

"Well," she drew out the word to add drama, "the thing is, the ambassador was so impressed by my translation of meeting minutes that he told the intern coordinator to offer me the post."

"Tori! Why didn't you lead with that? That's amazing! You have to say yes."

She laughed.  "I didn't lead with it because I needed to know I wasn't agreeing to the position because of ulterior motives."

"Most definitely not," I said. "Opportunities like that are rare. The boy becomes a bonus."

"Icing on the cake?" she asked.

"More like the little sprinkles on top of the icing. Because, wow, to have an ambassador notice your work is incredible. What did your abuela say?" Tori never did anything without her family's involvement, especially her grandmother's.

"She prayed, said a blessing, and then gave me her blessing to stay. It helps that she was born in Hermosillo. If I'd impressed the French ambassador, there would have been a fight."

I limped over to a recently vacated bench in the square as Tori explained the concept of interpretation. Translating conversations wasn't just a matter of knowing both languages. An art guided the interpreter, and not everyone could do it.

"It's like you and buildings," she said about my ability to look at a room and see architectural anomalies. A thought niggled at the back of my mind, but I lost it as I noticed Fred shaking DI Parikh's hand as Edward left him to find me.

"Perfect timing," I said to Edward as we disconnected. "Tori's going to stay in D.C. for the summer, too."

"I'm glad she's doing well," he said, helping me to my feet. "Can you make it to the car?"

Despite my earlier confidence traipsing around the Baths, my shin now protested with every step. "Is it in front of the Abbey Hotel?" I asked, referring to the nearby parking lot.

"Aye."

Assuring him that I was okay to go that far, I still leaned on him heavily all the way to Parikh's mom's SmartCar. Not the chariot of a girl's dreams, but better than a motorcycle for warmth and stability.

As we drove, my mind circled back on what Tori had said that triggered a reaction. Tantalizingly close but just out of reach, I couldn't grab hold of it.

When we arrived at Ash Tree Cottage on Greenway Lane, the house glowed with light; a sure sign the Priestlys were home.

Inside, scents of soup and freshly baked bread drew us to the kitchen.

"Maddie, dear," Meryl said as we entered, "you and Edward will join us for dinner, I hope."

"How can we help?" Edward offered.

I went through the pocket door to the dining room and set the table. Alone, I emptied my mind and allowed thoughts to flit at random. I was so wrapped up in not paying attention to anything that when Edward opened the pass-through disguised as a cupboard, I screamed.

"How can this surprise you?" Edward asked.

"I forget it's there," I admitted.

"How? You found a secret passage upstairs, and you've used this before."

Not a passage, but one room was smaller on the inside than the outside because a one-foot channel had been added to accommodate pipes and wires.

Between the lack of accuracy and the uncustomary exasperation coloring his statement, it set me off.

"I don't know if you know this or not, but I've had a lot going on lately," I said, taking the pot of what looked like hearty chicken soup and plopping it on the trivet.

Edward entered with a basket of sliced bread, which he placed on the table with unnecessary gentleness. "You cannae run off and put yourself in danger like that."

I thought he handled my warehouse disaster with noticeable calm. Apparently, not so much.

"I tried to text for backup. My phone got squished."

"Do ye have any idea what it does to me to get two cryptic messages followed by your phone going dark?"

When he said it that way, it sounded extra bad. Thinking back to what I typed, something about getting a dog and James missing, my heart went out to him.

"I'm sorry," I said, noting that just a few months ago, I would have never admitted to being at fault. "I—"

"Thank you so much for the spa retreat, Maddie!" Roger boomed, coming in the door from the entry hall. "Could not have been better."

Meryl entered from the kitchen with a dish of Brussels sprouts with mandarin oranges, saying, "Yes, it was amazing. Thank you so much, dear." Her smile was genuine, but a worried look crossed her face as she took in Edward and me.

Rather than a clipped and, frankly, English response, I called on my Arizona straightforwardness and said, "First off, you deserve it. You both do so much for the community and me. But my dad paid for it, so don't be too impressed. And I sent you away because I'd done something very silly and didn't want bad men to find you at home if they came."

Glancing shyly at Edward, I continued. "No one came to the house. Everything seems to be okay. But I charged off into the unknown without a plan and almost got myself trapped in a burning warehouse."

Other details didn't seem pertinent at the moment, but confessing brightened my mood. "You shouldn't have had to cook," I said, changing the subject. "You're supposed to be relaxing.

"Nothing relaxes me more," Meryl said with a smile.

We helped get everything to the dining room. Knowing they were safe made dinner all the more delicious.

As we cleared the table, I went into the kitchen, looked at the pass-through disguised as a cupboard, and opened it.

Edward handed me bowls, which I rinsed, and gave to Roger to wash.

Stepping around Meryl, who was on drying and putting away duty, I went back to the pass-through and closed it, then opened it again.

Tori had said I had a way of looking at buildings. Something at the warehouse caught my attention, but the threat of imminent disfiguration chased it from my mind.

I opened and closed the pass-through disguised as a cupboard again, triggering the image at the warehouse.

A room was hidden in plain sight at the forge.

# Chapter Thirty-One: The Warehouse Revisited

Several images from my time writhing in pain on the warehouse floor came to mind. James tied to the chair, the forge taking up more space than I thought it should, and Mac seeming to spin in slow motion.

Now I realized that it wasn't confusion or fear that slowed his movements, but cold calculation. Mac took in every inch of the situation, from the aristocracy to the reporter, his captives, and his knocked-out thugs. He had been figuring out if he had enough time to retrieve something.

And he hadn't.

Slamming the cupboard door closed, I said, "I need to see the warehouse again."

Edward shook his head no before the statement was out of my mouth.

"It hasn't been declared safe. Even the forensic team hasn't been able to finish their sweep."

"There's something there, but I have to see it in person."

"Maddie, love, it's been burned. There's nothing left."

"The forge is still standing, isn't it?" I put my hand on his arm. "It's important. I don't need to be close. And I'll have police protection." I squeezed.

His stony features melted after a minute, and he raised his eyebrows. "Pud?"

First off, dessert is dessert, not pudding and certainly not pud. And secondly, my theory needed confirmation.

But it's hard to say no to a handsome Scottish man with a hopeful expression.

* * *

After consuming a trifle, a layered confection that included elements that did actually taste like pudding, Edward and I thanked Meryl.

"You must have been cooking since you got back," I commented.

"Dolly sent the trifle home with us, so dinner was easy."

Said the woman who baked bread from scratch every day.

"Lavender and honey," I said, referencing the flavor of the dish. "I should have known it was from De Valence." Lavender from Simon and honey from the local beekeepers near the medispa.

Adrenalin at the thought of solving a piece of the puzzle muted my aching joints, and I practically skipped up the stone path and out the gate to the car.

"Would you care to share your theory?" Edward asked.

"Not really," I said. "I might be wrong."

He didn't press me, but instead took off toward the warehouse district. The stench of burned plastic hung in the air. Far from the delightful scent of burning wood, the building stank of random materials and chemicals.

The warehouse James and I had been held captive in was a charred outline. Windows and doorways were gone, the inner office a gaping hole.

Police tape blocked our forward progress, and Edward didn't have the authority to move me past it. He had a brief conversation with the officer guarding the site and returned with a monocular for me to use for searching.

"They won't chase us away, but you can't go in."

"Come on," I said after a glance through the scope. "This way."

I led the way to the left side of the building, toward the back where the forge sat.

Covered in soot, it maintained its clean lines, having been designed to withstand high temperatures.

Holding the monocular to my eye, I scanned it from this vantage, storing my estimation of dimensions in my head.

"Other side," I said, scurrying around back where I couldn't see in, and then over to the area for supplies I'd hidden behind the night before.

The inventory wall consisted of cheap metal intended for melting, which it had done. Not completely, but enough for me to see over it to the forge.

There was an accounted for space at the corner. Not that I was an expert on drop forges, but during my research on blacksmiths, I'd come across a few videos explaining how modern equipment worked. I visualized stripping away the walls that held the mechanism, revealing spaces for heating, melting ore, and pulling and dropping the weight. The front-right corner was too big and unaccounted for.

"It's a trapezoid, not a square," I declared.

Edward took the monocular and made affirming noises as I explained my logic.

"Hidden in plain sight," he said.

"Exactly," I responded, hugging him.

He called in the information to the various agencies dealing with arson, kidnapping, and forgery, and took me home.

"That was dissatisfying," I complained.

"I could do with you being a bit less the center of excitement. They'll let us know what they find."

"Tonight?"

"Patience, love."

* * *

The next day, I immersed myself in work to avoid obsessively texting Edward for updates, which he didn't have. I knew he would call as soon as he heard anything, but I wanted to learn what they found. Even if the chamber on the forge was empty, it still proved that Mac used hiding places for important documents. There might be similar enclosures in other buildings that he owned.

The call never came, but Edward appeared as I left the Baths, his heart-melting crooked smile firmly in place.

"They found something," I said, springing to him.

"Most of the day was spent arguing over who got to look. In the end, fire services convinced the SOCO team that it might not be safe inside, so they took apart the forge."

"Did they find a chamber?"

The grin widened. "Fireproof, heatproof, and large enough for storage."

I beamed. "And?"

"Is that not enough for ye, lassie?"

Much as I wanted to scream, "What was in it?" a certain decorum needed to be maintained. After all, a girl didn't want to appear impatient. Again. "How about we go to The Boater for a drink?" Calm and collected, that's me.

"Anything for you," he said.

Our conversation on the walk to Pulteney Bridge meandered aimlessly until I asked, "When will you have to go back on your assignment?"

Suddenly somber, he said, "As soon as Mac is arrested. Parikh got me back here to close out the drug ring, but I need to finish my work on this other case. It's rather a good thing, really," he said, sounding unsure. "The more detectives who know me, the faster someone will take me off probation with MCIT."

Edward faced many trials on his journey to becoming a detective. The first was getting past the screening system, which he did with the help of a chief inspector from Edinburgh despite his background. He augmented his work as a police constable by taking classes. While it wasn't required to have a degree, he felt his past was a strike against him that needed balancing out.

Proving himself as capable in the normally quiet city of Bath, DCI Bray recommended both he and Parikh move to the Major Crimes Investigation Team, essentially putting him in a position where he needed to prove himself again. However, once he was off probation, he should be eligible to be a Detective Constable.

To me, he already was. Determined described Edward best and if he set his mind to advance, he would. No question.

None of which was relevant, but I had to distract myself from the fact that he still hadn't told me what they discovered in Mac's hidden chamber.

"Have you heard?" Donny asked as soon as we ducked into the main bar from The Boater's entryway. He was bartending, looking affable and slightly dazed.

"About Mac?" I asked, unsure if he had any news of Lily.

Pouring me a half-pint of Bath Ale in a quaint barrel glass, Donny raised an eyebrow at Edward, who pointed at my drink and nodded.

Sometimes Edward was on the job and couldn't drink alcohol, so I was glad that he was officially off tonight. We needed downtime to hang out and relax.

Picking a table near the street window, we laced our fingers together and leaned close. Gazing into his deep brown eyes, I almost forgot about what the arson team discovered at the warehouse based on my tip.

Almost.

"So, the forge?" I asked.

Eyes dancing, Edward said, "If you'd waited any longer, I would have thought you were a changeling."

"Yet, still you avoid answering."

"Two forged rondels with fake bills of sale, a ledger detailing all the collectors and purchase dates, and, most telling, an Irish ID which will allow him to travel to any part of Europe."

"Wow," I breathed, "that's amazing. That's enough to put him away for forgery."

"They did point out that they would have discovered the hidey-hole on their own."

"Eventually."

"Maybe eventually," he said, lifting my fingers and kissing them one at a time.

"What's wrong?" he asked, a crease forming between his brows.

My excitement ebbed when I remembered that forgery was only one part of the problem. The drug ring and murder were critical, and Edward didn't list any evidence that Mac was involved. "We still don't know who killed Raibead."

The twinkle returned to his expression.

"What else?" I asked, hope returning and dragging exuberance along with it. My feet danced under the table in anticipation.

"In addition to the daggers and ledgers, they found—"

Glass shattered as a flaming bottle sailed through a pane of the mullioned window and exploded onto the floor beyond us.

Edward leaped up, heedless of shards big enough to sever an artery, and started stomping on the flames, which had the unfortunate effect of splattering gasoline around the floor and up his jeans' leg.

Appearing like a magician, Donny pulled a red gingham tablecloth from I don't know where and dropped it over the fire.

A man who'd been drinking across the restaurant rushed over with a pint glass.

"No!" I shouted, recalling the fire safety program from my grade school days. The high scorer on the test got to demonstrate using an extinguisher, and I studied like a demon for that privilege.

"It's water," he shouted and threw it at Edward's shoe, which spread the fire.

"No liquid!" I screamed as Edward took off behind the bar.

The cloth Donny used was starting to melt and smoke. It wouldn't hold the conflagration much longer.

I followed his lead and took off my beloved denim jacket to help smother the flames. The blue fabric covered the worst of the smoldering tablecloth, but black, acrid smoke billowed from underneath it in every direction.

Seconds later, Edward emerged with the fire extinguisher, ready to spray the floor.

"Wait!" I yelled, and unlike the random customer, Edward did. "Is it a B or C?"

"B," he hollered. I should have trusted he would have checked.

Woooft, woooooofffft, woooft. Noisy bursts erupted from the device.

"Jeans," someone yelled frantically, pointing at Edward as a blaze worked its way up the outside seam.

Wooft, the extinguisher exhaled again as Edward surveyed the damage to his clothing.

Sure he was out, he took in the room, and then me.

"Hand," I said shakily, indicating the stream of blood running down his fingers.

Lifting his arm, he examined the area and pulled a chunk of glass from his skin. He grabbed a napkin and wrapped it around the wound to stop the bleeding.

We made eye contact again. "Stay here," he said, and disappeared into the street.

# Chapter Thirty-Two: An Evening at the Pub

The patrons of The Boater stood in stunned silence, except for an old rock song coming through a much-abused speaker.

When chatter broke out in all directions, it was as though a dam burst.

I'd only seen Molotov cocktails in movies, and they always created far more havoc than they should. The bar hadn't exploded, but the effect was instantaneous and terrifying.

I blocked out the noise and focused on the fire-affected area, starting with the window. It gaped open, a single maw with jagged, clear teeth threatening from every direction. The remainder of the curved window appeared entirely unaffected. I always thought mullioned panes were decorative, but now I understood their practical aspect.

The table where Edward and I sat was littered with pointed fragments and bright red droplets.

Touching my face, I felt for liquid or pain and, finding none, continued my survey of the room.

The petrol-filled bottle had been brown, and I wondered if it once contained beer. Discarding the thought, I thanked the thief for throwing it with such force that it hadn't engulfed Edward and me, instead sailing to the unoccupied middle of the bar. Either the vandal's aim was perfect to propel it inside, or they had intended it to hit the front of the building and burst apart outside.

No more smoke came from the floor, and I crept over to my jacket. I felt around, gingerly at first, then with more thoroughness, avoiding foam that hadn't dissipated. No heat, no warmth. The fire was out.

From the top, my denim jacket looked fine. Hopeful that I would be able to remove the smoke and gas smell, I lifted it to check for holes in the sheepskin lining and discovered an abomination.

The cloth Donny had used must have been nylon or polyester, as it melted rather than catching fire. The spots where the extinguisher hit the gingham also congealed, and where it touched my jacket had become one, impossible to separate.

"A mighty sacrifice," I told it, replacing the mess the way I found it.

Standing, I backed away, retracing my steps, attempting not to contaminate the crime scene further.

Once I was clear, I sought out Donny, who was sitting at the bar. His expression had gone from dazed to bewildered. He swayed on his stool.

"That was some quick thinking," I said, pointing to the tablecloth.

"I've been working on it, you know? Turning a coin into a cloth. Practicing…" he trailed off, staring into nothingness.

Ignoring food service rules, I stepped behind the bar and fixed him a tea. I didn't see the sugar, so I uncorked a Highland whisky and added a dollop.

"Drink," I commanded, handing him the mug.

He downed it in one scalding gulp and returned the cup without looking at me. I fixed him another, this time sans liquor.

"Thanks," he said, his voice stronger.

"You're a magician and a hero. Not bad."

A little encouragement goes a long way. He achieved a small smile.

Not knowing when Edward would return, I checked on the other patrons. The man who threw the water hadn't set the pint down yet, clutching it in disbelief.

I returned to the bar and made a similar concoction for him.

When I returned, I removed the beer glass from his grip and wrapped his hand around the fortified tea.

"Thought it would help, didn't I?" He tried to sound belligerent, but it came out as a whine.

My first instinct was to explain how gasoline, like an oil fire, spread with water. Suffocation was the only way to put it out, which is why there are different types of extinguishers. A or E types wouldn't have worked, nor water.

But sometimes it's best if I don't go with my first response. "Of course you did," I cooed, and guided him to a chair. "Quick thinking."

The rest of his party hadn't moved, but didn't appear to be going into shock.

"Did anyone call nine, nine, nine?" I asked.

A woman from another table held up her cell.

"Smart," I told her. "Thank you."

With the immediate danger past, I planned to sneak out. Edward might need my help. But the second I reached the threshold, a barrage of questions hit me. Apparently, making tea equaled being in charge, and the pub patrons asked me what they should do next.

Except for Donny, who had grabbed a broom and dustpan, so I headed him off.

"Wait," I suggested. "Instead of cleaning, why don't you make pots of hot tea for the tables. I couldn't find sugar. You'll do it right." Not wanting to send him into a downward spiral, I avoided mentioning that he shouldn't touch the crime scene.

Head bobbing vigorously, Donny set to the task with renewed enthusiasm.

The water-throwing man and his friends were shrugging into their jackets, so I rushed to them next. "The police will need witness statements from you." Luckily, sirens raced closer so they couldn't duck out.

A police constable I'd seen before but whose name I didn't know entered and got everyone under control. Donny handed her a tea, and she started taking names.

"Madeline McGuire?" she confirmed when I told her mine. "I have a message for you." Removing her phone from her jacket, she scrolled and quoted, "Constable Edward Bailey," she glanced at me, waiting for confirmation that I knew him, "and Detective Inspector Parikh have requested that you stay here."

I nodded, smiling politely as I planned my escape.

"They included a note for me as well," the PC continued. "If she tries to leave, handcuff her to the bar." Returning her cell to her pocket, she met my eyes and smiled, waiting.

Faking an innocent expression that I used to practice on my mom, usually with little success, I finally blinked and gave in. "Okay, I'll stay."

"Ta," she said in such a friendly way that I couldn't break her trust.

Stuck, I needed something to do. Now that Donny had his host duties, he no longer needed my help. I stalked the areas not roped off by the PCs.

Without Mac's ubiquitous presence, the bar's atmosphere changed. He hadn't been there as long as Donny, but his big personality filled the nooks and crannies. Now, the pub exuded a less boisterous but friendlier aura.

Passing a built-in pedestal that supported a pot with fake flowers, I knocked on it. A hollow thud echoed back, which got me thinking about all the aforementioned nooks and Mac's desire to hide things.

Waylaying Donny, I search his face before questioning him. Color had returned to his cheeks, and his hands were steady.

"Now that it's over, kinda exciting, innit?"

"I know. You'll be able to keep patrons entertained for years on this story."

He brightened, so I brought up Mac.

"Did Mac do any repair work here?"

"Loads. Upgraded the toilets, added a supply cupboard behind the bar..."

Donny continued listing Mac's repair jobs, but I stopped listening. If the man knew enough to create a fireproof compartment in a forge, he could easily build one into a ramshackle building as old as The Boater.

"Thanks," I muttered as I allowed my architecture brain to take over and fit pieces of the room together. In the main bar, I found three hollow areas that supported statues. With Donny's help, I removed a panel on each. Empty.

"Excuse me, Madeline," the constable said as I pried a piece of molding off and discovered a disused fuse panel.

"Call me Maddie," I said.

"PC Linden." We shook hands. "What are you doing?"

I attempted to come up with a better phrase than "Looking for secret compartments," failed, and said, "Looking for secret compartments."

"Maybe we should wait for DI Parikh before you destroy any more of the building along with possible evidence," she suggested.

Good point. As she removed the hammer from my grasp, I said, "Can I go downstairs and look there? It might be important. I promise I won't leave through the garden."

My assurances didn't work. "You'll be staying here, where I can keep an eye on you. It's a rare day when a detective inspector with MCIT gives me a direct order."

I might have growled.

Hammerless and trapped, I surveyed the room again and noticed the head of a small animal above the bar. I couldn't tell if it was an otter or a beaver, but it wasn't something one would normally stuff and mount.

"Did Mac add that?" I asked Donny, wondering if it covered a hole.

"Nah, been there for donkey's years."

Mac had mounted a new dartboard downstairs, but I couldn't check that right then, could I?

Behind the bar was the only unexplored zone. I got PC Linden's attention and indicated that I was sitting out of sight, but still there.

"What cupboard did he install back here?" I asked Donny.

He pressed on a smooth, obviously new, and not hidden panel, and it popped open. Rows of shot glasses two deep gleamed.

"Super convenient for stag parties," Donny told me.

The compartment extended to about one-third of the bar's depth. Wishing I'd asked Edward how the team at the forge opened the hidden storage there, I set to figure out this one myself.

The panel utilized a plunger and a magnet system. Easy and effective, but too risky for someone to accidentally open. If Mac hid anything behind the glasses, the mechanism would be more intricate. The more I searched, the more I saw only glittering glassware.

Fed up, I removed two glasses in each hand, setting them on the bar while continuing to stare inside for a knob or keyhole. Clearing my head with a shake, I thought about the Roman era lock that Sam 3D printed for me at Chedworth. The keyhole was a simple round, almost invisible if you weren't looking for it.

Mac wouldn't want curiosity about a lever or knob. Changing my focus, I relaxed my gaze again without the expectation of what I was looking for. After four scans, I gave up. It was a cupboard for shot glasses.

As I finished replacing the first row of shot glasses, a squared-off edge caught my eye. Each shelf in the cabinet was held in place by pegs that could be moved to adjust the height of the shelves. Rows of circles an inch apart lined each side.

One circle at the top left was odd. The shape was the same size as a peg hole, but it was hexagonal, like an Allen wrench or hex key.

Every fiber of my being longed to grab a key and rip it open, the feeling almost as strong as finding an artifact when sifting debris from an archaeological site. But if it had evidence of any crime, my interference would ruin it.

"PC Linden?" I called.

"Done with your lie down, are you?"

Ignoring the implied criticism of my actions, I asked if she had an Allen wrench.

"Not on me."

"Donny," I said, pulling his attention away from performing card tricks for a table. "Do you have any tools here?"

After pulling a coin from a lady's ear, he ducked behind the bar, gave a distressed glance to the mess I was making with the shot glasses, and pulled out a leather roll. Untying it, the leather straightened, revealing a variety of tools. A collection of hex keys sat in a pocket.

Snatching them into my fist, I leaned into the cabinet and tried three until one slipped in.

Counting to five, then ten to keep myself from turning it, I addressed the constable. "Can you come over here? This may be nothing, but a known forger who worked here has a history of hidden compartments. I think I've found one."

Tight lips and clenched jaw showed her skepticism, but she came behind the bar and looked.

"You see, there is an opening for an Allen wrench. It might not be anything, but you should be the one who tries it for chain of evidence validity," I said.

Linden stood, and I thought she would simply ignore me, but she pulled out plastic gloves from her jacket, then her phone.

Her face still indicating she thought the endeavor a waste of time, she was nevertheless thorough. Taking pictures of every step, she began by removing the key, returning it to the hole, and turning it until the mechanism engaged. *Click.*

Excitement changed her expression. Eyes glowing, she turned to me. "Shine your flash in there, would you?"

Pushing my cell's flashlight and directing it at the wall, which opened half an inch, I warned her, "It might just be where he keeps his best liquor. You know, for special patrons."

Without answering, she opened the door.

We gasped in unison.

# Chapter Thirty-Three: The Final Discovery

I held my breath, staring at the open secret panel behind the cupboard of glasses. Donny continued to occupy the pub's patrons with free beer and an impromptu magic act.

PC Linden was already on her cell, calling in our find.

Stacks of plastic baggies lined the chamber, each filled with fine white crystals. Cocaine? Heroine? I didn't know enough about either, but no one hid little baggies of flour. Definitely drugs.

"Sorry I doubted you," PC Linden said when she hung up. "I'd heard a bit of your reputation for disaster."

"Not my fault." A phrase I said too often. "Trouble finds me."

Her skeptical expression returned, only this time accompanied by a smile. "I'd say you sought this out with action and forethought."

I couldn't argue. "The guy who put it there was a very bad man," I said in my defense.

Within minutes, DI Parikh arrived on the scene, taking control of the evidence and barking orders into his cell phone so forcefully that I thought he'd break it.

Waving repeatedly in his direction wasn't getting me anywhere, so I tried to approach him.

"I am sorry, Miss McGuire, but this is an active crime scene now."

"I know. I found it. My fingerprints are everywhere." Frustrated, I changed directions. "Where is Edward, and did they catch who threw the

Molotov cocktail?"

"Didn't you hear?" he asked in a way that implied I carried a police scanner around my neck at all times.

"Is he okay?" The longer I didn't get news, the more fearful I became. Edward has a habit of throwing himself, literally, at danger. I guess I could see his point about wanting me to stay safe. Constant worry wears on a person.

"Constable Bailey? Yes, brilliant actually. He borrowed Jones, and the fleeing arsonist collided with the PC. Michael MacMillan, or Mac as you know him, sent the perpetrator to burn down The Boater. The man is singing like a canary, as your American movies would say."

Not since, like 1940, but great news.

"It's nice to have you back in charge."

Parikh stilled for a moment, took off his glasses to clean them, and turned to me. "Thank you," he said earnestly. Replacing them, he transformed back into the Detective Inspector. "PC Linden, please transport Miss McGuire to her residence." To me, he added, "I'm afraid I will need Bailey."

It was, without a doubt, the most anticlimactic end to the evening imaginable.

* * *

At the Priestlys', I paced around the empty living room, waiting to hear from Edward. Roger and Meryl were at a community center function, and I needed to talk.

No one specifically told me not to contact Lily, so I called her.

Her greeting was tentative.

"I was calling to see if you're okay, but also to tell you that they've linked Mac to both forgeries and a drug ring."

"And?"

"What do you mean?"

In a small voice, she asked, "And Donny?"

From my eavesdropping, I recalled that she asked how she could trust her boyfriend. Since I didn't officially know he wasn't involved, I answered, "He was in shock. When he first heard about the antiquities forgers and the fire, he was sitting at the bar. He couldn't believe it."

A sob came through the cell's speaker.

"Lily, are you okay?"

My intention for calling was to dissipate my adrenaline, not provide comfort. Sometimes I needed lessons in friending. Certainly, now wasn't the time to mention hidden drugs at Donny's workplace.

"DI Parikh asked Donny to go to the station tomorrow for a witness statement. If they suspected him of involvement, I think they would have made him go tonight, you know?"

More snuffling. "The man worked with him," she said, her voice still quiet.

So much had happened since I last saw her that it took me a second to figure out what she meant. She witnessed Douglass's attack. "You saw someone who worked with Donny and Mac in the Abbey Square?"

No response except static.

"Are you nodding?" I asked.

Another sob, but this time with a laugh. "Oh, I don't know which was worse. Seeing Constable Douglass attacked or recognizing the attacker. And I thought…"

"You thought Donny might be involved, and that was the worst part."

"Oh, Maddie, it's awful!" she wailed. "Will he forgive me for not trusting him?"

"Please," I said, taking on a casual tone. "Simon had me arrested once, and I accused him of murder."

Lily gasped, then laughed in earnest. "You did that?"

"We weren't each other's biggest fans when I started at the Baths. If we can move past that, you and Donny will be fine."

I didn't add the part about how our bonding happened when the murderer sealed us in a chamber together. Nothing like a near-death encounter to form a friendship.

Changing the subject, I asked, "Have they told you when you can come home?" With all the chaos whirling in her quiet city, I hoped she still wanted to return.

"Nothing yet, but I can't wait to get back and see Donny."

The doorbell rang, and we hung up.

With paranoia born of experience, I snuck to the window and peeked. Edward, knowing my patterns, stood within view and waved.

As he came into the boot room, I gave him a ferocious hug, stepped away, and punched him on the arm. *Thwack!* Not that it hurt him with the leather jacket as a buffer, but as a not-so-subtle indicator that he shouldn't run off and leave me.

Holding his palms up in slow-down motion, exposed the bloody napkin wrapped around his fist.

"How's your hand? Are you okay? Shouldn't you have that looked at?"

"I wanted to look at you first."

Any lingering annoyance I had at being left behind dissipated in a puff of romantic joy.

Taking him by the arm, I led him up the stairs to the bathroom. Considering myself an expert on open wound care after the number of times I got hurt, I carefully washed the blood from his skin. After drying it, I added antibacterial cream and used two Band-Aids, which I refused to call sticking plasters, to hold the skin together.

Without speaking, the process became more intimate, loving somehow, and when I looked into his eyes, electricity sparked.

Our kiss, long and slow, built in intensity until I started to wonder how much longer the Priestlys would be out.

"Let's go upstairs," I whispered into his ear.

"You're sure?" he asked, knowing the only thing on the top floor was my studio apartment.

Before I could check in with my brain, his phone rang.

He blew out a huge puff of air, then shook himself before answering.

"Right…right…of course. On my way."

"Mac?" I asked, referencing the subject of his call, not the caller.

"Aye. The arsonist was caught, mostly through the efforts of Jones."

"I heard."

"Did you hear that the man ran straight into Jones, who stepped onto the sidewalk at exactly the right time?" Edward's mouth twitched, surprising a smile. "The impact caused Jones to stagger, and he fell full force onto the suspect.

I couldn't help laughing. "He has that habit." We headed downstairs and out. "Did Mac trigger an all-ports warning?"

Similar to an all-points bulletin, or APB, in the US, an all-ports warning was issued to trains, airports, ferries, and boats.

"Not an official detention, but the attempted theft of a pelagic fishing boat in Falmouth caught a bright official's attention, and he made the connection to our warning. The owners of the boat did not take kindly to the action and have the thief, who matches Mac's description, tied up in a boat house."

"I hope he's uncomfortable. Do you have to go?"

Shrugging on his jacket, he said, "Aye. Parikh is waiting outside." He kissed me again and said, "Be careful, Maddie."

Of all the things he could have said, that warning scared me the most.

# Chapter Thirty-Four: A Celebration

Several days passed with Edward in Falmouth, which I learned was in a deep harbor on the coast of Cornwall. In Arizona terms, it would be like going from Tempe to Nogales, which wasn't horrible, but I could hardly follow Edward there.

Sporadic updates included Edward's arrival, the identification and subsequent arrest of Mac, and Parikh's press conference. Douglass had been released from the hospital, and Lily was cleared to come home.

As soon as Edward made it back, we headed to The Boater to celebrate everyone's return. Donny, tending bar, couldn't sit with us, but he stopped by our table often enough to be part of the party.

"Who is in charge now? Do you know?" I asked him.

"Dunno," Donny admitted. "Someone from the company said they'd make sure payroll went through, so all of us bartenders and cooks are showing up based on Mac's schedule."

"What company? I thought it was locally owned."

"Fuller Turner and Smith. They franchise out, but they also have pubs that are company-run."

"I hope you spoke up and said you'd like to be the manager. You'd be great at it!"

Donny carried himself a little taller.

"Thanks for encouraging him," Lily said, watching him with a smile.

Once everyone had a round in them, tea included, Edward regaled us with adventures from Falmouth.

While he was gone, I had researched the area and made a note to visit the next time my mom came out. There is a castle there that Henry VIII built, and she loves Tudor history.

Edward didn't see anything so picturesque. The boathouse where Mac was detained included a launch, so it sat over water. The fishermen not only tied Mac, but hauled him onto a lift and suspended him over the stormy water. By the time Parikh arrived, Mac was so cold that he was happy to see him.

The process of getting Mac down soaked Edward, who didn't have anything to change into. Tonight, he ordered tea with a shot of whiskey and kept hiding a cough.

The arrest went smoothly, and Mac's lawyer or barrister, I never could remember who did what, focused more on deals and conditions than suggesting his client was innocent.

"Did he plant all that evidence to frame Parikh?" I asked.

"Your timeline and the people he used were spot on. A master chess player you are, my love," Edward answered.

I could feel the blush travel to my ears.

"You never told me what else they found at the forge," I said to cover my pleased expression.

"A saber, a replica of the one used to kill Raibead."

"The knight," I added for clarification, at which point Lily went pale, and Donny distracted her by rolling a coin over his fingers.

Edward whispered, "Circumstantial, but with everything we have on him, it should seal the conviction."

"Tell 'em your part," Donny said to Lily.

She continued with news about Douglass's attack. The constable had been knocked out and kept in hospital for observation to ensure he didn't have a concussion, but he hadn't been badly hurt.

"He called to tell me he was on the mend," she said. "But then he made me go over my statement again."

She'd recognized one of the stockers from The Boater as Douglass's attacker. "He always got all shirty with Donny, even though he was just supposed to be there to store food." Between the sudden violence and that recognition, she said, "That was me done. Couldn't think of what to do next."

"Mac admitted to sending the man, and we found him easily enough. He's at the king's pleasure, Lily, so you don't need to worry.

"Interestingly," Edward continued with a sidelong glance at me, "the only charge Mac didn't own up to was planting the forged rondel in Douglass's car. I believe his exact words were, 'That'd be a stupid thing to do.'"

I chose this moment to use the restroom.

When I returned, Edward excused himself to cover another coughing fit. At least, that was what I thought he was doing. Instead, he met James outside and brought him to the table, Milo by his side.

"How's the arm?" I asked, noting that Milo sat by James's wounded side, keeping watch so no one got too close.

"I've had worse," he said, cocky and obnoxious. Tonight, I didn't mind.

Milo looked at me and tilted his head, doggie smile inviting ear rubs.

As I scratched and cooed, I asked, "When were you released?"

"Me or the dog?"

"Both," I said to be polite. "How did Milo like staying with Jones?"

"Not as much as he likes my eejit brother," Edward said, muffling a sneeze. He needed to go home.

Switching places, I asked James quietly, "Are you okay getting back to the boat on your own? Edward needs rest."

"Aye, that's he does. I've got Milo here. I'll be fine."

Simon and Dolly arrived, and we couldn't leave for at least another round. Half-pints of beer were genius. Lily immediately engaged Dolly in details about wedding plans. Idle curiosity or hoping for her own day?

Making a homework excuse, which wasn't altogether untrue, I said my goodbyes and pulled Edward out.

We went down through The Boater's garden patio to the river. "Are you moored in the same place as before?" I asked.

"Close enough. We swapped with another boat," Edward answered, which caused a sneezing jag.

"Settle down," I said with a grin, knowing he wouldn't want me fussing about his health. His narrow boat was still within walking distance.

"Donny and Lily look serious," I continued, for something to say. Even though they hadn't been dating all that long, they seemed sure of each other.

I couldn't help comparing my relationship to yet another couple's. Lily and Donny were happy. And Tori's breakup with Scott brought her joy.

Where was I with Edward, then? Earlier that week, I was just about ready to do anything for him. With him, honestly, and I don't think I would have regretted it. Today I ached a little with every one of his coughs.

Tearing down the last of the walls around my heart and psyche, I pledged myself to him.

Silently, of course.

Just in my head.

But still, it was a big step.

With that, there was one more thing I had to do. Confess.

"So," I began.

"I cringe whenever you start a sentence like that," Edward said, then sneezed.

"You know how one of Mac's rondels—"

Stopping suddenly, he spun me to face him. "Don't tell me anything that would make me investigate situations that shouldn't be investigated," Edward said, all playfulness purged from his tone.

It took me a moment to process what he implied. Don't confess about my part in the rondel; that much was clear, because he seemed to know what I was going to say. My grand plan of subterfuge, uncovered without a whisper.

It was more than that, though. I'd ranted and joked about planting evidence on Douglass. Edward made the connection that the rondel was my idea.

If he concluded that, then he probably discerned who put the rondel in Douglass's car, as I didn't have a lot of pickpocket friends.

Of course, he knew it was Harold, or, as Edward called him, Gabriel. A thief and a conman, Harold nevertheless returned a significant artifact that he and his partner had stolen from Chedworth. I never disclosed his name or the Captain Kidd location to the police. Not even to Edward.

Grateful to keep Harold safe, I took Edward's face in both my hands and kissed him, ignoring the impending infection. "You are amazing."

Tucking a loose wave behind my ear, he said, "Not many thieves would give up a treasure for a girl they knew they couldn't have."

So, he knew. I mean, yes, he knew that the thief he called Gabriel had returned an ancient gold coin by hiding it in my pocket. But I thought Edward missed Gabriel's motivation. Of course, he hadn't. He understood Harold, aka Gabriel, better than I did.

One of the reasons Edward captured my heart was his intelligence. And broad shoulders. And the crooked smile and soulful brown eyes.

I kissed him again.

# Meryl's Multigrain Seed Bread (Bread Machine)

Ingredients:

- 8 oz water
- 3/4 oz olive oil
- 1/2 oz honey
- 1 3/4 oz rolled oats
- 5 Tablespoons Seed Topping, divided 4 and 1 (see note)
- 10 oz bread flour
- 1 tsp salt
- 1 tsp active dry yeast

Directions:

1. Place ingredients in the bread machine pan in the order suggested by the manufacturer.
2. Select Dark Crust on Basic setting, and press Start.
3. After the 2nd rise, sprinkle the top with 1 Tablespoon more seeds.

OR to finish in the oven:

1. Set the machine to Dough Cycle.
2. Remove the dough after the first rise, about an hour, and place the dough in a 1-pound loaf pan.

3. Remove the bowl from the machine, but do not turn it off. Set the loaf pan with the dough into the bread machine for the second rise. The machine acts like a proofing drawer. If not using a machine, set the loaf pan in a warm area and cover.

4. When it's close to fully risen (about 50 minutes), moisten the top, and add additional seeds. Allow to rise for an additional 10 minutes.

5. Bake at 350 for 35-40 minutes.

Notes:

Seeds - Any combination of seeds and nuts will work to reach 4 tablespoons if Seed Topping isn't available—pumpkin, sunflower, blanched almond slivers, poppy, sesame, flax, anise, etc.

Cup Measurements if you don't have a scale:

- 1 Cup water
- 1 Tbsp vegetable oil
- 2-1/2 Tbsp honey
- 1 tsp salt
- 1/2 Cup rolled oats
- 2 1/3 Cups bread flour
- 5 Tablespoons Seed Topping - divided 4 and 1
- 1 tsp active dry yeast

# Acknowledgments

My thanks to those in the UK and Ireland start with Tim Stuckes, retired Police Inspector formerly of the Avon and Somerset Constabulary, for his insights into the British police force—insights which I freely ignore in many instances. I also extend my gratitude to Yvonne Quinn, aka @hey_ontour, for providing me with Irish phrases and situations, and the best tour of the Cliffs of Moher and Galway one could ever have.

In America, my thanks go to the wonderful Shawn Reilly Simmons, Deb Well, and everyone at Level Best Books. Thank you to Sisters in Crime and Mystery Writers of America for their resources and support. As always, my heartfelt love and thanks go to Kim, Jade, and Alyn for knowing so much that I do not. Finally, my profound appreciation to the Blackbird Writers for their treasured support and wealth of experience.

# About the Author

Sharon Lynn was raised in Arizona but developed a profound connection to England when living there as a teenager, inspiring the setting of the award-winning Cotswold Crimes Mystery series. Nowadays, she spends half her time in Flagstaff, AZ. It is an International Dark City where lights are kept to a minimum so the Lowell Observatory can see stars. The nights are what she refers to as "werewolf dark" and provide the perfect inspiration for mysteries. The rest of the time, she lives on a boat in San Diego, where the changing ocean and foggy mornings conjure her muse. Sign up for updates at www.sharonlwrites.com and www.blackbirdwriters.com.

AUTHOR WEBSITE:

https://sharonlwrites.com/

SOCIAL MEDIA HANDLES:

https://www.instagram.com/sharonlwrites/
https://www.Facebook.com/sharonlwrites
https://bsky.app/profile/sharonlwrites.bsky.social
https://www.threads.net/sharonlwrites
https://www.x.com/sharonlwrites
https://www.goodreads.com/sharonlynnwrites
https://www.bookbub.com/authors/sharon-lynn
**amazon.com/author/sharonlwrites**

https://allauthor.com/author/sharonlwrites/
https://www.linkedin.com/in/sharonlwrites

# Also by Sharon Lynn

Novels:

*Death Plays with Fire: A Cotswold Crimes Mystery* Book 3 by Level Best Books (2024)

*Death Takes a Fall: A Cotswold Crimes Mystery* Book 2 by Level Best Books (2023)

*Death Takes a Bath: A Cotswold Crimes Mystery* Book 1 by Level Best Books (2022)

Short Stories:

"The Professor's Lesson" in Malice Domestic 16: *Mystery Most Diabolical* (2022)

"Final Curtain" in Malice Domestic 15: *Mystery Most Theatrical* (2020)

"Carne Diem" in Malice Domestic 14: *Mystery Most Edible* (2019)

"Death on Tap" in Sisters in Crime Desert Sleuths' anthology *SoWest: Killer Nights* (2017)

"Death on Tap" and "Carne Diem" are available as standalone short stories on Kindle